Thirteen

A Novel By:

King Jewel

Published by: New World Publishing

ISBN: 0-9769335-2-7

Library of Congress Control Number: 2006930128

Cover Design by: Candace K
Edited by: A Forrester

First Trade Paperback Edition Printing: November 2006

Printed in the U.S.A by

Dedication

DELORES L. SMITH

R. I. P

This accomplishment is solely dedicated to the strongest black woman the world had the pleasure to know and love "My mother". She came from a long line of beautiful, resilient, proud, intelligent, and above all loving women. She raised seven children who sometimes didn't want to be raised. She was the mother and father to all of us and the mother to any community she lived in. With the strength of a hundred men and the love of an entire village she taught us to fly in a flock and solo. A woman that can teach five boys to be men is a rare and precious gem. My mother and Ms. D to the community was truly a "SUPERWOMAN"

Acknowledgements

Growing up in a house with six other personalities, it always felt like things could be better. That's until you grow up and see that things were perfect. I received so much love from my brothers and sisters even when I didn't deserve it. I know now that love is bigger then three words. Love is more than a few hugs and kisses. Love is something I feel at every cook-out, holiday, birthday party, baby shower, wedding, and sadly enough every funeral. So I'm taking this opportunity to let *ALVIN, MARITZA, MONIQUE, GENE, WILLIAM, TWAN, AND YOGI,* know that I love you all so very much. I really cherish what we have and how it gets stronger with every second passed.

To all of my beautiful nieces and handsome nephews I can't believe how the thought of you guys just lights me up. You're all so different but in your own way. You remind me of your grandmother.

LaLisa-Caring
David-Leadership
Tennile-Glamour
Alvin-Brains
Lanette-Beauty
T.J-Compassion
Tyrell-Strength
Desiree-Forgiveness
Mike-Pride
Tydek-Willpower
Kayla-Toughness

Mehki &Elijah-Too young to tell but I can't wait to see what the future holds. I am sure they will uphold all that is great in the world. To the only great grandchild of the bunch Jordan, you're truly a joy to be around. With all that raw energy you're going to make a great athlete one day.

As I followed your growth over the years you never cease to amaze me. You are truly a gifted bunch and you apply yourselves. The world is your playground. I leave you with this: Rome wasn't built in a day. So just because your not where you want to be you still have a lifetime ahead of you to perfect it. Look how long it took me to write this. Keep your head up and reach back for a family member.

To Arron and Stink-a I know it's not easy going from a boy to a young man. Trust me I'm living proof of that. My only advice to you is keep your head high so you won't miss the blessing the Lord has for you. Personally if I had a penny for everyone I missed I would be living in the Hampton. Blessings don't come wrapped up under a Christmas tree but trust and believe they are always on time. I love you guys but more importantly I love what you're going to become. Any day can be your new beginning, so take full advantage of that.

When I think of the Smith family I can't do much but smile. This is a family that has more ups and downs than any roller coaster but that's not what makes me smile. The reason I smile is because each and every time they manage to bounce back. This family is a testament to the word strength. The list is so long but let me try and name a few. Aunt Loy who's always been there for me more times then I can count. To my cousin Susan who's always been like an aunt to me. Your words of encouragement have always inspired me to do better things. My favorite cousin Sabrina, we have been best friends since the Riverdale days and that will never change. To the rest of the clan *Allan, Moses, Peaches, Danny, David, Harvey, Hadith, Niema and Chicky*, I love you all and neither time nor distance can change that!!!

To my second family the Boyd's and *Lewis's*:

All the love and respect goes out to my aunt *Annie Mae*. Even before my mom passed away she treated me like one of her own. This lady is truly one of the great ones. Nothing can express nor compare to the love she's poured into me. Not to mention the countless hours she prayed for me. Thank you, sweetheart.

Celia Lewis ~aka~ Aunt Cel. I must smile when I think of this woman. She literally came out of nowhere in my life but now ranks at the top of the class. She's been there each and every time I needed her and made Rockford feel like home. Thanks auntie for everything. Also special thanks to *Aunt Etna, Aunt Janie, Aunt Maxene, Uncle George, Uncle Roger, Uncle Charlie, Uncle Red, Boss Hog, Scrap, Todd, Daryl Ray, Tiny, Reggie, Yogi, Vicky, Pez, Blade, Kennefa, Uncle Sonnie, Rockfish, Lisa, Scooby, the Garcia family, Tarsus , Derrick, Tabrese, Trone, Warner, Larry, Erickton, Dip, Big Joe, Geno, Annie, Dayvon, Troy, Mike Dog, Tyress, Smoke, Joey, Ray Your favorite rappers-favorite rapper, Chrisie, Johnna, Lee Martin, Margie and Darius.* If by chance I have forgot anyone it wasn't from lack of love. Trust me this has been a long process.

The Arnold family:

This family I've held dear to my heart for a very long time. From the love of *Betty* to the comfort from *Sarah and Bernard.* This family has put the S. H in southern hospitality. I've been to more restaurants in Maryland but the best food is on Monument St. at Shelby's. Much love to many. *Cootie, Lil Cootie, Manny, Justin Tisha, Lil Shelby, Nessia, and Bernard.* A special thanks to Betty Arnold for giving me Sarah. You did a great job and without her I would have been lost. So, thanks to the Arnold's for all the love it was certainly appreciated and it's right back to you.

All my love goes out to the great *Anna J*, the incomparable *Marlene Ricketts* and the talented *Dante Feenix*. You are a player and not a hater. When you pointed me in the right direction and didn't know me that was huge. Most people in the same line of work try to shut you out, but not you. Thanks. You're a class act. My mentor and homie *Marlene Ricketts* you have been a giant in this whole process. I've learned more from you in a month than in a lifetime. As a mentor and business partner you are priceless. Thank you for your time, effort and patience. Now where do I start with Philly's finest? *Anna,* you are simply the greatest. Not because of all your accomplishments in the book field. To me it's all how you embraced me as a young author and a big brother. With the world in its fragile state the little things in life goes unnoticed. Not in this case. I not only saw the love that you put into my book, but I felt it also. I know I almost fainted a few times but you never let me hit the floor. I guess you're my guardian angle!!!

Friends have truly been rare in my life. Has that been good or bad, your guess is as good as mine. All I can say is over the past twenty five years *Chuck Martin, Daryl Boyd, Mark Reily, Wise, and Gums* has stood the test of time and I thank you for it. In my eyes quality beats quantity any day!!!

164 street crew: *Reef, Sweets, James Joy, Alvin, Bread, Stacy, Mike Beman, Mark Dog, Chuck, Purse, Kev Simmons, Pooch…* the list is long but the love isn't.

Special shout out to the first solo *M.C Chief Rocker Busy Bee*, the teacher himself *KRS-1*, the Legendary Ice-T, Bronx finest Fat Joe, Mickey Benson, the Chiles family, Do- You-Couture and the brain power behind it *Pep and Frannie*, my brother from another mother *Black, zee and falon . Jay, One Shot, K.K., Prince, Ron, T.I, Chris Jones, Zoe Bop, Bird, Score, J.D.L, Tony Shoulders, Amber, Az, Doreen and Phenom clothing, Panama, Big E, Bubbles, Blue, Kareem, Brian, Toney Bey, Stone, The Do-U models, Dread, Angie, Vonne , The nanny of the year Jazzy Joyce, Tina, Juicy, Tonya Butler, Courtney, The Tank family, Cookie, Branches, Sharnetta, Chief Danny, Danta Feenix, Jody, Violet, Saleen, Lamont Wright(yoda), Maria, Nicky, Troy, Rom, Snoop, treasure Blue, Muff, Poodie, Tiny, T.T, Miz, Kia Neal, Boobie, VJ, Buck, Chudney, Buddest, Joe, Kia, Denise Varona, Rock, Buck, Rocket Rod Peters, B. Guy, Beato, Papers, Fat-Boy, Brooklyn Finest, Tone, Jeff, K-Born, High bridge, Purple City, To my main man Jason when the chips was literally down you showed me I wasn't alone. For that you go down in history as the last of a dead breed. Thanks kid! To all the Mr. Me to niggas you don't have to lie to kick it!!!!!!!!!!!!!!!!*

R. I. P. Saints
Delores Smith, Susie Carter, Renee Ash, Tanya Brooks and Barbra Chiles

R. I. P. Soldiers
Al Barnes, Rashid, Keith Black, Mice, Sammy Joe, Jimmy Dee, Sean, Avon, Jerome, Moses, Bubba, Jose Martin Sr.,

Malik Sealy, Blake, Damon, *Conrad Mcrae, Ant Grant, Carlton Hines, My father Amos Smith a special man by any standards. Thanks for all the years of love, respect, and support. You will truly be missed.*

Kenya Hooper and Colby Charley if I apologized a zillion times I know it wouldn't be enough. All I can say is that I was young and dumb and full of myself. A deadly combination by anyone standards. If by chance this reaches your ears or eyes try to witness my metamorphisms. Colby not a day goes by that you don't enter my mind. You've taught me more than words can express. Without laying an eye on you I know you are a blessing to all around you. You're both forever in my prayers!

Inspiring women:
My life as well as my book has had a fair share of ups and downs but if it wasn't for the love , respect, support, encouragement, nurturing, security, and above all belief in me as a person and a artist I don't know how I would have made it. *Sarah Arnold, Frances , Nicole, Kimberly, Lori, Ms. Barbra, Maritza, Paula, Monique,Ali True, Brenda Roper, Annie C., Angel, Donna, Tanya, Jackie, McKenzie, Kenya Jay, Shy, Shavon, Tia, Ivey, and Poochie.* Everyone that I mentioned and some that I didn't played a roll in my chaotic life. Which means we're forever linked in life. Some wiped my butt when I was a baby, others wiped my tears when I became a man. No matter the role big or small I love you all. Keep me in prayers as I do you. GOD BLESS!!!

~King Jewel

Granted the Devil is a Bad man but no matter how bad he is, he cannot take the credit nor the Praise for all of our shortcomings. We all are conscience men and women and have made bad choices in our lives. For me I apologize to all that I have directly or indirectly affected.

My comfort is in knowing that with each mistake, whether big or small, my wonderful God Lord and Savior was there to forgive me. Not only did He forgive me He gave me a beautiful Daughter to let me know I am still one of his blessed children. If it can happen for a wretch like me on a daily basis pay attention, it will happen for you also!!!!!

King Jewel

PART I

"The Game"

CHAPTER 1: Black

Hot 97 had our car rocking as we fought through the rainstorm on the F.D.R. Drive. Things could be better for the three of us but who are we to complain? We have jewels on our necks, and bank in our pockets. Anybody who's known us, knows that we've come a long way. Personally, I've had a lot of hungry nights as a kid. Not to mention having to celebrate Christmas in January or February, because mom didn't have the money. Now when we go into Dr. Jays we buy a new pair of sneakers and leave the old ones.

"We ain't caught no traffic tonight on the F.D.R., that's a first!" I said, while rolling that good shit from Branson.

"I guess not, stupid! We're the only fools out in a baby hurricane," Born replied, while gazing at the heliport to his left. Tip and I busted out laughing, while Born choked on the blunt.

"Could someone please tell me who's idea this was to be going to shady ass B.K. on one of the worst nights all summer?" asked Born in a reluctant tone.

"It was mine and I don't want to get into it again with you two fake ass thugs," I said. I leaned my head back with the blunt bouncing between my lips and showed my frustration in an irritated voice.

They never said that I was the boss, but to anyone outside looking in it was understood. It has always been like that ever since we all met in third grade. Tip and I hit it off from day one. From that day on we were like Siamese twins. I showed Tip how to look under the teacher's dress with a mirror on his shoe. A trick passed on by my uncle and gladly accepted by Tip. Tip was always the smallest out of the three, but he had a lot of heart. That was what I liked about him. We didn't meet Born until after the Christmas break when he transferred to our school from the Bronx.

From the first day, he was a hit with all the girls. He even had sixth grade girls sending him love letters. Like all good friends, we had a run in after school. The whole school was standing around waiting to see the big fight. Instead of giving them what they wanted, we decided to call a truce and join forces. Even when I was in the third grade, I was thinking about the big picture.

After that day, we were like the Three Musketeers. We were together from sunup to sundown. It was no big surprise to anybody when we got into the drug game. From the third grade to the day we closed the books on school we were into everything from setting off stink bombs in the girl's bathroom to extorting the school for money. It's true that we nickel and dimed in the game for a while. That's because all we wanted was to shop at Dr. Jays and Mart 125, buy Branson, and go to the Apollo on Wednesdays. It was not until the summer of 1989 that people started to big us up in the game.

It was 1990, and a big coke drought had swept New York. You can count on one hand how many people had it good. Although the prices were sky high and the profits were lovely, I think that the days of paying sixteen thousand a key was over.

At this stage in our lives, money wasn't a problem. I'm not trying to say we were on the same level as 'Big Dog' and his crew, who were hitting half the city before the Feds gave him life. Let's just say we were very comfortable. Although we were spending top dollar, nobody had anything worth putting on the streets. After about a week of ghost meets and dead ends, I was uptown at Jerry's Den. I was getting my blow out laced. When you walk out of the shop and you're fro is shining and slightly blowing in the wind, it made it look like mink when it was done, and I felt like a new man.

As I was leaving the joint, I saw my man Dust Head Red. He's been puffing that shit since I've known him. Nobody would call him that to his face, because of his passion for shooting people was right up there with his passion for getting high. His other passion was paper chasing.

Red had heard about my problem. Although this is a big city, word sometimes travels fast. For a small fee he put me on to a clown from Flatbush named Pepper. I'm sure he hit Pepper up for a fee also. I can't be mad because the game is sold not told. This guy is known for having it long and strong. Strong is exactly what I need right now. I wasn't really feeling this kid's style and I heard about his love for the fags up state. At this point it was him or sit home bitching like everybody else who didn't have it.

Nevertheless, desperate times called for desperate measures. I went and told Tip and Born what the deal was. It seemed like their dislike for Brooklyn was worst then mine. We argued for about an hour, which felt like the whole damn day. It seemed every word out of their mouths was on some negative shit. They made sense to a certain point but were missing the most important point of all. If we rode this drought out for another few weeks it would put a nice dent in our cash, especially with our spending habits. I hated handling business in Brooklyn too, but I hated being broke even more.

I think that was the comment that got through their thick skulls. When I got to the point where they had semi agreed with me I said, fuck it and beeped Tykim. Tykim was an old acquaintance of mine from Job Corps who deals with Pepper. With Tykim in the middle I thought things would go smoother. Tykim became a little bugged out after his little son died in that fire. The word on the street is that he fell asleep while he was smoking a blunt. He's not a crackhead or nothing, but those wollies are taking its toll on him.

After going back and forth with them I needed a drink and piece of mind. I was at the *Seville Lounge,* a little spot I hang sometimes, when Tykim called me back. Not a lot of guys my age hang out there. When you drive by it, you see a lot of mean Cadillac's. It's something about that car that makes an old geezer feel like a Mack. Tykim gave me just the help I needed and it was on and popping.

Once I spoke to Pepper, he made it clear that he wasn't coming to Harlem because he didn't feel like killing anybody today. I thought to myself, *he didn't feel like Kato and them kids from 19th Street putting a broomstick up his ass.* Kato vowed he would do that right before he killed him for grabbing his baby's mother's ass at the Freaknik in Virginia. Our conversation went from bad to worst in seconds. BK niggers had it in their mind that Harlem cats were not built for combat. By the end of the call I had held my ground and my tongue. It wasn't easy to do but the love of the dough makes all things possible.

I told Pepper that we would come out his way between eight and nine o'clock. Pepper told me not to bring a bunch of bitch ass niggers with me. I thought to myself, *is this the same nigger that was fucking homos, calling someone else a bitch?* Some things are better left unsaid, so I just hung up the phone.

I thought about stopping by *Club Cheetaz* while we're out there. On second thought, Tip gets the double dose of the "little-man complex" when he gets drunk and I don't feel like talking to the police with a bag full of money or coke. That would make for an uneasy conversation.

The weather was hectic out here and the boom from the thunder broke my daydream. I was thinking about my lil man while Tip and Born argued about who lied on their dick the most. It makes me sad thinking about my son. It's been about a year now since his mother ran off with some reject from New Jersey. Although she didn't leave an address for me or my family, I'm confident that I'm going to find the bitch one of these days.

I told Tip to turn down the music. He paused for a minute because that new NWA shit came on. He's been on their dick ever since we hung out with them at the Tunnel. Once he turned the music down, I told them to let me do all the talking when we get there. They had no problem with that because that was the regular. Not that I didn't trust them, but Tip can be hot headed and Born was only smooth around the ladies. The one thing I had no problem with, was trusting them to watch my back. I told them I wasn't sure how we would make the switch, but they had to be on point.

"If anyone of those Crooklyn niggas try to play themselves, I'm going to kill them, and anybody who knows them," Tip said with his lip turned up.

Born came right back with a quick, "Word is born." Sometimes I'm not sure if he says that so much because it's his name or because he's a five percenter. They all say it a lot but he runs it into the ground.

We had about another fifteen minutes before we hit Tompkins Projects and Born was rapping as usual. He always spit something when he's a little nervous. To be honest, he was pretty good. I would never tell him that because his head is already big enough.

As we pulled in front of Tompkins, it seemed like a horror movie with a little thundering and lightning added for good measure. Even though I don't believe in God, I felt like somebody was trying to tell me something. I hit the horn four times, just like Pepper told me to. Two minutes later, right before I was going to do it again, there was someone coming out of the shadows.

Oh, boy, its fake ass Jamaine, I thought to myself as I watched him approach our car. Every time I see him I think about the time he busted his ass on eighth Avenue trying to do a wheelie. Man, I laughed so hard I had to break out my asthma pump.

"What's up, niggaz? Oh yeah, I see ya'll got your game faces on, but it's no need. Life is good in the big boro. Now follow me to the man," Jamaine said with a smirk on his face.

We just gave him blank ass looks like we couldn't understand what he was saying.

"Lock up the Benz and bring up the rear," I told Tip after we got out of the car and proceeded to follow Jamaine down the street. It was about eight-twenty and our timing was perfect. The sky was dark and the air was so stale it made my skin crawl. As we walked into the projects, it made me flash back to my childhood and the days we spent running in and out of the buildings playing Ring-O-Leavia and Hot Peas and Butter.

As we walked down the dimly lit hallway, past all the crack head's apartments, it was hard to imagine a real family being forced to live here. The walls were covered with graffiti and *Decepticon* gang symbols. The floor was covered with broken forty bottles and gold top crack vials. It was a crazy sight to see that life in the projects hasn't changed one bit.

Jamaine informed us that the elevator has been broken for the last four months, so we had to take the stairs. The stairs reeked of piss and spilled beer. The smell was so harsh I thought I would throw up. The only reason I didn't cover my nose is because I thought it would be a bad time to show any weakness. To say the least, it was a long walk to the twelfth floor. Since my strive to be ghetto fabulous, I haven't walked up many stairs. As a matter of fact, in the last few years the longest I've walked was from my crib to my garage to get in my car.

When we opened the stairwell door, we were greeted by two unfamiliar faces. One had a long scar from the top of his eye to his neck. It looked like a Riker's Island Special. The other was tall, dark and bald-headed. He was trying his best to look intimidating.

"Yo, you search these niggas?" Scarface asked while trying to give us an intimidating look. His expression went from mad to worst, knowing Jamaine's silence meant he didn't. Scarface started with Tip first, of course, because he was the smallest.

"They have guns," he yelled down the dimly lit hallway. The first thing he felt was that big-ass Desert Eagle, and his eyes got big as shit.

"We got two hundred and fifty thousand, too," I said right after that to keep these dudes from bustin' at us.

"What's with these clowns?" Born turned to me and said loud enough for everyone to hear. The look on the two errand boys faces showed that the tension just got thicker.

I don't know about my crew or his, but I was hyped up. Everyone paused after Born's statement. It was silent for about thirty seconds, but you know when the tension is thick because the attitudes are thicker, thirty seconds felt like an hour.

"Hey, dumb and dumber, stop harassing our guests and let them by." The voice sounded a little funny, like he should've cleared his throat before speaking. Nevertheless, it sounded polite in a sneaky kind of way.

As we were escorted further down the dim hallway, Pepper's face got clearer and clearer. He was about 5 feet 10 inches, 190 pounds, with a low haircut. From the first time I'd seen him out in Vegas at the Tyson fight, the hype didn't match the man. The word on the street is that he's a mack with the ladies, but I couldn't see him fucking none of my hoes. On the other hand, they say he's a real thorough kid. He looks like he'd been doing push-ups right before he came into the hallway. I had to keep myself from cracking a smile. I wish one of them niggaz would tell homie he's not in jail anymore.

On a serious note, he still has that jail look, like when you look like your holding your breath all the time. Add that to a few dollars, a milked out 300CE, and Eddie the Monster widow's peak. I guess a Brooklyn bitch would go for him.

Our eyes locked halfway down the hallway, and from there on it was a stare. Number one rule for a man is never break the stare, so we didn't. When we got face to face, we both paused and then shook hands very firmly. I'm not sure what rule that is, but it's pretty high on the chart. The tension was still a little thick.

"Was it hard to find my crib?" Pepper asked after sizing me up. When Pepper managed to muster up a phony-ass smile, he had a mouth full of gold like he was from Miami or Baltimore.

"I'm out this way at least once or twice a week for some of Junior's banging cheesecake," I told him, returning the same phony ass smile. He teased me about how I didn't know about Junior's. I cut him off rudely with a stern look.

"How long do I have to stand in the hallway with a quarter of a mill?" I asked him with a straight face. I could tell he didn't appreciate being cut off like that.

Instead of saying something slick in return, he gave a faint chuckle and said, "Where are my manners? Come right in." Once we were all inside, the first thing that caught my attention was the smell. I didn't want to turn my nose up just in case it was his apartment.

"It smells like ass up in here!" Tip took the words right out of my mouth. I thought that was going to make all hell break loose.

Instead, Pepper said, "You're right, Shorty."

I knew Tip hated to be called Shorty, but the look on my face made him swallow his next comment. I was glad so we could get on with business and break out.

"If everyone doesn't mind, can we get on with it?" Born said with his face frowned up. My nod and facial expression showed that I was in agreement.

"If you feel that way, do you have the money?" Pepper said with the same tone from the phone.

"Of course. Do you have the work?" Born questioned him with a look on his face that said it all. Wasn't nothing poppin' off until we saw the product.

"Yes. It's one finger snap away." Even though this sounded like a scene out of Scarface, I didn't want it to end the same way so I opened the Louis Vuitton bag up.

I don't know if it was just me, but stacks of hundreds makes my dick hard. I didn't want to prolong this evening any further, so I turned the Louis bag over and dumped the money on the table. Pepper went to touch the money and I pulled the table towards me.

"Aren't you forgetting something?" I asked him, making sure not a dime was touched before I got my product.

"What?" Pepper said as he gently placed his hand on his chin. He gave me a real Elmira look like I was really trying his patience. I answered his question with a stern face.

"The stuff," I said in the memory of my man Al Pacino. Again, he gave me a fake laugh. Then cut it short by snapping his fingers twice in Jamaine's direction. You can tell Jamaine was in a trance from the money on the table. Pepper had to snap two more times to bring Jamaine around. Pepper was pissed because it looked corny to have to repeat the snap. I found the whole thing to be corny, but then again, so was Pepper.

Jamaine jumped up and left the room. I didn't really like that and by the look on Tip and Born's faces, they didn't either. I gave them the *be-on-point* nod. Occasionally, I gave the fake security a hard stare to let them know I wasn't fazed by their presence.

Pepper tried his best to make small talk while we waited for Jamaine. He asked me about a girl from Mart 125 that we both knew. He also knew the twins from the Polo grounds. When he told me that he was in love with freak-ass Lexus from Espanard Gardens, I almost threw up. I knew at least two different kids that had tapes of that freak. To be honest, I wouldn't mind letting the chicken suck my dick. Then he switched the subject and asked, "Can I start counting the money?"

"Why bother? If you can't produce the birds, the money goes with us," I said as I leaned back in his old Lazy Boy.

"Do you have any intention of coming back to cop?" he laughed in an uneasy tone without opening his mouth. The hatin' was so blatant it was oozing out of his pores, but fuck 'em. Business is business.

"The drought will be over in another week or so. By then, my man will be back in the mix, and the boat will be docking back in Harlem," I said with both hands together. "No disrespect playboy, but this was a one shot, one head crack."

"Huh! I thought as much. I'm giving you this crazy low price so you can take the PC elsewhere," he said while slowly nodding his head

"I never wanted to be added to your clientele list. This is purely out of desperation," I said while gently caressing the gun in my waist.

"A man should never put himself into desperate situations," Pepper informed me.

"Only if the man doesn't know where his ass is at," I informed back. At the same time, the front door busted open. We all jumped to our feet. Me, Tip and Born stood up at the exact same time our guns were coming out. Tip had the big ass D.E. pointed at the door, and I had the Berretta pointed at Pepper and his crew. Pepper's crew was a step slow so they had to look down the barrel of our guns.

To my surprise, Born had two 380's, one pointed towards the door and the other at Pepper's head. It was like a Mexican standoff. I found it a little strange that Pepper wasn't even reaching, but this wasn't the time to worry about it either.

Pepper had both hands up in the air. At that point, I was seeing and hearing in slow motion. It took me a few seconds to figure out Pepper was saying "WHOA!" As the sweat beaded up on my forehead and I clutched the butt of the nine with all my might.

By this time, Jamaine had dropped the Nike bag and had his hands sky high. He was light skinned, so out of fear, he turned dark red and I swore I saw a tear trickle down his face.

After a few deep breaths, Pepper ordered his people to not shoot, and put down the heat. At the same time I gave Tip and Born the look to do the same.

Born put down his twin 380's very slowly. I reminded myself to compliment him on how serious he looked with those two joints. He looked like he was playing in a *Die Hard* movie or something. I looked to my left, and Tip still had the heat pointed right at Pepper's head. I told him to put it away, but he didn't.

I recognized that face. The last time I'd seen it was down at Myrtle Beach at bike week. We got into it with some cats from North Carolina. He cleared the whole strip with that four pounds, and even after the clip was empty, he was still in the middle of the street clicking the hammer. I had to drag him to the bikes before the cops came.

I walked over to Tip and put my arm on his shoulder and lowered the gun. By this time he was slowly coming around. Once he looked me in my eyes, I knew he was back. The next thing I heard was Pepper blasting Jamaine for busting in the door like the police were after him.

Jamaine said a few words that didn't even sound like English, and before he could finish, Pepper slapped him to the ground. I was glad he did it because I sure wanted to do it myself. Then Pepper followed it up with a kick to the face. "Now, get your gay ass up and bring that bag over to the Don."

It took Jamaine a minute to gain his composure. As soon as he lifted his head up, the first thing you noticed were his puffy eye and the blood coming from his mouth. It's no doubt that he was redder than a slapped up white boy. I don't think a man can get anymore embarrassed than that.

After I calmed down from the whole ordeal, and the tension came down a notch, I kind of felt sorry for him. Pepper told Scarface to go and get the money machines out of the back room. Once he returned with them, Pepper proceeded to dump out his bag on the table. Ten small square packages fell out, and all you saw were little snakes printed on them. That was a good sign for me. I had some work that was out of Cali that had snake prints also and it was proper.

"Now may I count my money?" Pepper said in a very sarcastic tone.

I gave him a mob style nod while I proceeded to take out my switchblade. When that five-finger blade shot out of its case, Pepper looked up at me with a very annoyed look on his face. He immediately went back to getting the stacks ready to run through the machine. At the same time I was trying to cut a small window in the brick to give my personal test.

It wasn't easy because this thing was wrapped airtight. From the look of things, it had three individual layers. The first was a strong plastic with the snake designs. The second was a thick rubber wrap, which was pretty hard to cut. In between the second and last layer was some crude oil and Saran wrap. When you see some work wrapped in rubber like that, it's a strong possibility it wasn't hit up once it got here. Rubber means that wherever it came from, it was in danger of getting wet.

Once I got down to the goods, I scooped out a bit and place it on my tongue and gums. From being around it for so long, I know some good shit when I test it. I must admit this was some potent shit.

When I looked up, Pepper was running the money through the machine by the piles. By the way those machines were knocking off those stacks we'll be out of this pissy ass crib in no time.

I gave Tip and Born the nod to let them know it was all good. At that point, Born started to pack our property away in our bag. Pepper was down to about the last twenty or thirty grand. Once he ran that through, we were already standing and waiting for him to give us the okay. We knew the count was perfect, because we counted it twice.

"It was a pleasure doing business with you gentlemen," Pepper said making eye contact as the last bill went in and came out the other side. At that time, we shook hands and I turned to head for the door. Before we got a chance to turn the knob Pepper put his hand on my shoulder and said, "Are you sure you won't reconsider becoming a regular customer?"

"I thought we told you our man will be on in a few days. We're not like you Brooklyn niggas. We don't stab our friends in the back," Tip jumped up and said, with aggravation clear on his face.

"Is that right?" Pepper said with a smirk on his face. "If we stab our friends in the back, imagine what we do to our enemies." He broke out in a sinister laughter and his boys followed suite. Those words went right through me, and the laughs made the hairs on the back of my neck stand up.

When he stopped laughing, he told Dumb and Dumber to go downstairs and make sure the coast was clear. They left Pepper's side and headed for the door. I don't know why, but I was picturing them getting stuck between the doorway. Something you would see in an old Woody Woodpecker cartoon. To my disappointment, it didn't happen.

"Give them a minute and we'll go down," Pepper said while he cleaned up his work area. I didn't like the way that sounded, but I went along with it anyway.

"Don't worry, if there is any trouble, you have my permission to use Jamaine as a vest." He showed us his gold teeth with a smile, but I don't think Jamaine found that amusing.

At once we all piled into the hallway. Born was first, then me, then Jamaine, Tip, and Pepper was pulling up the rear. As we walked back through the dimly lit hallway, my beeper started to vibrate. I was going to look at it, but I needed to keep my eyes open for what was ahead. I thought that was more important than knowing which bitch was pressed to give me some head.

As we all marched down the stairs, all I could think about was my son. My mind was flashing back and forth on him, but I was still on point. We sounded like a football team running down those steps. When we were right between floors eleven and ten, a housing cop was entering the stairwell on the tenth floor. We already had our guns drawn and that was the first thing he saw when we ran into him. I was at a lost for words, and by the size of his eyes, so was he.

"Oh, shit!" Tip yelled out, breaking the silence. At that instant, the housing cop started pleading for his life.

"Please, I didn't see anything. Just please spare my life." By this time, we were up close and personal.

"What are you waiting for? Kill that cracker!" Pepper was asking Born. The cop was bent over with his face into his hands. He was doing a lot of whining, which was making it harder to hear. He was telling us he had a wife and three kids. Pepper was not compassionate to any of that shit.

"Don't make your problems mine. Now, kill that cracker! Stop acting like a scared bitch and pull the trigger," Pepper yelled at Tip, who seemed to be stuck on what he should do next. In an instant, Tip turns his gun off the police and placed it right on Pepper's forehead.

"I love my man and I can't stand you. Now, who do you think is in more trouble, bitch?" Tip asked him very calmly, and actually waited for a response. It was like everyone else was frozen waiting for me to tag them.

I told Tip to put the gun down and let me think. The officer was still chanting the same thing, "I don't see anything." At this point, I was feeling a little desperate. I knew it was him or me and I weighed my options, but they were feeling kind of slim.

So, I took two steps towards him with my gun raised. That's when the man looked up and started pleading for his life louder. That was the last word you heard from *'Officer Friendly'*. That blow to the temple was so hard, I thought I killed him, but I didn't.

"Damn, if you were going to hit him that hard, I should've shot him," Born said attempting to lighten the mood. That might have been funny if we weren't five minutes away from going to jail for the rest of our lives.

I bent down and took the cuffs off his belt and placed them on him. I've never touched a pair of handcuffs before in all my years of living. One time, I scooped this half Korean chick out of Club Rolex in Miami. We went back to my suite and this crazy ass freak broke out some fuzzy handcuffs. It goes without saying that my dick got soft and I threw Agent Skully's ass out.

"Okay, Mr. Nice Guy, what are we going to do with him now?" Pepper asked with a hint of sarcasm.

"Fuck, you can't leave him there or else don't make no plans for the next twenty or thirty years," Tip said in an agitated tone.

"That's for sure! As soon as one of these old bags comes out to buy a pint of thunderbird, they're going to call the law," Pepper said, and ran through the door onto the tenth floor.

"What is that fake motherfucker doing?" Born said, mirroring the thoughts of the rest of us.

"What do it look like, he's breaking on us," Tip said. Before he could finish his thought, Pepper came flying through the door.

"Drag his ass this way," he said while holding the door open. We bent down, and grabbed his arms and legs, or should I say leg, because Tip didn't help since he had the bag of cocaine. We walked for a second then Pepper pointed to an abandoned apartment. We kicked the door open and threw him inside.

"You better hope the rats get you before I come back," Pepper said before he closed the door.

We bounced up out of there like somebody was chasing us. We headed for the stairwell and proceeded down the stairs. It seemed like I was clearing four steps at a time. All I wanted to do was get out of dodge. This has been one hectic night, and after these next three floors, it will be all over.

I was beginning to smell a little fresh air from the lobby door being open. I could feel myself starting to breath a little harder, not because I was tired, but because of the anticipation. It's over now anyway because I see the word *Lobby* written on the red door ahead of us. As Born approached the door, he slowed his roll and put his hand up to signal to us to do the same. As he peeked out of the door, all he saw was an old lady standing there pressing for the elevator. He said, in a very soft tone, "Grandma, the elevator is broke."

"Thank you, young man," she said and started towards the exit.

"Are you sure? Because I visited my bingo buddy, Agnes, here a few weeks ago. Then again, it could've been a few months ago. My memory is getting so bad. I think I have Alzheimer's or something like that," she turned and asked Born once she got to the door. I knew if Born didn't cut her off we would be in the stairwell for another hour. He listened a little while longer then cut her off by telling her to have a nice night and wished her good luck at bingo.

"God bless you and be careful around here, these projects can be very dangerous at night," she said and went on about her business.

"Thank you again, and I'm about to leave as soon as my friends come downstairs."

She was mumbling something I couldn't hear, and as her voice faded away, he repeated *"okay"* a few times so he wouldn't seem disrespectful. Then he ran back to the stairwell to let us know that the coast was clear.

"Damn, man! What was your bitch ass doing? Holding church service?" Tip said, pissed because it was taking us forever to get out of the building.

"Fuck you and come on," Born told him and made his way out of the building.

We piled out of the building one by one with Born leading the way. As I looked over the parking lot, I was wondering why the Bopsie Twins weren't down here looking out like Pepper told them to.

Before I could turn to ask him where they were, I felt something splash on the back of my neck. It was warm, but at the same time, sticky.

"What the fuck!" I said, out loud, and as I was turning I heard a girl screaming. When I turned all the way around, all I could see was Tip grabbing for me with both hands, with his face blown off. I never saw so much blood in my life! I couldn't believe my eyes.

I grabbed Tip and gently lowered him to the ground. At the same time, I saw Pepper turn the black gun with the silencer away from Tip and turn it onto the girl. Her screams went silent. Although her mouth was still wide open, there wasn't a sound coming out of it. Before I could blink, he had shot that young girl twice in her chest. I knew I had to snap out of it or I would be next. As I started to reach for my pistol, I remembered I still had Tip resting in my arms. I couldn't bring myself to drop him, but in another second I would be just like him.

As mine and Pepper's eyes locked, I saw the devil in him and I was scared. I guess this is the time where everyone says your life starts to flash before your eyes. I was in another world at this point. All I could do was look down at Tip and imagine Pepper doing the same to me.

It seemed like an hour had passed, but I'm sure only a few seconds had. The next thing I heard was a loud thunder that brought me out of my trance. It made my whole body tighten up because I thought the shot had just entered my body. Instead, when I looked up I saw Pepper clutching his stomach. Then the next shot I heard was going straight through his chest. I looked over my shoulder and saw Born holding those two 380's. That's when I saw a lot of movement in the darkness.

"Born, watch your back!" As soon as I said that, all hell broke loose. Gunshots started to come from both sides of us. By this time, I had my own gun out and it was time to go to war. I laid Tip down as gently as I possibly could, like he was just hurt and not dead. I grabbed that Dessert Eagle and my own joint and started banging back.

It was real dark out here because the lamppost was out. They probably knocked it out when they were busy rapping those forty pairs of sneakers around it. Bullets were getting closer and closer, so we headed for cover. We took cover behind a black Chevy Blazer with big chrome crash bars. We heard the truck getting hit up, but that didn't stop me and Born from getting at these clowns. We were blasting at the darkness. We knew they were there because we saw the fire from their guns.

After a minute or so, one of the guys tried to get to Pepper. He tried to pull him to safety, but to no avail. No sooner had he tried than Born came over the top of the roof and lit him up. He really hit that kid up and all I could think was don't hit Tip. I knew I sounded crazy, but my heart really was hoping he's alive. Even though I know I have pieces of his brains still in my afro. All I know is that there are two down and one to go, and his time is coming to a close.

Born looked at me with fire in his eyes and told me that he was out of ammo. I started to pass him the DE, but I snatched it back and gave him mine. I felt drawn to it because it was Tip's. The way Born looked at me and I looked at him, I think he understood my pain. Born was checking the rounds I had in the gun when I heard footsteps coming our way. It sounds like more than one person though. I should have known that those fake ass niggas brought in reinforcement. I immediately rose up to let my anger be known. I guess they thought we were out of bullets because those cowards were trying to rush the car. Too bad for them, because they were very wrong!

The next thing they saw was me coming across the Blazer's wheel in the back with the D.E. The timing couldn't have been more perfect because when I rose up, his face was right in front of the gun. A five year old couldn't miss this shot, so I squeezed. The bullet hit him right in his forehead and flipped him onto his back. When his man saw that, he tried to break for the building. It was too late because I hit him right in the back. It knocked him down, but he was starting to crawl away. That's when I took aim and hit him in the back of the neck.

Suddenly I heard sirens from everywhere and Born was tugging on me saying that we had to get out of here.

"I'm not leaving without Tip," I told him as tears began to form in my eyes at the lost of my childhood friend.

"Black, that was my best friend also, but he's dead and we have to save ourselves now."

"Born, you're crazy! Tip's not dead. Look at him. He's waiting for us to pick him up."

"He's gone and we got to get ghost!"

Although I didn't believe the sirens were getting closer and closer, I went along with his tugging. As we made our way back to the car, these motherfuckers are still blazing at us. When we got back in the car, we stooped lower than low. Then it hit me-the coke!

"Oh, shit! I gotta get that bag!"

"No way! Do you hear the sirens and the bullets flying? Don't be stupid! I already lost one brother Black, I can't lose you too. We can always get that back, but we can't replace each other," Born said trying to make sense of the situation.

"Born, let's ride."

Suddenly, the passenger window burst into little pieces. When I looked back it was a kid no older than sixteen or seventeen screaming, "YOU KILLED MY BROTHER!" As we drove further and further away, I can still see the tears in his eyes and the gun in his hand. I took a deep breath and thought to myself how I had to leave my best friend in an off-brand project lying in his own blood.

As we mirked around corner after corner, I felt the tears rolling down my face while the car threw me from side to side. Strangely enough, I found myself daydreaming about the time we were backstage at the Survival of the Illest Tour and Tip was about to shoot the whole Death Squad. It was funny as hell. Him and Red were both drunk and high. Neither one of them could land a punch, everybody was laughing so hard. Well, that was before Tip pulled out the trademark DE. I never saw a bunch of gangster rappers run so fast. I'm going to miss him.

"I wonder whose brother that was?" Born asked breaking the silence. I didn't even bother to reply. I didn't care.

CHAPTER 2: Born

"Born ... Born ... Born, wake up! Are you all right?" Lia asked with a frightened look on her face.

"Yes. I was having a nightmare about last night. I can't really call it a nightmare because it really happened. The only thing that was different was that I was the one that died," I reluctantly said, with my eyes wide open now. I think that was the reason I was tossing and turning in Lia's arms.

When I came in last night, she knew something was wrong. I told her "No" several times, but she knew me better than I knew myself. We've been dating since high school, but we started living together once my daughter Ashley was born.

It's only 9:15 in the morning and I can't believe how drained I am. I can't remember the last time I was up this early. My mind is saying get up and beep Black, but my body is numb all over, I just wanted to lay here with Lia's head on my chest and think about Tip.

After a moment or two, Lia asked what I was thinking about. I lied and told her nothing. I was thinking about the time me, Black and Tip were at the Tyson vs. Berbic fight, and a girl out of nowhere started screaming at the top of her lungs. Being from New York, I started to look all around like someone had a gun, but no one did. Me, Tip and Black, just looked at each other with a dumb look on our faces.

We were looking at her screaming while tears were running down her face. We were about to walk off when she grabbed hold of Tip's leg. Tip was about to kick her in the face until I told him to chill.

I asked her what was wrong. She stuttered for a moment, but when she got it out she said that she loves Tupac and she was his number one fan. When she got up and asked Tip for his autograph, it dawned on us. I felt a sharp elbow to my side. Needless to say, that wasn't the first time that someone said he looked like Tupac, but it was the first time someone was totally convinced. It didn't hurt that it was a red bone dime piece from

Rio. We didn't see Tip for a whole day. When we did see him, he was all smiles.

"I tried to tell her I wasn't Tupac but she didn't believe me. That's how us fifteen percent guys do," he said with an amused smirk on his face. We just cracked up laughing at his crazy ass, and continued with our day.

I really hated that I showed him that article in Maxim where it said fifteen percent of men are nine inches and better. Nevertheless, we laughed our asses off all the way to the airport. That's how I want to remember my man, smashing hoes and making us laugh.

The ringing of the phone made me jump. My nerves are really on edge right now. Lia asked me if I was alright once again. I didn't answer but nodded "yes". She tried to get up to answer the phone, but I wouldn't let her. I held her tighter than I think I ever did before. She didn't make any effort to get up again, she just laid her head back on my chest and rubbed my stomach.

She had her special way of relaxing me. Even though my mind was on Tip and the problems ahead of me, Lia was making my dick hard as hell. I don't think she was doing it on purpose, but the combination of her Victoria's Secret body splash and her soft little hands had me ready to go.

Just as I began to slide her hand down to feel what she created, my beeper went off. This time Lia jumped, which made her grip tighten up. The vibration was very loud because the beeper was on the nightstand.

By the time it finished vibrating, it had almost fell off the nightstand. I slid from under Lia and looked to see who was calling me at 9:30 in the morning. It read, "tone only". I hate when that happens because it always leaves me wondering.

I was about to put it down when another beep came through. I was hoping it wasn't that tone only shit again. When I pressed it, it was a strange number, but the code was oh, so familiar. Black has been using the same code for years. 381 was his favorite number. He played it everyday and also had it on his plates. I asked him one day why it was his favorite number. He told me that if it wasn't for P.S.381 that he wouldn't have met his two, long lost brothers, me and Tip. If I wasn't a hundred percent man, I might have cried. It took me a moment to call Black because at this point I couldn't stand anymore bad news. I knew that this was going to be a very long and trying day.

When I called Black back, he paused before he asked if I were screening my calls. He sounded okay, like last night never happened. Maybe I'm the one bugging. Maybe I was dreaming about last night, is that possible? I don't think my luck could be that good.

"Are you there?" Black asked me, bringing me back to the present.

"Yeah, Black, I'm here. What's really good?"

He told me how crazy shit was right now. He didn't want to get in depth over the phone, so we agreed to meet at Copeland's at one o'clock. He told me to stay up and then I heard a dial tone. That was perfect timing because I had to take Ashley and Lia across the bridge to my mother's house at twelve. Ashley's first birthday is in three days and her grandma wants to spoil her to death.

I can't believe that my little momma is one year old already. It seems like a few months ago when she was covered in blood and I was cutting the umbilical cord. I was so scared because the last thing I wanted since the day I knew Lia was pregnant was to hurt my child. I don't think I'd ever been more scared than the first time I held her. Once I overcame that fear, the only thing that scares me now is not holding her.

My mom didn't like that when Ashley was born, Lia and me moved to Hackensack, New Jersey. It's only about twenty minutes away from her. When I moved, I tried to get her to come, but she refused. She started talking crazy about how she's going to stay right there. She was one of those old ladies who were a Harlemite. She was born there and had no intentions of leaving.

She'd seen Harlem at its best, when guys like Nicky Barnes could've ran for mayor. When there was an after-hours spot on every other corner, and they partied at the Cotton Club seven days a week without fail. I told her that was thirty or forty years ago and it's never coming back. Harlem is a different place now. A place that only the strong can survive.

I cannot, or will not, complain about my childhood, because with two jobs and a dead papa, my mom showed me what the word strong meant. I just can't see something as sweet and innocent as Ashley being spoiled by something as rotten as Harlem. Although I'm not feeling my mom for not moving with us, I understand and love her that much more.

Me and Lia snuggled back and talked about Ashley's first birthday. We were wondering if that big rat at Chucky Cheese was going to scare her. We also talked about adding a little boy to our clan. If we did, I would name him Terrence after Tip, but I didn't tell her that. I thought she was going to bring up the marriage subject, but she didn't. I dozed off with Tip and Black on my mind.

With two or three magical touches I was up, but almost two hours had passed. Damn! It was eleven fifteen and I still hadn't showered yet. I jumped up and ran around the house like a chicken with no head.

As I clutched my daughter close and we sped out the door, I was praying that there wasn't any traffic on Route 4. To my surprise, we made it across the bridge in record time. I'm not sure if it was my new 7501-L or my skills. Nevertheless, we made it to my mom's block shortly after twelve.

While I was un-strapping Ashley from her car seat, Black was blowing my beeper up. I knew it was important because he put a few 911's behind his cell number. As I stood up with Ashley in my hands, a chill ran down my back. You can call it a hustler's spider sense, so I looked over the block very carefully. Although I didn't see anything, I knew something wasn't right.

As I rode the elevator to my mom's floor, the butterflies were still floating in my stomach. The doors opened on the fifth floor. As we started to walk out we noticed that it was the wrong floor. We stepped back in with a grin. When we got to the sixth floor, the first thing I noticed was that my mom's newspaper was still in front of her door.

I bent over to pick it up, which wasn't an easy task with Ashley's fat butt in my arms. As I went to place my keys in the door, the door swung open violently and my mom dove into my arms. She was thanking God and Jesus at the same time.

I didn't understand what was going on. She was kissing me repeatedly with our cheeks clinched closely together. It wasn't until she switched cheeks when I tasted the salty tears on my lips. That's when my heart started racing and the room started to spin.

I tried my best to pry her arms from around my neck, but she had the "kung-fu grip" on me. Finally, after a few moments went by, I understood what she was saying. She was thanking God that I wasn't dead, thanking God for bringing her boy back home safe. I asked her to calm down and stop crying. She said she couldn't because she's too happy. Finally, she got herself together, but she was still shaking like a leaf.

Once I sat her down in her favorite chair, I told Lia to get her a cold rag and a drink of water. She picked up Ashley and said she didn't know where to start. I told her to take her time and start from the beginning.

She took a sip of the water and then took a deep breath. Lia reclined her chair and gently laid the damp rag on her forehead. I could tell by the way her eyes batted that it felt good to her. She said that Detective Sullivan just left here and told her that Tip and four others were murdered in Brooklyn last night. My eyes immediately went to the floor.

Lia, who was right next to me, fell to the couch with tears running down her face. My mother told me to look at her, and I did. She asked if I knew about Tip, God rest his soul, I haven't lied to my mother since I forged her name on my report card in the fifth grade.

"Yes. I was with him." I lifted my head up, looked her in the face. I could see the disappointment in her face. Although she knew the life I lead, she didn't think it would lead to this.

"Sweetheart, that motherfucker Sullivan was talking a whole lot of shit. He said that he's been on you and Raymond's heels ever since Mr. Smith got beat up in his liquor store," she said, her concern quickly turning to anger.

Usually I laughed when she called Black Raymond, but this wasn't the right time. Sullivan told my mom that if it was the last thing that he did, he'd see to it that we fry for those bodies. I tried to console my mom saying that everything was going to be alright.

I kissed and hugged three generations of Thompson ladies that I would be lost without either of them. I took out a stack of money and gave it to them. As I turned and grabbed the

doorknob, I felt three pairs of worried eyes burning in my back. I closed the door behind me and my hands were shaking too uncontrollably for me to lock the door. When I finally got in the elevator, I took a really deep breath. Some say it's a sigh of relief, but I don't feel like there will be any relief in my life for some time to come.

As I hit my mom's stoop, I looked around for Sullivan and his crooked ass task force. Although I didn't see them, I smelled them in the air. I put the key in the car door, opened it up and the blare from my air horn alarm made me jump back. At the same time, my pager started to beep out loud. I don't know how it got off vibrate, but I hated that.

I finally got my alarm to cut off and beeper to shut up. I heard Lia yelling from the sixth floor that she loved me, so I waved and pulled off. Black was blowing me up like crazy, so I picked up my cell phone and hit him back. Needless to say, he was pissed.

"This is not the time to take your time calling me back," Black barked into the phone angrily.

I told him it was unavoidable, I couldn't really talk in front of my mom's and Lia. He asked me if I'd seen the noon news. Tip and the rest of those suckers' faces were on there. They were saying it was a drug deal gone bad because they found fifty pounds of pure cocaine, street valued at seven million dollars. All I did while he was talking was shake my head like he could see me.

"When it rains, it pours," I said cutting him off.

"What else is new?" Black responded nonchalantly, and then the phone got quiet because we were both in deep thought.

"Sullivan and his goons were at mom's house this morning, and Sully said that he's going to tie us in and make sure we fry for those murders they talked about on the news." I knew those BK cats was going to try to come across the bridge but that was the least of my worries. My main concern was Sullivan trying to play super cop.

"Yo! You know this fake motherfucker is still heated about Mr. Smith's liquor store getting robbed," I said trying to make light of the situation. Black just chuckled in disbelief.

"Where you at?" he asked as I listened to him fiddle with the dial on his radio stations.

"I just made the left at Willies on my way up the hill to Amsterdam."

"I just pulled out of Espanard Gardens, so wait for me on the corner of St. Nick," Black said.

"Alright."

I hung up, and pulled over on the corner, reclined my seat once I was parked. They were letting a hot beat ride on Hot 97, so I decided to spit a few bars. Then I slipped into a freestyle about Tip. Before I got too sad, Black pulled up behind me and hit the horn and we both pulled off. Outside of Copeland's, the parking was crazy. The best we could do was double park. Once we were seated we ordered right away, even though I wasn't that hungry.

"I didn't sleep all night because I kept dreaming about Tip. What's up with you?" Black asked as he browsed the menu trying to decide what he wanted to eat. I told him it was a rough night for me also, but I didn't tell him I had bad dreams of my own. I didn't want to sound phony with that "me too" shit.

I asked him what our next move was. For the first time in all the years I've known Black, he didn't have an answer. To be honest, that scared the shit out of me. When I was younger and I had a problem, I would just get into bed with my mom and it would all go away. This is one time where I don't think if mom kissed the boo-boo it will disappear.

"You remember where Tip's aunt lives?" Black asked breaking my trance.

I couldn't recall. She is Tip's only living relative. Although he gave her money on the regular, you could tell he didn't care for her. I think he was just civil to her because it was his mom's sister. She didn't come to his parent's funeral when they died in that car accident.

"What about that fake bitch Michelle, his baby's moms?" I asked trying to think of someone we could contact for him.

"She didn't leave a change of address when she took off to Atlanta with that basketball dude. She stayed in touch with him, but after Tip shot her brother in the ass cheeks for yelling at Jamal it was over between them. Right now, we're Tip's only family and we gotta handle everything."

"Once that's done, I think we should put the operation back in affect mode," he said.

It was easy for him to say because he didn't have a child or a steady girl friend, and his mother moved once he graduated from high school. So there was nothing for him to protect in New York. Now, me on the other hand, everything I loved and wanted to protect was in New York. I couldn't get my mother to move to Jersey, let alone out of town.

"As of now, our finances are on zero, but there is nobody that can put us at the scene." Black said in an effort to formulate a plan.

"Speak for yourself. I was talking to Grandma Moses for a few minutes. She seen my face as clear as day," I said, and busted out laughing.

"You might be right," Black said, "but she didn't live in the building."

"So what? I'm not taking any chance!" I exclaimed.

"For the sake of argument, if we did leave town, what are we gonna use to start over? Are you forgetting that we lost all of our dough last night?" Black asked.

I was about to reply but the waitress walked over. My big head was racing a mile a minute but my little head zeroed in on those hips. I knew this wasn't the time but I was a sucker for a pair of Edwin jeans. We placed our order and watch her walk away in amazement. Reality set back in and Tip's face was hovering over my head.

I can see it in Black's face that he wasn't feeling the idea at all. I was all out of sad looks as he was out of sighs. Lucky for the both of us, shorty with the fat ass was bringing the food back. She came over with my grilled salmon and Black's smoked turkey wings. Suddenly, my appetite was alive and kicking.

"With Sullivan trying to shove five bodies down our throats, we're just sitting around waiting to go to jail," I said trying to reason with him.

Black said nothing before digging into his food.

"You have a point, because this clown is still upset about a robbery that happened ten years ago. Nevertheless, I can't leave New York," Black replied after a few second of silence

I tried to make Black understand, but he wouldn't.

"Black, I love you like a brother, but I have to roll out for Ashley's sake. It might be the biggest mistake you'll make in your life by staying. My money is light as a motherfucker, and I decided not to mess with the street anymore."

"What you mean?" Black asked, his eyes getting wide.

"I mean as of today, I'm out of the crack game. The game killed my brother and I can't let it get me. I have a daughter who needs her daddy and I can't let the streets make her an orphan."

That hit home with Black, I could tell by the way his eyes sunk. Black told me he can't leave the game. He sounded confused, but sincere. "Hustling is all I know," he said.

We got up from the table and I left the waitress a nice tip. Something I couldn't afford at this point. Once we got outside, we smacked hands and I gave Black a hug before I hopped in my whip and drove off.

CHAPTER 3: Detective Sullivan

"This is the 24th Precinct, how may I place your call?" the soft voice stated while popping her gum and flipping through a Vicky catalog.

"Hi, good afternoon. This is Detective Bryant from the Brooklyn 17th," he replied in his best Billy Dee voice.

"Good afternoon, Detective. How may I help you?" she replied, his voice making her stop slouching and take notice.

"I'm trying to get in touch with Detective Sullivan from Robbery." Detective Bryant stated, hoping he didn't have to jump through any hoops once he was connected.

"If you can hold for a moment, I'll connect you right to his desk. Before I connect you, do you mind if I ask you a personal question, Detective Bryant?"

"No, I don't mind. Shoot."

"Are you the same Detective Bryant that caught that monster that killed that twelve year old girl last year?"

"Yes, one in the same. How did you know?" Detective Bryant replied by saying in a modest voice.

"The trial was on Court T.V everyday for a month. I missed my stories because of you. I'm glad you caught the bastard. Oops! Excuse my language. I meant to say that you did a great job. Keep up the good work. Sorry, Detective, I didn't mean to hold you up," the desk sergeant replied in an apologetic voice.

"Don't worry, it wasn't a hold up at all."

"Please hold Detective." Two rings later Robbery Detective Sullivan answered.

"Is this the same Detective Sullivan I beat five times in the obstacles at the Academy?" Detective Bryant said while laughing between words.

I responded by saying, "Yeah! Yeah! Yeah! Is this the same Detective Bryant that couldn't get any pussy until he started working vice?"

Bryant didn't have much to say after I said that. He wanted to know if I had anything on the stiff that was left in his backyard. I told him that I knew everything there was to know about his stiff. I could tell that he was excited.

"Oh really?"

"That guy's name is Terrence Jamal Jenkins, a/k/a Tip, a/k/a Bad News. He's twenty-four, no known relatives. He hangs around 139th with two other pieces of shit. His rap sheet is a mile long, but never did any time. The little bastard has more attempted murders than you and I put together. So, why hasn't he done any time is probably gonna be your next question."

"That had crossed my mind," Detective Bryant said sarcastically.

"Well, we can't seem to get a soul to show up at the trials, or if they do show, they can't seem to remember a damn thing." By this time, I was pissed, just telling the story.

I wanted to tell him how slick they were when they were barely teenagers. I didn't want to get into it because it always makes my ulcer hurt. If Mr. Smith didn't bitch up because he had the hot's for the boy's mother, four people wouldn't be dead in Brooklyn. I must've been thinking out loud because Bryant asked me to repeat myself.

"What did you say?" he asked while taking notes on what I knew.

"Uhhh…nothing," I said clearing my throat. "What about the money and drugs they found at the murder scene?"

"Two hundred and fifty grand is a lot of money, but anything is possible."

"Those little bastards have been selling drugs since they were in high school."

"It looks like they graduated," Detective Bryant said nonchalantly while clicking his pen wildly.

"I bet my pension that whatever happened that night in Brooklyn that these two crimmies were on the scene. I know for a fact that they don't shit without each other."

"Do you know anything a little more concrete?" Bryant asked, ready to get at them at that very moment.

"When I get something, you'll be the first to know."

Just like all cocky detectives, Bryant reminded me that it was his case and he didn't want anyone to blow it. There are a lot of eyes on this one. I made it clear to him that I don't blow cases I break them, but I would stay out of it just the same.

Once I hung up, I put up my middle finger at the phone and said, "Fuck you!" out loud. That's why I didn't tell him that I paid a visit to Born's mother's house. Some cops might think I jumped the gun on that one, but I call it a pressure tactic.

See, when you let a fucking nigger know that you're on to him, he begins to panic and make all the wrong moves. When a motherfucker starts thinking about being "Bubba's bitch" for the next twenty years, believe me, he starts to fuck up. I think I'm going to pay those two a visit after my two o'clock meeting with Internal Affairs. I'm going to ride through their turf and shake shit up a little bit.

Damn! I need a shot of some good *Irish* whiskey right now. Look at the time. I've been in there with those stuffed shirts for almost three hours. They're crazy as hell if they think I'm going to wait this late in my career to see some shrink. I got more sense than both of them put together.

They think that because of that fancy piece of paper on the wall that they are better than me. His black ass wouldn't last five minutes on the streets of Harlem, let alone seventeen years. And his partner, Opie Tayler, forget it. I wouldn't have let that freckle faced queer back me up while I was turning off a fire hydrant. I didn't make this many years in these streets without being tough. Those sissies call it "excessive force," but sometimes you have to rough up those young punks to find out what you want to know.

Take my badge and gun if I'm doing something wrong by making the streets safe. Let me get out of here before all this pussy rubs off on me. I hope the frank man is outside because I'm hungrier than a slave on a ship.

The ride uptown was hot and muggy. As I cruised up the FDR, I noticed some crack dealers in a brand new Mercedes Benz. It made me sick to my stomach to see all these motherfuckers killing people and at the same time benefiting from it. Here I'm doing all I can do for the city and where does it get me? I'm on a traffic filled highway in an old ass Impala, sweating like a sumo wrestler. On top of that, I have to live in a cheap, roach infested apartment.

Between alimony and child support, I can't afford to live anywhere else. And here you have these scum buckets that probably never gave their kids two nickels to rub together. Where is the irony in that?

I would love to hit my siren and pull them over and kick the shit out of them. I.A.D would love that shit. I could see the report now. *Only forty-five minutes after Detective Sullivan left our office, he beat the shit out of three choirboys who never hurt anyone.* BULLSHIT!

I was happy my exit was coming up. I swear I didn't know how much more of that loud music I could take. As I came off of my exit I couldn't help thinking what if these motherfuckers have skipped town already? I know I would if I had one of the baddest detectives in Harlem on my ass. Then again, they're not me. I would bet my mother-in-law they don't have a smart bone between them.

I decided to get off boring Lennox Ave. and ride up St. Nick for a while. I wonder if the Sugarhill war death toll reached double figures yet. These savages have been killing each other for about six months now. Chief Spangler told homicide to keep a close eye on the situation but until someone innocent gets killed, let them slaughter themselves.

I heard that the whole briefing room stood up and clapped when he said that shit. I've got to admit that they're neither worth the time nor the paperwork. If I didn't think, five generations of Sullivan's would turn over in their graves if I went to jail, or even worse, get a dishonorable discharge, I would become a modern day Charles Bronson. Thinking of those scum buckets getting picked off one by one made a slight smirk come to my face. Seconds later, that same smirk disappeared quickly because of the thought of Attica. Shit! Up there, a snitch or a child molester gets treated better than a cop.

It was still muggy but the scenery was nice as hell. These young girls really know how to strut their stuff. They're famous for walking up and down the same block a million times with hardly anything on. The ones that do decide to put something on, it's so tight, I wonder if they can breathe. Don't misunderstand me; I live for the Harlem summer.

Every year around this time they have a Harlem celebration and the big booties really come out. I tried to hit on this Puerto Rican girl once. I went to her apartment after her ex-boyfriend decided to rob her and kick her ass. I tried to let her know that the jailbird wasn't worth crying over. At the same time, letting her know she needed a working man like myself. This girl was so pretty that even with the busted lip and runny make-up she was still getting me hard.

It might have been bad timing, but I was really dropping hints. Just when I thought I had her attention, she let me have it. She let me know that before she messes with a pig faced white boy, that she would start eating pussy. I could've slapped the shit out of her, but I kept my cool. As a matter of fact, I hope King Kong is over there beatin' her ass right now.

Okay, it's show time. Once I make this right I will be on the Black Top Boys turf. Although they stretch over a four-block radius, building 6407 is the main headquarters.

I circled the block several times to no avail. I didn't want to discourage myself, but it wasn't looking good for the home team. There wasn't a sign of Born or that cock sucker Black either and I was starting to think they did the smart thing and left town.

I parked down the street in hopes to see anything that would lead me to them. After about an hour or so, I was ready to go home. I've been up since five o'clock this morning filling out backed up reports. Something told me to take one more pass before I called it a night.

After I circled the area twice, I'd seen one of my old stool pigeons named "Cat." They call him that because in his day he was the best cat burglar around. After he graduated from free-basing to smoking crack, he let Scotty take his booty. Now the only thing he can steal is Tylenol out of the Rite Aid to get high.

My timing was perfect because he was walking very fast. That meant he was on his way to buy crack or just bought some. When I pulled up beside him I could see he was high and wasn't in the mood to talk. He stuttered as he said my name and gave me a fake smile. I didn't return it, I just told him to get in. He lied and said there were too many people around for him to get in.

"I don't care if the Virgin Mary is watching. You better get in or spend the next three days in detox," I told him while unlocking my door, and not waiting for a response.

"My mother is sick and she's waiting for me to bring her some aspirin." He got in and told me while looking around nervously to see if anyone saw him talking to me.

Like I gave a fuck. I just laughed and slapped his leg very hard. I could tell it stung, but it also got me his attention. "I'm not in the mood for games, and I'll run you in for one wrong answer. I'm looking for the Black Top Boys."

"I ain't seen them," he said nervously as he watched me play with my handcuffs. I knew he'd seen the seriousness in my eyes, so he recanted his statement.

"Black is in the lobby of 6407 waiting for Fingers to finish washing his car."

Finally my day was shaping up. I kicked Cat's crackhead ass out of the car and sped around the block to 6407. I didn't want to give myself away by pulling up all fast, so I parked a block away. As I approached the building I saw how everyone's eyes got big when they saw me. It looked as if they wanted to scream, but sound wouldn't come out of their mouths.

I pulled my badge and let it hang from my chain before I entered the building. Like all good crack spots, the lobby door was busted. As I pushed it open slowly, the door squeaked like a Stephen King movie.

Once I was across the threshold, I felt the urge to grab for my gun. It was a chrome snub nosed 38. It was only one of a handful in the U.S.A. It belonged to my Uncle Patty, who was killed in the line of duty in the Bronx. I feel like Uncle Patty is watching over me as long as I have his gun.

As I walked further into the building, I didn't see a soul. My instinct said Cat lied to me. When I see that motherfucker I'm going to break him in half. As my blood started to boil I crept to the back of the building and halfway up to the first landing. I saw Black sitting on the steps. He had his elbows on his knees and his face in his hands. I couldn't tell if he was crying or not, but I didn't care. I slowly lifted Uncle Patty and aimed it at the top of his head.

Once I was comfortable in my stance, I cleared my throat and said, "You look like you lost your best friend." I thought that was pretty clever for a white boy. Instead of him lifting his head up he spoke right through his hands.

"What in the fuck do you want Sullivan, or should I call your funny ass 'Bob Hope?'"

I didn't find that funny, but I was kind of shocked that he knew who in the hell I was. "That was pretty cute. Now, how did you know it was me?"

He tapped his jacket lightly and said, "White people never heard of a cell phone?" Then he looked up with his eyes blood shot, and said, "Do you think you could sneak your white ass down my block without somebody letting me know? On top of that, I'm Muslim. I can smell a pig from a mile away."

"You called me Bob Hope, but you're turning into a regular Richard Pryor. Now, Mr. Pryor, can you get the fuck up before I blow your head off and plant a rusty 22. on you?" With that statement I think I got his attention. He slowly got up with a lot of hatred in his eyes. Once he stood up and walked down the stairs. I slammed him into the wall and searched him from head to toe

Unfortunately, he didn't have anything on him but a little weed. At this point I would've loved to run him in for a switchblade or something.

"Even if your Hunt's Point hanging mother calls you, do not take your hand off that wall." Once I had said that, I guess he knew I was trying to trick him into getting his ass beat. He didn't bite. I asked him a few questions, which he played dumb like he didn't know anything. I could've asked him his name right then, and he would've said he didn't know.

"What do you want from me? I got things to do," he finally asked me.

"You have all day to sell crack, but Tip's brainless ass won't be with you." No sooner had I finished the sentence this young punk swung around and tried to take my head off. I guess I tricked him into that ass kicking after all. I ducked the wild haymaker and slammed Uncle Patty upside his temple. When his head bowed, I hit him again on the back of his neck with the gun. He went to one knee, but I could see he was out on his feet.

I didn't let that stop me. I yanked him to his feet and gave him a few knee lifts to his mid-section. I was really fired up at this point. I've been waiting for this day a long time. I went to give him another Rocky gut punch when I saw blood spilling out of his mouth. So, instead of hitting him again, I slammed him back on the wall.

I explained to him that I knew he was on the scene in Brooklyn when those guys were murdered. Of course, he said he didn't know what I was talking about. I let him know that he can play stupid all he wanted, but it was going to catch up with him.

He told me that he hoped a sniper catches up to me. That little smart-ass nigger had me looking like a smacked red ass. I drew my hand back to break that smart-ass jaw of his, but he covered it up. So, instead I kicked him in his nuts with my cowboy boots. If it didn't make him sterile, it shut his ass up.

"Now listen to me Tough Guy. I got all the pieces to that night's puzzle and, although I don't know where you fit, I'm going to make sure you and that bitch Born will fit somewhere. If I have to frame you my damn self, you're going to fit. So, watch your back, watch your front and still none of it will do you any good. This is big news right now, and one of your brothers, Mayor Dinkins, wants it solved. Me being the good detective that I am, I should get a few points for bringing your head on a silver platter. Once I charge you for murder, you will tell on every crack dealer in town. You could just save yourself and put the puzzle together for me."

Instead of answering me, he spat blood on my boots. I started to give him one more kick for the road, but figure I got my point across. I went into my pocket, took out my business card and dropped it on the floor. I told him, "Go clean yourself up because you're starting to look like one of your customers." I laughed and walked out of the building. When I looked back, I noticed that the card was no longer on the floor.

As the fresh air hit me I looked up and saw about twenty-five or thirty black guys blocking the courtyard entrance. Some of the faces I recognized from working this neighborhood for so many years. Maybe a scar or two, or a few missing teeth. Maybe even a gold tooth. There were a lot more beards and mustaches, even a foot or two difference.

Nevertheless, these were the same hoodlums stealing fruits from the Associated Super Market and robbing each other for those funny looking gold glasses. Their faces have hardened over the last decade or so. Although I'm twice their age, I know their capabilities. On that note, I removed Uncle Patty from my holster and pointed it straight at the crowd. For a moment I thought I was Moses himself the way the crowd parted in half. As I walked with caution I heard people calling me white boy, cracker, Opie Tayler looking motherfucker, pig, and honkey. I've heard all that and more since I started working at the 24th.

As soon as I made it past the mob, they all rushed into the building. I guess they thought I killed that piece of shit. As I approached my car, to my surprise, all four of my tires were flat, all of my change was gone out of my ashtray, and somebody pissed on my front seat. All I could do was laugh and call for a tow truck.

CHAPTER 4: Black

As I went to sit up I remembered why I laid down in the first place. Every bone in my body was screaming with pain. I should've gone over to Harlem Hospital last night, but I didn't feel like waiting in the emergency room for ten hours. On top of that, the Hospital of Death has had more than its share of accidents, if you can feel me. My grandfather went there for a bullet wound in his leg and never came out. They hit the family with a bunch of bullshit, but it never brought him back.

I eased myself back down to my soft mattress, a place that I might stay all day. I knew I had to hip Born to what went down. I also knew that this would be the straw that broke the camel's back. Once he heard that Sullie was on the warpath, he would lose his mind. He already thinks that leaving is the best thing for us right now. After that ass kicking yesterday, I might have to agree, but I can't leave the Mecca. I would be lost without the bright lights, big buildings, and crowded streets. Even the sweet sounds of fire trucks and police sirens are enough to put a man to sleep.

Once I started breathing hard, I heard a loud knock on the door. I was reluctant to answer because I was in so much pain, but it could've been Born. So, once I made it over to the door, I asked who it was because for some strange reason my peephole was missing.

The voice on the other side of the door answered with a faint "It's me." Being that's what Born says all the time, I unlocked the door. As I turned the second lock I saw the door fly towards me. It all happened so fast I couldn't get out of the way of it.

The door hit me right in my face and all I saw were stars when I flew back. As I laid on the floor holding my face, I looked up and saw Sullivan standing in my doorway. I was unsure of what to do because he already had his gun drawn. He walked in with all black on and an insane look on his face. I knew he came to finish the job. So I slowly made it to my feet, at the same time trying not to anger the pain that had control of my body.

I finally broke the silence with a simple question, "What do you want, Sullie?"

He replied in a deranged voice, "Some answers or your life."

I don't know if he'd seen it, but I took a very nervous swallow. I tried to explain to him that me and Born were at the movies the night Tip got murdered. I could see by the look on his face he wasn't buying it. I was running out of lies and options at the same time.

He started to talk, but for some strange reason, I couldn't understand what he was saying. He was sounding like Charlie Brown's teacher, which scared me more. The sweat started popping up on his forehead as I watched him fidget with that 44. Magnum. By the time I figured out what he was doing, it was too late. He took all the bullets out of the gun except one.

I was thinking that this was my chance to rush him, but I could see clear as day the one bullet going through my chest plate. His eyes were cutting right through me. This felt like something out of the Twilight Zone. His eyes were black with no pupil, and he still sounded like a cyborg. I didn't know if I was just scared to death or I was losing my mind. It felt like a combination of both.

Before I knew it, I was looking down the barrel of his gun, so I dropped to my knees and pleaded for my life. It seemed like with every word I said he took one step closer until the barrel was right between my eyes. After I felt that cold gun I became speechless. At first, I thought he was jut trying to scare me, but this motherfucker must be drunk or something. I decided to close my eyes and say my prayers.

Right before I could give all the praises due, I heard a "CLICK," which made my neck jerk back. I couldn't believe this nut was playing Russian roulette with me.

Finally, I heard him say, "Do you want to tell me about the murders?" Although I was two seconds from shitting on myself, I still didn't tell him anything. He clicked the gun again and this time I almost fainted. I knew that I had to make a move real fast. There are only three chambers left and one of them will spell my death.

Without thinking, I hit him in his dick with all of my might. He dropped to his knees, but didn't drop the gun. So, the next thing I saw was that barrel point straight at my chest. I grabbed the hand that clutched the gun and tried to point it away from me.

As soon as I pointed it away from me, he pulled the trigger again to no avail. As we wrestled back and forth on the floor, all I could think of was dying, which was good because I held on with dear life. He punched me right in my face, but I still didn't let that gun go. That kung fu grip was the only thing separating me from life and death. The struggle lasted another second before the gun went off. I felt warmth from the barrel and thought that would be the last thing I felt.

I looked into Sullie's eyes and saw them begin to roll into the back of his head. I wonder if it could be that he was the one to get shot? I stood up and looked down at Sullie and the hole in his stomach.

The phone ringing made me jump up out of my sleep. I reached for the phone I didn't know what scared me more, the crazy ass dream or the phone.

CHAPTER 5: Born

When I picked up the phone, all I heard was Black on the other end, babbling about something. I told him "Calm down, I can't hear a word you're saying." Once he calmed himself down he was telling me about what happened between him and Sullie. My jaw dropped to the ground. He told me every detail about the episode between the two in the building. I couldn't believe Sullie said all of that bullshit.

I take that back, I can believe he said all of that. That just makes leaving New York that much easier.

"Have you thought about leaving town any more?" I asked him hoping he had. I didn't want to leave my best friend here, but what choice did I have?

He remained silent for a second then he got hyped about a dream he had. He told me how Sullie busted in his house and tried to kill him, but instead he shot Sullie in the stomach. I told him "That was one hell of a dream. Don't forget what they say about dreams, they are part of the truth. Yo Black, I still think skipping town is in our best interest. I don't want to bring our dirt to my mother's house and I would never forgive myself if anything happened to Lia and Ashley. I have a Aunt down south that will take us all in until we get straight," I said in a pleading tone.

Black let me know how he's bigger than any hick ass town. Black said, "If I had to get a job at the Gaucho gym passing out basketballs, I'm not leaving New York."

I told him he was the same old Black and would never change, and that's why I loved him. I told him I would hit him later because I had to get a present for Ashley's birthday. Before I hung up I asked him about the funeral arrangements. He told me that April had taken care of everything. The wake would be at Johnson and Son on Friday.

"What will he be wearing?" I asked already having an idea. Tip stayed flashy, and wore nothing but the best.

"What you think?" he replied, confirming my thoughts.

"Okay. Hit me when you crawl out of bed. Peace," I said, then I hung up.

I knew by his expression that Tip was going to blow up the spot with some mean Hugo Boss shit. Tip was real big on Hugo Boss. He got so many bitches down in Miami, he fell in love with Boss. I must admit he was shining like a diamond.

I knew I had better hurry up down to FA&O Schwartz before they closed. They close those doors at 7:00 pm sharp. I should know, because before Ashley was born I spent fifteen grand just on stuffed animals alone. It was worth every penny because Ashley will kill to go in her room. That was good for me and Lia because once those six weeks were up, I was more than ready. To be honest, we only waited three weeks before we got busy. I felt funny about making love while she was pregnant. I was afraid that I might hurt the baby. Although the doctor said it was okay, I wasn't cool with it.

I need to call my cousin Keith and iron out a few things before we bounced up out of here. I didn't tell him why I needed to come to North Carolina, but I was sure he would get around to asking. I would make up some bullshit story about getting out of the big bad city.

As far as family down south goes, they think I'm working some fake ass nine to five and going to college part time. My mom told my aunt Anne Mae that because they both go back and forth about how great their kids are. Me and my crew call it fronting. I guess it's my fault because if I did something with my life for her to be proud of, she wouldn't have to lie. I just hope that this little move will help my life from getting any worse.

My only problem now is money. Besides from the few stacks I got left, I'm dead broke. I was real leery about putting all my money into that move, but since Black and Tip was a little short, I had to. That was going to be a major score with that drought sweeping through like that. Instead, one third of me died that night.

The biggest plus about moving down to North Carolina is every street corner won't remind me of Tip. It's crazy how things were all good just a week ago. Now, the only thing that hasn't changed is my love for my family. I think the only way for me to get over this hump is by selling my car. It's still in great condition and the miles are still light. I paid a little over 50 grand for it so I should be able to get about forty for it. I don't want to take it to Broadway because all they want to give you is a bunch of beat up coke for it.

I'm going to make a plane reservation for the Saturday morning Red Eye, and I'll go see Tricky Nick the car man on Friday. He supplies all the hustlers in town with major whips. I know he has about forty grand on hand. Once I finish rubbing elbows with the so called rich at FA&O Schwartz, I'll break the news to my mom that I have to leave town for a minute.

CHAPTER 6: Black

Damn, that was one hell of a dream. I woke up with a sweat on my face, throwing punches. When I jumped up I grabbed my stomach. Why? I don't know. Once I stopped breathing, like a bunch of big niggers were chasing me, I just laid in my bed staring up at the ceiling and thinking about the direction my life has turned in.

An hour or two had passed without me blinking and I thought to myself that this house is really starting to depress me more than I already was. I need to get out and get me some fresh air, and on top of that, I could use a bite to eat. I'm going to see Ms. Delores at M&G's to get some of that smothered chicken with macaroni and cheese. If that don't make me feel better, next stop is going to be Bellevue.

Once I breezed through the Throggs Neck traffic I pulled up in front of M&G's. As usual, I couldn't find a parking spot in front. I didn't want to double park because the last thing I need right now is a fifty dollar parking ticket. Right now fifty dollars will feel like five thousand if I had to take it out of the stash.

A nigger like me is broke for real. Sometimes you hear a street nigga say he's broke and he still has like ten or fifteen thousand stashed somewhere. In my case, I'm broke and this thirty-seven hundred I got isn't going to magically flip itself into some real doe. It will crush me to sell my Cuban with the Jesus piece. It wouldn't make too much sense to be walking around with eighty-five hundred on my neck and don't have gas money in my pocket.

I don't want to go back to putting that pistol in niggas faces. That was cool back in the days, but running around with a price on your head can get dangerous. I had to laugh at the thought of me working side by side with my grease monkey Uncle Lloyd. I've taken minor set backs before, but sixty-nine thousand dollars isn't minor. Born's riding around like he's Shaft or something because I know he has a hundred thousand or two tucked away.

He used to preach to me and Tip daily about fucking up our doe. I didn't want to hear that BS because the spot was still pumping. I never thought this day would come. I would borrow a few stacks from Born, but I don't feel like hearing the "I told you so" speech.

I didn't know my next move, but the rent and insurance isn't gonna stop adding up just because I'm fucked up. Damn! I hate parking across the street next to the fire station. I always imagine one of these drunken firefighters smacking my whip.

I'm only going in for a quick minute though, so it should be cool.

It's a luxury being able to call Ms. Dee on the phone and give her my order. Especially when I walk in and ten seconds later she's bringing my food over to me. I can see the kids from Drew Player hating from the sidelines, but I love it.

Soon as I walked in, I sat at my favorite table next to the window. I waved at Ms. Dee and she waved back with a big smile. Like always, Tyreek and his Drew Crew were in the back looking extra dusty. I wonder if I looked that dirty when I was street grinding?

Like clockwork, Mama Dee brought my food over to me and planted a wet kiss on my cheek. She told me how sorry she was about Tip, but glad that her son in law and I were alright. She called Born that because her twelve year old granddaughter loves him to death.

I guess Tyreek and friends were getting a little restless because they shouted out "Can we get some service, too?"

Mama Dee shouted back, "If you pay like your fat ass's weighs, you could get all the service you want."

The crowd of eleven people all busted out laughing. She had taken the words right out of my mouth, but I wasn't laughing because I didn't like that bitch talking to Mrs. Dee with no respect. Nevertheless, Mrs. Dee is an old gangster and handled herself just fine. I could see that fat boy didn't like being laughed at. If he wasn't so black, he might have turned red from embarrassment.

I got up from the table and gently placed a napkin over my plate. I walked by Tyreek and went to the bathroom to wash my hands. When I got in there, all they had was that stinky green soap. I hate using that and then eating. Instead, I just used water.

When I looked up to dry my hands, the first thing I saw was my reflection in the mirror.

It caught me by surprise because I didn't have my same look. It looked like I'd aged five years in a three day span. I had bags under my eyes and I could see my facial skeleton clear as day. I've never worried about this many things so hard in all my life. As a matter of fact, I've never worried this much in my life. It's crazy how it was all good just a week ago.

When I walked out I noticed that Tyreek and company were gone. They must have gotten tired of waiting. I also noticed a lone body standing at the counter with an Underworld Records jacket on. That's the biggest label on the west coast. As I started to walk to my table, the guy turned and looked at me. When we made eye contact, all I could see were those two big rocks in his ears. Those things were really saying something.

I broke the stare and continued to walk to my table. I noticed that the napkin wasn't like I'd left it. It made me wonder if those kids tried to hit me with some bullshit. When I looked up to tell Ms. Dee to give me another plate I noticed this fake Russell Simmons walking my way. Although he looked slightly familiar, I wasn't in the mood to talk.

Kurtis Blow walked over to me and put his hand out, but I didn't return the gesture. I gave him one of those looks that let him know that I was a real gangster and not one of those studio gangsters that he was used to. His hand quickly faded out of sight. With a stern look on my face I asked, "Do I know you?"

"That depends" he replied in a real proper voice.

"Depends on what?"

"If your name is Binky or not" he said. I just stood there with a puzzled look on my face. No one has called me that since my grandmother died. I made everyone stop calling me that because it killed me when I thought of her.

I was angry because I still didn't know him. I told him, "You better have a real good excuse for calling me that."

"I'm Daryl, I used to live right next door to you," he said. Then he went on to explain how we used to be friends. Once he said that, it all came rushing back to me. We weren't really friends. I used to bully him all the time. Not to mention, he didn't have those thick glasses on either. He was a good kid, but boy, was he green as a pool table top.

He told me how his pop joined the service and they moved out to California. To make a long story short, him and his UCLA degree were here to start up Underworld East Records. They were hot out there, but I know New York doesn't want to hear none of the Jherri Curl shit. They don't even button their shirts all the way down.

I told him point blank, "That's not going to fly out here."

He said, "I'm not trying to bring Cali to New York or New York to Cali. I just want them to know that they're brothers in this game, not enemies."

"That Martin Luther King stuff sounds good, but I can't see it," I said while shaking my head.

He gave me his card and told me, "You're the first person I've seen from back in the day. I want you along for the ride."

I wasn't trying to hear that Hollywood game, so I just took the card and told him I would call. Mama Dee interrupted with another hot steaming plate of smothered chicken with macaroni and cheese. I offered Daryl some, but he said he was waiting for his order. I asked him about some of those model chicks in the videos and inquired if they were coming to the Big Apple, too.

"They are one phone call away," he replied.

"How about that fine ass red bone that was in the Casanova video?"

He blasted her and called her every name in the book. I told him, "I like them like that."

"You can have her if you can stop her from charging me child support," he said to me with a smirk on his face.

We laughed our asses off for about four minutes. He was hitting me in the head with all this Cali shit like I never left New York. I dropped a few names and places so he could know I was official. I told him about the fights in Vegas and the whole nine.

"I was there one year when some guy was faking like he was TuPac," he said cracking a smile. He then went on about how the girl blew their phones up for four months straight. I never laughed so hard in all my life. He must have thought I was crazy, but it was an inside joke. One that I will take to my grave.

Finally, his food came and Mama Dee presented his fried pork chops to him. That took the smile right off my face. I asked about the swine, but he just shrugged his shoulders and headed for the door. Right when he had one foot inside and one outside the store, he said, "Call me."

"Alright."

When I looked down at my food I saw that it was cool again, but I didn't let that stop me. I tore into that like it was my last meal on death row. Once I knocked that off, I let out a mean burp and slid away from the table. I paid for both of the plates and left Ms. Dee her usual $10 tip. I wanted to break it down to $5, but after Ms. Dee made her pay like you weigh speech, I couldn't. I bounced up out of there feeling like a stuffed cow.

As soon as the light turned green I got to the middle of the intersection I saw Tryeek and Co. standing across the street. I tapped my pocket to make sure my little friend was there, and then I continued to walk towards them. The eye contact was crazy, but I didn't break mine.

When I was passing, I heard one of the cowards call me a bitch under his breath. I was tempted to turn and say something, but I didn't. I thought to myself that it's nine of them and one of me, and they're the ones who're mumbling. If I let them trick me into harming one hair on their heads, I would be brainless.

CHAPTER 7: Born

"DAMN! This *Bad Boy* beat is off the hook."

I love to rap to this shit. One time I free-styled over this same beat for about an hour straight. Its funny how rapping just takes the weight of the world off my chest so I can breathe again. I think it's because I put all my pain into my lyrics.

I remember when I was small how many raps I made up about my dad. As a matter of fact, my first rap was about my dad. I've got to give him credit for at least that. Even though my mom did a great job, part of me wished pops was around.

That's enough of that mushy stuff. I still got a bunch of shit to do today. I really need to call the florist to double check the order for Tip's funeral. Although we're keeping it real small and low, we want it to be perfect. The time and place are only for those who need to know. We thought that would be safe for everyone there. This would be a bad time for surprises. We don't want no re-enactment of the movie *Colors*. Although there will be plenty of security on hand, I don't want to leave it to chance. Trust me, to a grieving family member, an Uzi can cause a lot of havoc. Havoc is the one thing that we already have enough of.

Speaking of which, this Sullivan thing is really starting to get out of hand. I've never seen him on such a rampage. He's running around like he's homicide for real. If he concentrated on robbery like he does me and Black, the freckled face motherfucker would know who stole my Benzi Box three years ago. But does he? Hell no, but he knows I killed thirty people in Brooklyn.

Give me a damn break. This clown can mess up a wet dream. It's just not going to be my wet dream, though. That's why North Carolina is really looking good right now. Black is acting like I want to live down there forever. I don't want my daughter to grow up a country bumpkin. I'll be back before Ashley turns two. Damn! That's my shit ... I'm really feeling this kid Biggie Smalls.

CHAPTER 8: Born

"Ashley, sweetheart, could you please stop crying for daddy? I know you don't want to get up this early, but we have to go see your Uncle Tip. If you're a good little girl in church, when everything is all over, I'll take you to Mickey D's. I know you love to play with those colorful balls. Who am I kidding? If you can cry all the way through I'm still taking you there."

"Lia, please don't take all day, the limo will be here any minute." She didn't answer me so I asked sarcastically "Did you fall in the toilet?"

"Where is your Uncle Black?" I asked Ashley, not really expecting a response.

The limo picked him up almost an hour ago. I would love to page him, but we decided to leave all of that stuff home. All the people we love are going to be with us and all the rest can wait. "Black has fifteen more minutes and if he is a no show, I'm jumping in the whip and..." At that very moment the limo driver honked his horn out front. It's show time.

"Damn, it's about time! Lia, the limo is out front." She still didn't answer, but five seconds later the bathroom door crept open. I didn't even have to ask, I could see she was crying. This whole thing has been rough on her and my mom. They were both close to Tip.

Instead of asking the obvious, I just told her how nice she looked. That made me see at least two teeth out of thirty-two. When she really smiles, she can light up this whole room. I broke our stare and told her that I was going to call my mother to let her know we're on our way. The limo driver starts beeping the horn again.

This motherfucker is an hour late and he wants to rush me? Ain't that a bitch? "Hey mom, we're on our way out the door, are you ready?"

"I've been ready for two hours" she replied.

"Okay Miss, we're on our way."

Finally Ashley stopped acting cranky so, I picked her up and gave her a strawberry on her neck. That was to ensure her good mood. I noticed Lia out of the corner of my eye with a slight smile. She loves the way my daughter and I get along. I turned and gave Lia a peck on the forehead and asked her, "You ready?" I saw the sorrow in her face when she gave me an innocent nod. I picked up the baby and we all headed for the limo.

CHAPTER 8½: Black

"Hit the horn again, Driver. Oh, never mind, here come the Cosby's now."

I must admit they do look good together. I'm a little envious of how happy they are. Not saying that I'm jealous because jealousy and envy are two different things. All I mean is that all the women I run across ain't shit. Now I just go to places where I know they're not shit.

I mess with all the strippers. It's easy, we fuck for a few months, and then I replace them. I also keep me a flock of chickens that I can call after the Tunnel. All they wanted was a pair of Reebok freestyles and they were happy. If they were happy so was big daddy.

The door flung open and the first thing I saw was my goddaughter's big head. Born was passing her to me so they could get in the limo. Once I had Ashley in my arms, she melted me right into my seat. She was so cute it didn't make sense and she loves her Uncle Black.

Then her twin got in next. She gave me a faint "Hi" and slid over for Born to get in. Before Born had a leg in the car, he was flipping about me being late. I sat there and zoned him out while I talked baby talk to Ashley. She lit up like a light when I started flying over her head like a plane.

Born was still trying to let me have it, but his voice was slowly fading away. I looked slowly over my left shoulder and gave the driver the address. When I turned back, I made sure I made eye contact with Born to signal that I was getting a little attitude.

After a moment of silence and Ashley putting out her arms for her mommy, I asked Born, "Did you get any sleep last night?"

"No" he replied. That would explain his cranky attitude.

I'm glad that broke the ice because it was getting a little stale up in here.

"Is that new?" I asked to break the ice. I had to make a comment on that mean tie he was wearing.

"What was I going to buy it with, my good looks?" he laughed, but I felt his pain. He told me that he was selling his car tomorrow and my jaw dropped. He loved that car. I mean love in a sick sort of way. It's not like it's the first machine he ever had, but for some reason he acted like it was. I never guessed one day it would come to this. I asked why he was selling it and he looked at me in disbelief, like he couldn't believe I asked that question.

He went on to tell me how plane tickets cost money and so do apartments. I refuse to believe that things were that tight for Born. All our lives Born was real good with a dollar. Now me, on the other hand, I know perfectly well why I'm broke. Jewelry hoes and clothes. Not necessarily in that order and I can't live without any of them.

I wanted to ask Born who he was selling his car to. I didn't because I could see the hurt in his face. He didn't even feel Ashley pulling on his suit jacket. Although I don't want him to leave, I don't want to see him like this. I wish I had some money to give him, but I'm probably worse off than him. I can't see me selling my whip.

"Driver, it's the first brick building on the left."

Chapter 9: Born

I just came out of the back of the church talking to Tip. I know he wouldn't want to see me cry, but I've been like a faucet since I got here. I had to check myself one time because after Ashley wiped a tear from my eye she started to cry. Although she doesn't understand what's happened to her uncle, she knows when her daddy is sad.

My mother and Lia were holding up pretty good. That was until Black's mother walked through the door. They cried and hugged the whole time. They were real close before she moved out of town. Like always, she was looking like Black's older sister. She was only 14 years older than Black and hated what he has become. My mom hated my lifestyle also, but she didn't rub my face in it daily. She won't even take a Christmas or birthday card from him, but don't get it fucked up. She would kill half of this church for him.

I wish the service could get under way. I haven't been in a church since Ashley was baptized. Even then, I felt that constant tap on my shoulder. The same tap I've been feeling all day. It's like each individual bone in my body is tingling at once. It's hard for me to explain it. I'll be glad when this day is over and we're out of this place.

Where in the hell did Black slide off to? Damn! Is that little Candy from 19th Street? I remember teasing Tip about hitting her, but now I see why he was on her. Oh, there's Black. His eyes look a little reddish.

Either he slid off to smoke a blunt or he was somewhere crying. Only Black would try to hide his tears at a funeral. I'm not much of a crier. At my grandmother's funeral, I didn't shed a one tear, and me and granny were tight. My mom told me that she hasn't seen me cry since I was eight months old. Lia just put her arm around Black. I think she can tell he was crying. Women can spot sensitivity a mile away.

CHAPTER 9½: Black

I really don't know how me and Lia got so close. I remember back in the day, I couldn't stand her. Back in high school we used to argue like cats and dogs about silly shit. I think because I had a crush on her in grammar school and Born stepped right in and stole her. I never told her or Born, I thought it would be best that way. Nevertheless, I'm glad we're cool now.

When she walked over to Born, I watched her body sway from side to side. I hated myself for that. Whenever I looked at her with lust in my eyes, I felt guilty. Not because Born was my best friend, but because I know if I could I'd fuck her.

My mom snapped me out of my trance by calling my name. I didn't want to answer because she used Raymond. I knew if I didn't she would call it twice as loud. She met me half way and gave me a big hug and a peck on my cheek. She wanted to know how I was holding up. Of course, I put on my macho side and let her know I was fine. She replied by asking me if I was smoking before I got here. I told her, "Hell no!"

"Well, why are your eyes bloodshot red" she asked. All I could do was laugh and hug her. She tiptoed and said in my ear, "A true man is in touch with his sensitive side."

"A true homo is in touch with his sensitive side, but thanks for the hug. I needed that."

She slapped the side of my face softly and said "You're just like ..." then she paused and squeezed my hand with the love of a mother. She turned and took one last look at me before she walked back over to my other mom.

No one in this world knows me like my mother. We'd grown up together like no one could imagine. I knew she missed my pops. There'd been times when I missed him too, but she missed him in a whole different way. Although she denied it, I knew that was her reason for leaving New York. I see everybody making their way inside the church. I guess it's time to send Tip off.

CHAPTER 10: Born

I never was a big fan of funerals. Ever since I can remember, I tried to duck them. I made it clear to my mom that funerals weren't on my things-to-do list. A few times she saw it my way, but sometimes she didn't. Like the time I wanted to stay home when my aunt died. She was my father's sister and I didn't see her much. My mother didn't think it was a good excuse.

At first, she didn't want to force me, I could tell because she was talking to me in her 'social worker' voice. She would say Rico after every sentence. Every time she sounded like that I knew she was trying to trick me into something. Till this day, I'm still leery of that voice. Once she'd seen that all the McDonalds, Pro-Ked's, and movie bribes weren't working, she went back to what she knew best, being a strong black woman.

She put her foot down so hard it should've gone through the floor. I knew at that time the best thing for me was to put on that ugly clip-on bow tie.

The Preacher cleared his throat then tapped the microphone. I could tell by his age that this wasn't going to be a short sermon. You know how those old school preachers are. Once they get on a role, they can go for hours. Not only can they go for hours, they know how to make every eye wet.

Speaking of that, there goes the first to let loose, Lil' Candy. She's not putting on a big show, but she is letting all those who are looking know that she and Tip were more than just friends. That one outburst set off a chain reaction. I just saw the whole church put up a hand to wipe their eyes.

I don't know whether the chain reaction hit Black, but I was one of the people who were wiping tears away. It felt like it was planned, but my mom and Lia grabbed my hand at the same time. I tried real hard to keep my emotions in check, but I was doing a poor job of it. Fifteen minutes into the service my mom and Lia were in full gear. To hear them two cry made my tears fall even faster. Sometimes it was hard to tell, but Tip was really loved by many.

My eyes focused on Black, but I couldn't see his face. He had his head slightly tilted towards his lap. I started to wonder if he was crying or not. I'd only seen him cry one other time. It was the weekend after his mother left town. We were both drunk as hell after about twenty shots between us of Hennessy and Coke.

We were downtown at Tavern on the Green eating and drinking up a storm. I was feeling a little down because my mother turned my offer down to move to Jersey. We left *TOG's* and grabbed a seat on the park bench. Black let me know that I should stop tripping, at least she would only be twenty minutes away.

Then it hit me how much he missed his mom. I really heard the pain in his voice. I looked over to let him know that things were going to be alright. That's when I'd seen the tears running down his face. To this day, he denies it. He told me I was so drunk that I couldn't tell that there were two men kissing two benches down. In Central Park, anything is possible. All I saw was long blond hair and two motherfuckers wrapped like a pretzel.

Now, that's a surprise! Mama Dee just walked in. I don't know who that guy is with her, but he's holding her pretty close. I know after all these years she's not stepping out on Mr. Jenkins. They both went and sat next to Black. Without hesitation Mama Dee put her arm around him and the guy shook his hand. That was strange to me because there aren't too many people that Black knew that I didn't.

I was grateful that Ashley was sleeping. She's just like me. She can get a little cranky before twelve o'clock. Not to mention, with all three of us crying, I know she would join right in. She's a real sensitive kid that can feel emotions.

It's almost time for the Preacher to have us come on up and take a last look. I've never had a friend die on me before. Let me rephrase that… I've never had a friend this close die on me before. That is an all time fear of mine. I always imagine the body jumping right up and grabbing my hand. I know I'm being silly, but it seems so real to me. Maybe he'll forget to say for all to come forward. The odds of that are very slim, so I might as well prepare for the worst.

Just when I thought the worst was on the way, it arrived. The Devil himself walked in God's house without a care in the world. Was I the only one that saw this lily-white motherfucker? Everybody was so into the service to notice that a snake just slid in.

I was unsure what to do. Should I slide down or try to sneak out with the crowd? The last thing I wanted to do was panic. If my mom wasn't so broke up, I would've tried to warn Black. Damn, I had to take a deep breath because I was starting to panic. I'm trying not to lose my cool. It would kill my mom to see me get hauled out of here. I don't want to turn around, but I must know how deep he and his crimmies are.

I didn't want to give away my location by turning around, so, I did it in slow motion. As I turned from right to left, I saw the tears running down the face of the queen that brought me into this world. I didn't have time to stop and comfort her because of what was happening around me. The next blurry face I saw was the Preacher. Although his mouth was moving nonstop, I couldn't hear what he was saying. I didn't have time to focus on his words, nor did I care what he was saying.

The last face I saw before my chin connected with my shoulder was Lia. She did not look like she was in her right state of mind. With that slight glance I could've taken her for a Bellevue escapee. In that split second I had trouble knowing two very important pieces of my life's puzzle. Even though I knew it was temporary, it was still a very weird feeling.

As my head turned all the way around like the Exorcist to scan the back of the church, I didn't see anything. I quickly shot my head around the other way to my opposite shoulder and I saw the same thing … nothing. I focused my attention up front with a puzzled look on my face. The tears had dried and the puzzled look felt very deep. I guess it was very visible because Mom Duke asked me if I was alright while she wiped her tears. I paused before I opened my mouth to answer her, but she faced back forward. I closed my mouth and did my best to fix my face.

Trying not to alarm anyone, I took one more quick look with the same result. I want to run over and tell Black, but I wanted to be sure. As bugged out as I am feeling right now, I could've been daydreaming.

With no feeling at all, I realized that the two lovely ladies on my side still had a hold of my hands. I gave them both a light squeeze and lifted myself up. Slowly, of course. Lia was the last to let go the very end of my fingertips.

As I cleared the last person, I took a long and reluctant stare up the aisle. From the fifth row on back the church was empty. Although I knew that while I eased towards the door, I could still imagine Sullie jumping out on me. As the door got close and closer, my heart beat faster and faster. It took every ounce of courage I had not to turn and run. The white person inside of me had to find the monster.

As I got to the big double oak doors, I paused while I thought about what was on the other side. The thoughts were a little off the wall, but they ended the same. My young ass strapped to a chair with a million volts running through my body.

I placed my sweating palms on the oak door and tried to push, but it didn't budge. My arms felt like rubber bands from being so scared. I took a real deep breath to try and pull myself together. This time I put my back into it and it began to ease open.

Immediately, I felt the warm air outside mix with the air conditioning of the church. The glare of the sun was too much to take. I had to look down for a second like I was a vampire. Once my eyes adjusted, I continued to push the oversized door. My heart was still hitting my chest at an alarming rate. The last thing I wanted right now was to get dragged off to jail and my heart was letting me know.

By this time, the huge doors were almost halfway open and someone grabbed my shoulder from behind. I nearly jumped out of my skin with fear. I knew this was the end of me. I spun around like a mad man with my teeth and my fists clenched.

I couldn't believe my eyes! It was Lia standing there. She apologized for scaring me and asked what was wrong with me. I opened the door the rest of the way and stepped outside. I scanned the block by looking up and down a few times. I didn't see a soul except for a bag lady in the middle of the block.

I took a deep breath and thought to myself that I must have been daydreaming. I walked back into the church and grabbed Lia by the hand and walked back to our seats.

Once I slid back onto my seat, I tried to focus on what the Preacher was saying. He scanned the church while he was asking who was going to read the eulogy. I was shocked because this was the first time I gave it any thought. I was stuck for words as I made a lame effort to stand.

Before I noticed what was going on, the guy that was with Black and Ms. Dee was making his way to the alter. I was really stunned because no matter how hard I stared, his face was still unfamiliar.

CHAPTER 11: "The Eulogy", Crack Head Tom

I was as nervous as I'd ever been. That walk from my seat was one of the longest in my life. Even though I hate talking in front of crowds, this is something I must do. The only other time I felt compelled to stand up was at one of my meetings.

I took a deep breath and cleared my throat in the microphone. I was trying not to be nervous, but it wasn't easy. I said to myself "here goes nothing" and started my speech.

"As I look over the crowd here this morning, I see a few familiar faces. Some that I haven't seen in years, and some I see every night in my dreams. Let me introduce myself for all that don't know me. I'm Thomas A. Cooper, affectionately known as 'Crack-head Tom.'" I heard a few sighs from the crowd, but willed myself to continue with my speech.

"I get that a lot for two reasons. One, I haven't been around the neighborhood for almost five years, and second of all, the last time any of you saw me, I was getting beat to death by eight guys from Polo-Ground housing" I looked around the crowd again to see the looks everyone's face. The last face I landed on was Ms. Dee, and she gave me the encouragement I needed to keep going.

"I know it is a shock to a few of you because you thought I was dead. Well, I was dead as long as I was getting high. On that vicious day a person did die and his name was 'Crack-head Tom'. Since that day I haven't touched any crack, or any drugs for that matter. I've been clean for over four and a half years. I was in a coma for about three weeks."

"For those three weeks, Tip spent countless hours by my bedside. It was a shock for me also. The first person I saw was Tip. We're all here because we know and love Tip. But, to be honest, I thought he was there to finish the job. Sorry, Ladies and Gentlemen, I didn't mean to laugh, but the whole thing tickles my heart." As the entire audience brought forth a quiet laugh with me I began to feel a lot more comfortable, and the rest of my speech flowed effortlessly.

"We all know that Tip had a mean side. What I didn't know was that he had a heart of a saint also. Once he saw I was in stable condition, he disappeared for a day or two. I couldn't tell one day from another, thanks to that medicine. When he did return, he brought me Wendy's and McDonalds because he didn't know which one I wanted. Even though my jaw was broke in two different places and I couldn't eat anything, the gesture was priceless."

I tried to urge them not to cry because this was a blessed day. I went on to tell them that after a week or two of him treating me like a long lost brother, we were sitting in my room watching Martin. During the commercial, he cut the TV off. You know the commercial; this is your brain on drugs commercial. I guess that led to his next question. He asked me what I planned on doing after I got out of the hospital.

"Up until that point, I never gave it a thought. At the time, getting high was the easy way out for me. If I was high, nobody expected anything from me, and I loved that. Then Tip gave me a million and one reasons why hiding behind that glass pipe wasn't my only option. Every reason I had to go back, he had five why I shouldn't. After he tore me down and built me back up, we were seeing eye to eye. Now all I could think about was taking the world by storm. This brings me to why I'm able to stand here before you and sing the praises of this special young man."

"Although I wanted to do right, I had no foundation, nor did I have the support I needed. Tip told me that if I were serious that he would come up with something. It took me two long months to recover from all of my injuries. In the course of that time, not only did me and Tip become good friends, he visited me just about every day. He might have missed seven out of sixty days, but when he came back, he brought me a hat and a shirt from the All-Star Game in San Antonio. That was the closest I had ever been to leaving town."

As I stood on the podium and told these strangers about the new me, the help and encouragement I got from Tip, and my new will to move on I knew after today my life would be different. It had to be, for both Tip and me.

"When I was getting discharged, Tip showed up with a slick sweat suit and some shoes. To this day I can't pronounce the name. All I knew was the word Sergio on the front." I heard a few chuckles and that made me feel a lot better.

"To make a long story longer, that wasn't all he brought. He looked in his pocket and pulled out a plane ticket. I was puzzled and couldn't understand why he was holding it out to me. He told me to take it, but my hands were frozen to my sides. The next time he said take it, my hands drifted towards the ticket. It took me a second, but I had to ask him what the ticket was for."

"He explained to me that it took him a while, but he found the perfect place for me to go. He told me about a Christian Rehabilitation program that would be great for me, but it was in Chi-Town. At first, I was really scared, but Tip reassured me that this would be the perfect beginning to the rest of my life." I took a look at Tip, and thanked God for the blessing he sent me at that very moment. Without God sending him to me, I might have been in that casket a lot sooner. I struggled, but I continued with my story.

"I couldn't leave my mother, but he knew I hadn't seen her in years. Then I asked about my son, but he knew that I hadn't seen him in years either. Finally, Tip pounded it into my head that there was nothing to stay for and everything to leave for. It was the biggest truth that I ever had to swallow. I think if he didn't walk me all the way to seat 15E, I would have headed for the nearest base house.

Once I got there, a lot of things unfolded right before my eyes. I found out that although this was ran by nuns and priests, that it wasn't free, to say the least. No, let me rephrase that. It ran Tip $40,000.00 a year for me to stay there. Not to mention, the money he sent me without fail through Western Union. God worked a miracle through Tip, and to this day, I don't know why. He never complained and never once mentioned that I owed him a red cent. God I know you're listening right now, so please let him rest in peace. I know that my friend lost his life in the street for the love of money, but I want to let all of you out there know that I'm living proof that something good came out of it." By then I couldn't hold my tears in any more and I just let them flow freely. Although my heart hurt for Tip, the tears I cried were tears of happiness because in my heart I knew he was in a better place.

"Please forgive my tears because I promised Tip I wouldn't cry. These aren't tears because I miss him, these are tears of happiness. I'm happy because now I know he's got that big mansion he's always dreamed about." As I wiped the tears away from my face, I told Black and Born, "he really loved y'all like brothers. He talked about you guys like no other. But, please, do me a favor, all those in ears reach. Please remember him just like I remember him, with a big heart and an equally big smile."

As I headed back to my seat, I thought to myself, *There, I did it.* Ms. Dee met me in the aisle and gave me a big hug.

CHAPTER 12: Black

I don't believe I can't stop crying. I was fine up until the part when he said that Tip loved me like a brother. That really touched home. Damn eyes! Will you please stop running? I can't take feeling like this. Shit! I know if Born sees me crying he's going to bring up that night in Central Park.

I feel like shit. I know that my death would destroy my mom, but why couldn't that be me up front in that pine box. I see now that Tip and Born had a purpose for being on this Earth. All I do is chase strippers. The whole time I was filling up their g-string, Tip was saving lives and making a difference. I can't believe how selfish I was being. Now I'm sitting here feeling sorry for myself. For what?

"Baby, you okay?" Mama Dee asked with a concerned look on her face. I didn't want to worry her so I gave her a lame excuse.

"Mama Dee, I'm fine. I just still can't believe he's gone."

"He's not gone. Instead of having him watch your back, now he's watching over you," she replied. She had a point, but I still wanted him by my side. I know that was being selfish on my part, but I miss him.

My mind was racing at lightning speed, going nowhere fast. By the time my head stopped hurting, the heavy set lady to my right excused herself as she tried to slide by me. From the sound of her voice, it wasn't the first time, she said excuse me. Although I didn't recognize her big ass, she did look familiar. As I looked around I noticed that everybody was moving toward the front of the church where Tip was resting. My mind and body were saying get up and pay my last respects, but my face was on a different page.

No matter how much Tip called me, I couldn't seem to get up. It was crazy because it seemed like each person that went up to see Tip would look back at me. I wasn't sure if they were showing their respects or wondering what was taking me so long to come up. They were more than right if it was the second one, but my feet were still numb.

As I looked around for Born, I couldn't see him because the crowd was too thick. It didn't look like there were a lot of people here while they were seated, but now it looks like the whole uptown is in here.

I looked down at my feet wondering why they wouldn't take me to my brother. While my head was down looking for a reason, I felt a gentle hand rest on my shoulder. The first thing I saw when I looked up was a long strand of slob hanging from Ashley's lip.

I couldn't hold back the smile and I reached for her. Born asked me if I was alright in a soft voice. I wiped my face dry and shook my head no. He gave me a half smile and said that he knows the feeling. He asked me if I was going to say good-bye. I paused for a second, but I still didn't answer him. I just nodded my head yes.

Without think about the numbness in my legs, me and Ashley rose to our feet. As I focused on the church I noticed how many people were grieving. It was a lot of people and they were all grieving in their own way. Born tapped me and pointed towards my mom. She was standing at the foot of the coffin singing that song from Cooley High. She wasn't singing loud. It was something personal between her and Tip.

As Born and I walked past her we both planted big kisses on her cheeks. She offered to take Ashley, but Born said "No thank you. I want her to say good bye to her Uncle Tip."

The coffin was only open half way, which I had a problem with.

I picked out that Boss shirt, and for what those big block gators cost me, the whole house is going to see them. I went to lift the lower half of the casket up and Born stopped me by placing his hand on mine. I told him "It is only right that he floss for the last time." He didn't answer, but he let me know that he was with me by lifting his hand.

Once I had it propped open, I got a chance to focus in on Tip. I said out loud "Damn, kid, you look like a million dollars."

Born replied by saying, "No Doubt!" The casket was filled with everything from lipstick to basketball cards. It seemed like everybody that passed left him a token of their love.

I had to laugh when I saw the Magnum condom. I guess the nine and a half inch mystery was true. I reached in my pocket and pulled out a flick of me, Born and Tip on jet skis at Wet & Wild. He always said that was the most fun he ever had.

I held Tip's hand for a moment or two and told him how much I miss him. I felt my eyes begin to burn, so I stepped to the side to let Born and Tip say their good-byes. As I stood to the side, I saw the grief that was leaking out of everybody in the place.

On one side it was very sad, but on the other hand, it was wonderful.

Wonderful to know that one person could be so loved. I hope I have half the love at mine. I could see that Born was starting to lose it, so I placed my hand on his shoulder for support. He turned around, looked me in the eyes and gave me a hug. I was speechless for a moment, but I took this opportunity to ask Born not to leave me. He didn't answer me, but when he squeezed me tighter, that was worth a thousand words.

We tried to pull ourselves together so we could take Tip to his new house. We gave the Pastor the nod to let him know that we were ready. Born called the crew up to the alter, so we wouldn't have to use any strangers for pallbearers.

As the church began to clear out, we took our positions. The whole time we were carrying the casket, all I could think about was dropping it. I know that was crazy, but that's how tense I was. Thank God it all went as planned and we got him safely in the hearse. I knew this was going to be one of the longest rides in my life.

Once the hearse doors were safely shut, I tried to place one foot in front of the other to make it to the limo. At that point, it was easier said than done. As I looked around and everyone was screaming to get to their cars, my whole world started to spiral. It felt like someone pressed the turbo button on the merry-go-round. As my head spun out of control, the ground got closer and closer until I was sitting on the curb with my head in my lap. Then everything went black.

CHAPTER 13: Born

Every time I look up I find myself drifting off into space. I wonder how long it takes for that effect to wear off. It's overwhelming my days and nights. I have a feeling that it will be around for a very long time.

I peeked out the back of the limo and I saw Mama Dee's Fleetwood right behind us. She's been an angel through this whole ordeal. I wish she would've brought my little girl friend with her. No matter how bad I'm feeling, she always brightens up my day.

Damn! Is Mt. Holly really on top of a mountain, or what? I asked the driver how much longer and he replied that it wasn't long, so I sat back and began to replay the eulogy in my head. Tom looked like a new man. It was wonderful what Tip did. It was also wonderful that Tom didn't forget it or blow a good opportunity. The question I must ask myself is when did Tip have the time to play *Gandhi*? We were together each and every day. I guess where there's a Tip, there's a way. I got to have a talk with Tom before he flies back to Chicago. There are still a few things I want to hear about.

As I relaxed and looked out the window, my fingers glided over my cufflinks. Then it hit me. I could've put them inside the casket. "Why didn't I think of that earlier? Shit!" I don't think anybody heard me because no one looked at me.

As I looked around the limo and saw all the sad faces, I was speechless. I wanted to break the silence with a word or two, but I couldn't think of anything to say. As I focused in on Black, he was looking like shit. He hasn't said a word since we helped him up off the curb. I didn't realize that he went down until I heard the screams come from over my shoulders. When I saw him laying there, my heart fell. Physically he's alright, but mentally, I'm not so sure.

One thing I can say is that it seems like we've been driving forever. I never heard of Mt. Holly, New Jersey before today. The driver told me he's been there hundreds of times and assured me that it wasn't much farther. Then again, he told me that 45 minutes ago and all I see is highway ahead.

Earlier, I saw a brochure of the cemetery and my mouth dropped. I never saw anything more gorgeous before. This wasn't on Lifestyles of the Rich and Famous. The thought of my best friend spending the rest of his days there made me feel real good. That's probably why it seems like we've been on the road for hours.

I was anxious as hell to see this dreamland that was laid out in the brochure. Although my hope was high, I know how those brochures can be misleading. Nevertheless, I'm hoping for the best, for Tip's sake.

Ashley tossed and turned on my mother's lap, but she didn't wake up. I was glad about that because I knew this day was nowhere near over. *Did I just see a Mt. Holly marker?* I asked the driver if my mind was playing tricks on me or were we really almost there?

He replied "We'll be pulling up to the golden gates in a few minutes." Once he said that, Lia started to fix her makeup. My mom started stroking Ashley's head and my man Black took a deep breath and I hoped that Mt. Holly knows what they're doing.

"There's only one man that can wake the dead and he's on his way." I had to laugh at that. It eased my mind a little bit to see Black laugh. Before I could take the smile off my face, the driver was getting off the Mt. Holly exit. The butterflies in my stomach began to take flight.

I've rehearsed this scene in my mind over and over, yet I'm still scared. We follow the snake road for a few minutes, and then I notice a big fortress up ahead. It was gated all the way around, but the gates didn't say stay out, they invited you in. The whole look just pulled us closer and closer until finally, we were right in front of the golden gates.

Now I knew just what the driver meant. I thought he was using golden gates in a heavenly sense. Maybe that's what Mt. Holly wants you to feel. I must admit, these gates are just like I pictured the afterlife.

As we passed through the gates, it only got better. Although there were flowered graves as far as my eyes could see, my butterflies began to disappear. The further we drove inside the more I was at ease. I can't explain it, but nevertheless, I was grateful. By the way everyone's faces were smashed to the limo's window, they were just as taken by the scenery. They were staring out the window like we just entered Happy Land House or Graceland (Elvis' crib).

There were trees the size of buildings and the grass couldn't get any greener. Not to mention, from the top of the hill to the lowest gravesite, the grass was all even. It must be a bitch to keep this joint right.

We stopped at the information house to check in. The driver exited the car and said he would only be a minute. When the door shut, it seemed like that was the signal for everyone to talk. The bad part was that they were all trying to talk to me.

My mother blurted out that she wants to be buried right here. I needed to hear that like I needed a hole in my head. My mom often talks about her death and it makes me sick. She talks about it like hitting a number. Ever since she started listening to that honky on the tube, she acts like dying is the best thing since white bread.

Me on the other hand I see no glory being cover in dirt and eaten by worms. Forgive me for being so naive, but what's taking the driver so long? He said a minute and it's been almost ten already.

Then I heard Black say, "It's about time!" When I looked up, he was entering the car. He pulled off and went around a sharp bend. Just up ahead I couldn't believe my eyes. Just when I thought this place couldn't get any better, I was wrong. To the left and the right were two great big lakes with a bridge that connects them both. When I looked to get a better view of the bridge, I saw a family of five looking over at the graves. That took the words right out of my mouth.

I wanted to wake Ashley up because she gets a kick out of seeing any kind of water. She loses her mind when you try to take her out of the bathtub. When she's in a really cranky mood, I take her to the Bingaton to eat French fries and wave to the water.

The driver broke my trance by saying, "DAMN! Did they switch the map? Last month's map was much clearer and had color to it." I didn't understand what he was talking about.

Black beat me to the punch when he asked the driver "What are you talking about?" The driver replied how the cemetery is so damn big that if you don't have a map, it will take forever to find your site.

When we finally approached the gravesite, the first thing I noticed was the golden tent with five men sitting underneath. When the limo and the rest of the procession pulled up, they stood up to greet us. The first two were pretty well dressed. The other three looked like they got their suits from Alexander's two-for-one sale. You could tell they were just there for the labor, and the other two were there to represent Mt. Holly.

As the cars began to empty, they were posted up greeting each and every person with a smile. I was hardly in the mood to smile, it's only been a few hours into the day and I'm already drained. All I want to do is move my man into his new mansion and watch my daughter play in the balls at McDonalds.

As we all sat graveside waiting for the preacher to say a few words, Black asked me if I was alright and I said, "I guess." He asked to talk to me alone, so we started to walk in the direction of all the cars. He put his arm around me and asked if I remembered the first time we went to Disneyland in California. I remembered the day like it was yesterday. We had just got in the game no more than a year ago. The money was alright now that I think back.

We were splitting up about $2500 a week. That was good for three teenagers. We had planned this trip for weeks. We knew this homo named Buns that worked for a travel agent and he used to hook us up.

The problem came the day before we were supposed to leave, Tip couldn't make it. To our surprise, the judge gave him thirty days in Sparford for getting caught with the gun in school. The lawyer told us he wouldn't do a day. That whole day we all spoke to Tip over the phone. After he stopped talking about killing the lawyer, he asked us about Disneyland. Of course we both said we weren't going without him. After we said that, he went crazy. He told us that we better go and have some fun. We couldn't believe that he was saying that.

After we hung up, he called back three times. We then agreed to go and have fun. The whole weekend we were there all I could think of was Tip. I had more guilt on my chest than when I slept with my girlfriend's sister. Nevertheless, I went through the motions and made the best of it.

Black said, "That's what Tip wants us to do now." It was kind of strange hearing this from Black. I thought I was going to be giving this speech to him. To know he feels this way is a real load off my chest.

I looked Black right in his eyes and asked "What are we going to do without him?"

He replied and said "Keep his memory fresh in our minds." That made plenty of sense to me, so I gave Black a faint nod and put my arms out. We hugged and Black whispered in my ear "Don't go." That made me hug him even tighter while I felt my eyes swell up. It killed me not to answer, so I took a deep breath and walked away with a tear in my eye.

CHAPTER 13 ½: Black

It's been a day that I'd love to forget as soon as possible. I just left Born and his family downtown at the McDonald's playground. A lot of times I find myself being envious of what Born has. The calmness he has at all times and the support of his family would make any man want to take his place. Once he's gone I won't let anybody get that close to me again.

For years I've heard of the streets eating people alive and leaving their family to pick up the pieces. I took the whole thing for granted because it wasn't me. Now that it is me, I understand and I'm feeling the pain for all that have lost a friend.

I know that my next move will have to be a sure fire hit because my funds are looking crazy. It's never easy to make a dollar out of fifteen cents, but stranger things have happened. As long as I'm riding around doing nothing I should shoot across town and see what Manny would give me for my chain. I've been dealing with him since I bought my first hollow rope chain. When I walked in the place, he always treated me with mad love, but that's business. I've heard from a few people that he really squeezed them when they were in need. I guess that's business, too? My motto is, 'expect the worst, but hope for the best.'

I just heard my beeper vibrate in my cup holder. When I picked it up I saw my favorite code - 69. I gave that code to Pamela who dances in the *Foxy Lady* in Queens. This has got to be the best pussy I ever had. She was originally from Baltimore. She came up here with her baby's daddy, but when he went to jail the Apple swallowed her whole. I can't say that I'm sorry it did. Although the pussy is good, I know the nature of a woman, and as much as she tries, I would never let them tie me down. I'm going to marry somebody when I'm about seventy or eighty, so I can have somebody next to me when I die.

"Shit! You stupid African, watch that fucking cab before I beat the shit out of you."

I can't stand those motherfuckers. They will crash a fifty thousand dollar machine for a five-dollar fare. I can't see the logic in that. I've been riding around these cold streets for the past five hours and the only thing I can remember is how much I miss Tip. He's been in that ground for about seven hours now and all I want to do is go back to Jersey and dig him up. I know that won't help my loneliness any, but…

Damn! There goes Pamela beeping me again. This time she put 911 behind that lovely 69. That's crazy because my man has only been in the ground for a few hours and I'm here thinking about some head. Maybe that fat ass can ease my mind for the rest of the night.

CHAPTER 14: Born

It's been one hell of a day. Between putting a third of me in the ground and chasing Ashley around in Mickey Dee's, I feel like I've been up for twenty hours already. It's good to be home now. Lia didn't say one thing during the ride home. I know from years of experience that this night is far from over. My daughter's last act before the sandman hit her was to push me back onto the couch. That was the first game we started to play after she started walking.

I started to take my shoes off and before I had a chance to wriggle my toes on the carpet, the phone rang. Me and Lia both looked at it with the 'should I answer it' expression. I told her to answer it and if it's my Mom, tell her I'm taking a shower.

I sat there in silence while Lia's sexy voice filled the room. I could tell by the things she said that it was Mom Dukes. After a brief conversation, she said good night.

She turned and looked at me with an expression I couldn't read, so I said "What! What?"

She replied in a very low tone that wasn't nice "You know, your mom is very upset and she is really worried about you right now."

"I know, but I'm exhausted. All I want to do is take a long bath and sleep until my problems are all gone."

"Since when do you take baths?" she said, with a confused look on her face.

"Since every bone in my body called out for relief. This week has been the longest of my life. I feel like the weight of the world is resting on my shoulders and my legs are beginning to wobble."

Lia offered to run my bath water. I told her thanks, but not too hot. The last time I tried to surprise her by getting into the tub with her, I almost burned my balls off. I jumped back so fast it wasn't funny.

I cut the TV on while I massaged my toes in the carpet. I rolled my eyes back and took a really deep breath in hopes to relax. When I opened my eyes, I saw that fake cool motherfucker from BET trying to talk all sexy. *Doesn't he know that men watch this show, too?*

I looked over at Ashley. She was cuddled up in a ball on the loveseat. It's been over a year since God blessed me with her, yet every time I lay eyes on her I get goose bumps. To think I prayed day and night for a little boy.

I heard Lia call out my name from the bathroom. I was hoping that meant my bath water was ready. I got up and walked in the bathroom. I was very surprised to see Lia in the tub. I didn't want to hurt her feelings, but I told her I wasn't in the mood.

She sighed and said, "Can't a woman hold her husband without it leading to sex?" It always scared me when she talked like that, but this time it didn't even faze me. I felt about four inches tall. I told her she was right and I apologize for being a jerk. I told her to hold that thought and ran and got my lil princess. I tucked her in bed with a kiss. I came back to the bathroom, got undressed and climbed in the candle-lit bathtub.

When the water hit my skin, I knew the temperature was just right. I slipped right between Lia's legs and rested all my troubles on her soft breast. She wrapped her legs around me and massaged my temples. She whispered in my ear and said, "is there anything I can do for you?"

I said, "Just keep doing what you're doing." I think that was the last thing I said before I fell asleep.

CHAPTER 15: Black

I hate fucking around in the Bronx, especially around the Highbridge area. Even though Beanie and Mark are crazy cool with me, those kids up there just don't know how to act. They will shoot at you because you got a hot car. I remember when I first met Pamela. I slid her back to her crib, and by the time I came back downstairs, there was an oil spot where my Wagoner was. Needless to say, I was past mad.

I went back upstairs and called Beanie and Mark. Mark was the first to call back. I told him the situation, and within two hours I had my baby back. Anyway, two honks later and Pamela was in my car. She was looking like she just got off a pole, just like I like her.

I shot across the G.W. to Route 4, to the Holiday Inn. She says the rooms there make her horny. Once we got upstairs, I left Born a voice message on his phone to let him know where I was at. I sat on the edge of the bed and began to flip through the TV. We usually watched triple X movies and fucked all night. Tonight felt a little different.

I stopped at the rerun of *Married with Children*. Al Bundy is a trip. He treats his family like shit, but when somebody else tries it, he knocks them slam out. While I was focused on the television show, Pamela found time to reveal that perfect body. All I saw was that sexy tattoo of a butterfly at the crack of her ass. When I'm hitting it from the back, I swear it looks like its flying.

She walked with the grace of a runway model and shortly after I heard the shower running. Normally, that would be my cue to go in there and take out the frustration of the street on her. Tonight is very different. This type of frustration will not disappear with a few strokes. I know that being alone now would only make it worse.

I finally slipped out of my suit and walked over to the mini bar. While I was standing in front of it in *ACA* boxers and my party socks, I couldn't decide what to drink. All they have in here is vodka, rum and bourbon, but all I drink is Hennessey or Moet. I guess a double shot of rum and coke will have to do.

While I was in the process of making it, Pamela called out to me. I knew what she wanted, but I was still tense and feeling much too guilty to go into the bathroom. I told her to hold on and I would be there in a minute.

After I poured three minis in the glass instead of two, I went back over to the bed. I tilted my head back and poured the monster shot down with one gulp. After my chest stopped burning, I took off the rest of my clothes and climbed into bed. *Married with Children* was still on. Kelly is such a freak. I wonder if Daryl knows her. They say everybody in Cali parties together. If he could get her into my bed, I might work for him.

I could see Pamela exit the bathroom through the mirror. Her nipples were rock hard and her body was perfect, without one stretch mark. That's amazing for a woman with a child. She still had water glistening all over her body, which made her even sexier.

What was strange to me, hands down, was that this was the best pussy I ever had and her body was the best I've seen. Now the question is: why ain't I hard as hell? I guess it's going to take me longer than I thought to relax.

Next thing I knew, I was being mounted from the back like I was a black steed. The ironic thing was, she was the only stallion in the room. I closed my eyes in effort to relax. I felt her warm body sliding up mine. When she rested her body on my lower back, all I felt was heat. Her pussy was still wet and her inner self was wetter.

She ran her nails up and down my back, ever so lightly, until it gave me goose bumps. She whispered in my ear, "Does that feel good, Daddy?" It felt so good that I couldn't respond. I just nodded. She started to massage me with a lot of intensity, so much intensity that it started to break my tension. I felt a calmness come over me.

She should quit dancing and become a professional masseuse. I wanted to turn over to see if she's as wet as she feels, but I couldn't bring myself to stop the massage. I figured I would let it ride for another five or ten minutes before I stop her. I got this dime piece on my back that will do anything I ask, and I do mean ANYTHING, but all I can think about is Tip.

I can't believe it. Guilt is starting to fill the room again. I guess the triple shot of rum is starting to wear off, so I closed my eyes and tried to enjoy my massage.

I don't know when it happened or why, but somewhere between the massage and thinking about Tip, I fell asleep. I don't know if it was the long day or the massage, but I went out like a light.

I don't know whether it was hours later or minutes later, but I woke up with Pamela between my legs doing her best to wake me. I can't think of a better way for a man to get woken up, but not tonight. As I pulled my semi-hard dick away from her, I explained to her that tonight was a bad night for me. She must have understood because she came up and kissed me on the cheek. I wanted to ask her if she wanted to go home, but I was too afraid she would say yes. Instead I pulled her close and tried my best to find the sandman.

CHAPTER 16: Detective Sullivan

"Excuse me, Ma'am, can I talk to you for a moment?" *Damn! I know that bitch heard me.* "If I were one of these murderers or drug dealers, she would have ran to the car. That's another thing, if I was in a foreign car instead of this piece of shit, it would've been different. That's why their lives are fucked up now. They were looking for that short cut to the top." There's an old Irish saying that my grandmother used to tell my uncle Ryan, she said, "the only short cut in life is death."

"Hey, pervert, why are you talking to yourself?" a voice cried out breaking my thoughts. My face got so red my freckles disappeared. I wanted to get out and throw these cuffs around someone's wrists or put *Uncle Patty* in somebody's mouth.

I don't want to lose focus on why I came down here. It's two a.m. already. Time only flies when you're having fun, but I don't call filling out reports at the station for five hours fun. As a matter of fact, that would fall under the bloody heading of torture.

I don't believe that these low lives are still running up and down the streets like it's mid-afternoon. I guess if I was on dope, coke, or heroin I would still be going strong too. I just want to complete my mission and head on home.

"Hey, Miss! Ma'am, do you have a minute?"

"I don't talk to cops," she shot back in a sarcastic tone.

I tried to convince her that I wasn't a cop, but she wouldn't go for it. She sped down the block like Jack the Ripper himself was driving by. As I blended in with the circular traffic I saw one guy selling crack to a pregnant teen. The rage was trying it's best to take over me, but right now a pregnant crack whore wasn't high on my list. *Oh, yeah! That's her right there. She's going to act right or I'm going to lock her chinky-eyed ass up.*

As I pulled up on her I knew she was more than I expected. I could tell that she was one of those half-breeds. She looked like she had a touch of nigger in her. Not that I'm complaining because whatever she had it was to my liking.

Instead of using my conventional "excuse me", I went with the forceful finger and with a demanding look on my face. I commanded her to the car with just one finger. When she walked to the car our eyes locked. I didn't say anything, but I looked her up and down like I was buying a racehorse.

She broke my stare by saying, "What can I do for you, Carrot top?"

"It's not what you can do for me, it's what I'm going to do to you."

"That sounds exciting," she said, looking around to see who was watching. Probably looking for a cop.

After I told her to get in she gave me a funny look, but she got in. Once she got in, I took off like Internal Affairs was after me. I hit the bridge in a matter of seconds. She had a puzzled look on her face, but I didn't pay her any mind. I could tell she wanted to say something, but she was like a rat cornered by a cobra.

By this time we were about ten minutes away from Hunts Point heading for the G.W. Bridge. I didn't want her to jump out at the toll, so I asked, "Are you alright?"

She took a deep breath and said, "Yes, but do you mind telling me where we are going?"

"To get a motel room." She didn't say much after that. I could tell she's new to the streets.

"Do you mind if we discuss money?"

"Money isn't the object."

Through giggles she replied, "Okay, Donald Trump. I charge a hundred for a blowjob, another one-fifty for this good ass pussy and one seventy-five for a half and half. I don't get with the kinky stuff and my ass is too small for a finger, let alone a grown man's dick. Oh, yeah, since money is no object, Mr. Trump, it's two-fifty and hour or fifteen hundred for the night." She then smiled and said, "Can you handle that, kind sir?"

I wiped the smile off her face when I said "I wonder if the tape recorder got all that."

"What tape recorder?" she asked, stunned.

"The one that's been on since you've gotten in the car."

She started banging on my dashboard and shouting at the top of her lungs. Then I guess she thought she had me when she calmed down and said, "You ain't no cop."

I laughed for a second and said "This is the part where you ask to see my badge."

"You got that right."

So, I reached into my jacket pocket and pulled it out. When I did that, it seemed like all her hopes and dreams jumped out the window. As she put her head down I reached over and smacked her with the back of my hand. Her face flew into the passenger side window. She tried to get as far away from me as possible, but my matchbox of a car wouldn't allow it. I could see the tears start to run down her face.

"What was that smack for?" she asked in between the sniffles

I simply said, "You are prey and I'm the king of the jungle."

"What are you going to do to me?" she asked.

"Ain't it obvious? I'm going to fuck you until I pass out."

She sounded relieved when she found out jail wasn't in her future. Well ... not tonight, anyway. After all, fucking was her business. She just traded her body for a get out of jail free card.

As we pulled up in front of the *Courtesy Motel* on route four, I told her to go and get a room. She opened the door, and then reached back for the cash. I told her, "Don't press your luck." She dipped in her bra and pulled out some money. She tried to mumble "crooked bastard" under her breath. Little did the whore know, I heard her ass. I'm going to bang her head extra on the headboard for that smart remark.

As she floated back to the car with the room key, I was undressing her with my eyes. The thought of those young, tender breasts in my mouth had me ready to burst through my pants.

We went upstairs to the room and, like the good detective I am, I let her go in first. I guess its just force of habit. No matter how many times I come to this motel, I'm always speechless.

These rooms are so sleazy that I feel like getting naked in the doorway. I don't know if it is the wall-to-wall mirrors or the velvet bedspread, but I'm always in the mood when I come here.

The first thing I did when I came in is turn the television to the XXX videos. Yeah! This is a good one right here. Vita Parks is getting the shit banged out of her on the pool table. I said, "Yo! Half-breed. Are you going to stay dressed all night or what?"

She sprung right into action just like I like it. The first thing to come off was the super short leather skirt. She wiggled from side to side a few times and it fell to the ground. I focused my eyes between her legs. I was surprised to see that she had on panties, but I was equally surprised to see that crotch was missing. I guess in her line of work, easy access is better. Nevertheless, they made me get that much harder.

The next thing she revealed were those golden brown breasts with her erect nipples. This little girl was getting better by the minute. As she took off her thigh-high stockings, I noticed her feet were a little worn out from all the walking she does. I don't have a foot fetish anyway, so that didn't block my erection.

She went to take off the crotch less panties, I stopped her. She looked puzzled, but she did what I told her to do. In the process of watching her I heard that slut Vita Parks moaning in the background. When she's whining like that I know someone is really putting it to her. I guess the little half-breed didn't like the fact that I wasn't paying her naked body any attention because she screamed at me, "Are we going to fuck or what?"

I looked at her with a rage and said, "Oh, yeah! We're going to fuck, but first let me show you a trick my ole pappy showed me."

I got up and walked over to her with my manhood leading the way I stood right in front of her and asked her while pointing at my prick, " You want this?"

She replied in a sexy voice "Yes, Daddy, I want to love you a long time." When she reached for my zipper I slapped her with all my might. Her eyes widened like a deer in headlights. When she fell back into the bed I jumped on top of her and slapped her until my hand felt swollen. She screamed, kicked, and scratched, but my two hundred and seventeen pound frame was too much for her.

When I got off her I took my clothes off like a schoolboy virgin. I didn't want to miss the moment. Once I was naked I sat back in the chair and masturbated to my young whore and Vita Parks the best piece of black ass ever.

CHAPTER 17: Born

An hour ago when I left Lia in the bed I felt so good. I love it when I wake up well rested. For that split second I felt like I didn't have a care in the world. Now that I'm moving around, I know that trouble is all I got. I'm running a little late. I told Nick I would meet him at *Yolanda's* ten minutes ago. I wish I knew his cell number so I could tell him to order me the linguini with clam sauce. I hope Lou's not having one of his noisy Gauchos banquets. The last time I was there the noise ran me out of there.

I pulled in front of *Yolanda's* a half of an hour later to find no parking spot. I double parked, hit my hazard lights and jumped out. As I entered the door the scent of fresh tomatoes woke my taste buds up. I love Italian food with a passion. I just don't like riding to the Bronx to get it.

As I looked passed the first table I saw Nick to the left of me. Although he had his back to me, I knew that stupid 70's afro from anywhere. When I got to the table I touched him on his shoulder and sat down, he moved his cell phone away from his mouth and told me, "I'll be right with ya in a minute." I knew what I wanted to eat, but I still scanned the menu. Surprisingly, the restaurant was fairly empty. The waitress made her way over to the table with a cocktail.

I guess Nick just beat me here.

"What would you like?" she asked flirtatiously. I ordered some water and my linguini. She went to turn and I told her to also bring some warm rolls.

After a minute or two Nick hung up the phone. We shook hands and gave each other a hard nod. Nick said, "These freaks are crazy as hell. Every time the first comes around Tabitha tries to give me some pussy. I got her into a brand new Acura for nothing. Now, I guess she wants me to pay for it also. Not to mention, she's fucking Kurt from 3333 on the regular. She can't get five hundred dollars from him for a month's worth of work? I'm not the herb she's looking for. Anyway, fuck that squeezer, what's up with you, Born?"

"Well, Nick, like I told you earlier, this week I need to get rid of my car and I need cash."

"Well! Born, I have some good news and some bad. The good news is that I got this kid out of Queens that wants your car. He's an up and coming kid who's getting a nice piece of change." He paused to gauge the reaction on my face. Something was telling me I didn't want to hear the rest.

"Now, the bad news. I could only get thirty thousand for you not counting my sales fee." I sat back in my chair and after I figured out his sales fee was a smooth three thousand I was sick. I knew that I wouldn't be able to open my store off that chump change, but I was stuck between a rock and a hard place.

"Yo, Nick! What kind of games are you playing?"

He gave me a dumb ass look while I was screaming at him. He tried to give me some lame excuse, but I wasn't trying to hear it. I lost my appetite and needed something stronger than water. Without shaking his hand or breaking my stare, I got up from the table. I could've slapped him right out of that chair, but it wouldn't change a thing. As I walked out all eyes were on me. I guess I was a little louder than I thought.

I focused in on my car as she was looking like a million bucks. How could I let her go for twenty seven stacks? I'm giving the three things I know, hustling, New York, and my whip for twenty seven stacks. I'm worse off now than I was when I came here.

I knew I was being robbed but what choice did I have? If I didn't take the money, then me and my family couldn't start over around the corner let alone a new state. I walked out the restaurant with a light breeze behind me. I tried to slam the door but all it did was close in slow motion. Once outside, I noticed New York's finest in action. They were pulling some guys out of a grey 4-Runner.

My heart went out to them. Not because they were getting harassed, but because that could've been me and Black. My stomach locked up and that moment I knew my families future was inside. I was so mad at this point I could've done anything.

The more I scrambled for the keys the madder I got. With the blue and whites lurking I didn't want to go back inside but my future was pulling me back.

I stormed back into *Yolanda's*. When the customers noticed I was back, their eyes got twice as big. Nick didn't see me yet, and his big head was there for the slapping.

When I walked in front of him, the first thing I saw was him digging into my linguini and clam sauce. My first reaction was to knock the plate on the floor, but I had more important business to handle. I reached toward the table and he nearly jumped out of his skin. With that I knew my point was made, so I dropped the keys on the table and extended my hand for the money.

As I hit the G.W. to go to my house, I had a lot on my mind. The biggest thing was staying out of jail. Although my options were narrowing down by the minute, I knew something had to give. As if my mood wasn't already on zero, it started to drizzle. I looked out of the window and watched the rain connect. The driver broke my train of thought when he asked me for two-fifty for the toll. I reached in my pocket and pulled out a five. I told the cab driver to keep the change.

CHAPTER 18: Black

I'm starting to get lonelier by the day. I can't believe how overnight my life has changed to shit. A week ago I couldn't get rid of Tip and Born. Now, a moment doesn't pass that I don't wish they weren't by my side. Life can be a funny thing. One minute you're in Vegas buying five hundred dollar bottles of Moet, the next week you can't afford to go to Atlantic City and buy salt-water taffy.

For the first time in my life I'm lost. I remember the days when I could throw a dime across the street into a phone. Now I don't think I could hit the side of the projects with a shotgun. I refuse to believe that my "golden boy" days are over. Yes, I'm lost, but I would be more lost if I follow Born to *Butt Fuck, North Carolina.* New York is all I know and all I want to know.

On the other hand, every place I go they say Sullivan's just left. I can't live my life like this. I also can't wake up every morning to roosters crowing. I'll be a fool if I stay and a God damned fool if I go. Why couldn't I be the one who died that night? If I could do it all over, I would take Tip's place. I know he would be a lot better without me than I am without him. I always knew God worked in mysterious ways, but now I see it first hand.

I should go to 86th Street and catch that new Wesley Snipes movie. Maybe that can get me out of this stinking mood. A little Jackson Hole wouldn't hurt either.

Okay, Born just beeped me. Just like old times, we can ride together.

CHAPTER 19: Lia

I can't believe Born. He walks in with a coach bag full of money and gets on the phone. Although he does that all the time, this time he called information for the airlines. I found that strange because every time he went out of town, he would call that faggot boy from downtown.

He confirmed two coach seats in Mr. and Mrs. Lewis. I wanted to ask whose bitch got these tickets, his or Black's? Although when I'm jealous I don't give a fuck but I knew it wasn't the time. 8:45 A.M Born shouted from the bathroom. Did I hear correctly? Eight-forty five tomorrow morning? Could he have been serious about leaving our families, friends, and home to go to North Carolina? I love him very much and want our family to stay intact, but I don't want to leave my family and friends.

Men can live anywhere as long as they got a bitch on the side. Men are crazy! No matter what mess they get into, they expect you to be there. The good for nothing ones want you to sweep it all under the rug. They go to jail after you beg and plead them to stop, then what? Then they want you to get molested three times a week by some dyke guard to visit them. Born and I have been through a lot in the last ten years. Even though I fucked around on him twice, I still know he's the only dog for me.

Maybe the country won't be so bad. We might even get closer with all the distractions behind us. Hopefully he will marry me before I try and give him a junior. I know that's wishful thinking, but I pray too hard not to get something out of life.

CHAPTER 20: Born

After all we've been through in the past few days, I really hated breaking the bad news to Black. I think going to North Carolina is the best thing for me and my family. When I started to think of how my next decision would affect me and my family, I became a smarter man. Even though I know Black never thought of me and Tip as thinkers, this is one time I must stand up for myself. When he calls me back I'm not going to beat around the bush.

It's crazy how I can say what I want to who I want, but when it comes to Black, I get tongue-tied. It's been that way since I can't remember when. It's weird because I'm not scared of him. It seems like I can't make a decision while he's around. Although he makes most of the decisions, he's never steered me wrong… that's the up side.

It's going to kill me being five hundred miles away from him. There hasn't been a day since the sixth grade that I haven't seen Black. To lose Tip and to leave Black is going to be the most painful decision of my life.

As I daydream about my decision and what it means for me, my mom screamed out, "Boy, its Raymond on the phone." My heart skipped a beat and I didn't know why. I picked up the phone and took a deep breath. When I opened my mouth it was like a floodgate. In three minutes I said I was leaving, the day, time, and where. When I was about to tell Black how much I was going to miss him, he hung up.

Keith interrupted my thoughts by barging into the living room. I guess my mom must have let him in.

Keith said, "Nigga! What are you running your mouth about?"

I felt about three inches tall, and my temper quickly rose. I snapped at him with a harsh, "What do you want?"

He reminded me it was Saturday and asked if I was going to shoot ball today. I told him no and he left.

When I went to turn around, the phone rung again. I picked it up on the first ring and it was Black.

The voice on the other end said, " I'm sorry kid. I lost my head for a minute," Black apologized.

"No problem man. What are you up to?" I asked him.

"Are you trying to see that new Wesley Snipes flick?" Black said all hype like he really didn't want to be by himself.

I was speechless and all I could do was take a deep breath.

"What's up, dog? Wifey won't let you out to play?"

"You know, I run shit around here. Yeah, we can catch the flick. It's been a minute since I've been to the Steak House. Then I have to come home and pack."

CHAPTER 21: Black

Sleeping was out of the question. I tossed and turned all night. Even though I had Rachel by my side, it still didn't work. To be honest, that made it worse. Those tits were looking so right, but my heart wasn't in it. All I could think of was taking this long ride to Born's house.

When he asked me to take him to the airport, I almost fainted. I wanted to tell him to take a cab. I knew it would've killed me to say it and killed him to hear it. It made me sick to know for sure he was leaving. It made me sicker to know there was nothing I could do to stop him. I hate when I feel selfish. Deep down I know he's doing the right thing by leaving town. At least until all of the heat blows over.

What really scares me is that he'll like that country ass life and stay. That would be the crazy shit. Part of me is glad that he's going because I would hate for anything to happen to him. The other half wants him by my side no matter the outcome. If I had a purpose in life, maybe I would run also, but I don't, so fuck that.

CHAPTER 22: Born

"Lia, can you please get Ashley while I pack this last bag? You know Black should be pulling up any minute. He's already pissed that I'm leaving. I don't want to make it worse by making him wait on us. If worse comes to worse, I'll just sick Ashley on him. If anyone can get a smile out of him, it's her," I said while looking around to make sure I had everything. Lia never answered she just looked at me with a sad face and went to tend to Ashley like I said.

"Lia, have you seen my blue Yankee's hat? This packing shit can give a brother gray hairs. Last night it took two hours to find my Bernard King autographed jersey." I'm, hunting all over the place trying to beat the clock and make sure I had everything, then I heard Black beeping his horn all crazy out front.

"Oh, shit. There goes Black. Lia, Black's out front. Are you ready?" All of the suitcases were in the middle of the living room. Now all I have to do is run them down to the car.

As I was thinking that, I heard Lia talking to Black. They were laughing about something, which was a good sign. Black entered the living room with Ashley wrapped around his neck. We kicked it for a minute, and then we loaded the car up with what we decided to take.

I knew I was leaving a lot behind but when its time to go you must put the sentiment to the side. I was talking like a real big man but it was easier said than done. With each trip I passed Black in silence, the last trip I made by myself. When I went in the empty apartment for the last time it was still full. Not so much with the material shit but with the memories.

Memories of me and Tip wrestling after the knick game. My daughter's first Christmas. The New Year Black got pissy drunk off the Moet, and could barely see let alone drive home. Not to mention all the sleepless nights me and Lia had. I'm glad my moo-moo is still young and can make her own memories elsewhere with no interruptions. They say what doesn't kill you makes you stronger, well I guess I'm superman. I turned to hear a hollow slam of the door and some lonely footsteps leaving the building.

CHAPTER 23: Black

I knew the ride would be just like this. Everyone was sitting back looking out the windows. It was quiet as hell up in here. If I didn't know any better I would think Born and Lia's jaws were wired up. I guess I wasn't any better because I didn't say shit either. I knew if I would've opened my mouth that I would regret it. I didn't have anything good to say, so I stayed quiet. The airport was just up ahead anyway, so it won't be long.

As I pulled up in front of the double doors I felt my stomach bubbling. That always happens at times like this. Born tried to make small talk by saying, "I hope they have something more than peanuts." Of course, Lia agreed with him, but I was still showing no emotion.

The doors opened up and the fresh air swept in. I couldn't believe how close I was to losing my best friend. I would've never thought in a million years that I would be alone. First my mom, then Tip, and now Born. I'm starting to think somebody put a curse on me.

While I drifted off watching the guy in the Camry getting a ticket, Lia made me jump by tapping the window. She asked me to hold Ashley while she got the bags. Instead, I declined and opened the car door.

When I rose up, me and Lia were eye to eye. Every time I get that close to that girl I feel weak in the knees. If I had a dollar for every time that girl made me fell like putty I would be the Black Donald Trump.

I told her to keep Ashley and I would get the bags. As I opened the trunk and began to remove the bags, Born put his hand on my shoulder.

"You alright?" he asked with a concerned look on his face. I didn't answer, but I nod my head yes. I didn't believe myself, so I knew he didn't believe me. I continued to unload the bags without making eye contact with anyone, especially Ashley. I felt my eyes burning already, but I refused to let go.

Lia and Ashley were standing off to the side with an older lady. I'm almost sure that she was sweating Ashley, like everyone else who comes in contact with her. Born went to the left giving the information to the sky-hop for the bags. I never thought it would come to this. Even though he said he was leaving on more than one occasion, I didn't take him serious.

What am I, some kind of black cat? Did I break a mirror and didn't know about it? Damn! It sure feels that way. Everybody that I ever truly loved has been taken away from me.

I feel my eyes burning more and more with every thought. Black, pull your self together. The more I try, the harder it's getting. I can't let them see me cry. Especially not Lia, so I closed the trunk, jumped in the car and sped off.

I couldn't believe I did that sucker shit. As the tears rolled down my face, Born got smaller and smaller in my rear view mirror. I saw Born standing there with his arms held high. I know he's thinking all kinds of bullshit, but the truth is, I am really going to miss him.

CHAPTER 24: Born

The stewardess brought me back down to earth. She reminded me that I was in front of my seat. I was really spaced out. I don't even remember boarding the plane. The last thing I can remember was letting my arms down after Black drove off.

After I got my two girls strapped in I placed my face in my hands. I can't believe how terrible this trip has started. The only way this flight gets any better is if we're hijacked by a bunch of madmen.

Lia touched my hand and asked if I was okay. What she really wanted to ask me if I was crying. I told her, "as long as our family stays together, I'm alright." She gave me a bright smile and went back to Ashley.

I knew that I was far from being alright, but I knew she needed to hear that lie. The best lies are the ones that make people smile. I wish somebody would tell me a good one right now. In just a few hours I'll be in a foreign land with Sullivan one step behind me. I can run, but I can't hide and that's what scares me the most. I'm too tired to think right now. First thing I need is to take a nap.

PART II

"ON THE RUN"

CHAPTER 24½: Born

Damn! I think that landing gave me whiplash. I'm no doctor, but it's not normal for pain to be rushing through my neck. These beat up ass cabs weren't helping it none. These cabs in North Carolina are nothing compared to the O.J.'s in New York. At least if you don't got a whip, you can still ride in a Benz or a Lexus. I guess I better get used to it. I've got to understand that this is not New York and the days of shitting outside are over.

The driver and Lia have been running their mouths ever since we left the airport. He sounds like one of those country guys who has never left his state. Some of the crazy questions he asks are a dead give away. Like some people are glad to be an American, I'm glad to be a New Yorker.

The driver said, "Excuse me, ma'am," then asked me for my family's address again.

With a slight attitude I said, "225 Division Road."

The driver said "Oh. I thought you said Division Place."

"I had a long flight and just want to get to 225 Division Road, please," I told him with annoyance evident in my tone.

Him and Lia picked their conversation up and ignored my frustration. Fifteen minutes later we were pulling up in front of a yellow-shingled house. The same one I pulled up in front of every summer when I was a kid.

Not much has changed, except my uncle's old ass Cadillac isn't sitting in the driveway. I guess my aunt couldn't bear to look at it after his death, although, he got killed in another woman's bed by her husband. Nevertheless, she still took it pretty hard. Now all I see is my aunt's Sentra boxed in by my cousin's hoopties and motorcycles.

Couso' and his crew are real big on motorcycles. There was a kid around my way that would wheelie from the Apollo all the way to the State Building. When I told them, they went crazy. Like all things, they can ride, but we really ride.

"That will be thirty eight dollars," the driver said, as he smiled up in my girl's face like I wasn't sitting there. I started to smash his ass and not pay him shit, but I didn't want to here Lia's mouth.

"Damn, nigga! Thirty eight dollars? What did you do, drive me all the way from New York?" I reached in my pocket and threw two twenties his way. I can't knock the hustle because money is power all over the world.

While I'm unloading my bags, the broken down screen door swung open wildly and my aunt came running out. Without putting on the breaks she ran up to Lia and grabbed Ashley. I must admit I was a little upset because those are the greetings I used to get.

"What am I? Chopped liver?" I asked her, acting like I was hurt. She didn't pay me any attention and kept wetting Ashley's face with kisses. She has never seen Ashley before, so I figured she would act like that.

I left the ladies out front while I took the luggage inside. After the third trip outside my aunt knew I was alive. She slapped me on my ass, and said, "Stop pouting. You're not my baby anymore."

"Oh, yeah? One look at her and I'm history?" I asked while acting like I would cry.

She came back with, "You were history a year ago when you sent her picture." I'm glad she said it with a smile on her face because she sounded serious. I knew before the day was over I would get my cheeks pinched.

I heard a rumble behind me, so I spun around. It was the Bad News Bears in the flesh. They were all trying to get down the stairs at one time.

My aunt has fourteen grandchildren and they were all screaming "Cousin Rico." Nobody down this way calls me Born and it would be too much trying to convert them. I remember when I told my mom my name was Born, and I don't eat swine anymore. She laughed until she was blue in the face. When she finished laughing she packed all of my belongings. She said "My son's name is Ricardo Colby Smith, and if you're not him I want your ass out of my house." I sit back and laugh about it now, but it damn sure wasn't funny when I was sixteen.

My little cousins are still screaming my name. The little guys are pulling me to play video games and the girls want me to play tag in the back yard. I don't want to hurt anybody's feelings, but all I want to do right now is chill out.

Luckily for me my aunt took time out from kissing Ashley to say, "Leave your cousin Rico alone. You will have plenty of time for all of that." Thank God for small favors. If my aunt didn't step in I would've been out back making mud pies, and playing John Madden or NBA Live.

What the hell! This big greasy motherfucker just walked out of my aunt's kitchen. He looked straight out of the Beverly Hillbillies. He had on an old pair of oily overalls. I looked down and he didn't have on any shoes or socks. His feet looked like he had been walking on hot coals all his life. To top it off, he was eating a sandwich with a greasy pair of hands that could choke a horse. My aunt sprung up off the sofa with Ashley close to her breast.

She addressed him as sweetheart and my face went blank. She introduced me as her favorite nephew. I think that was her way to soften the blow. She introduced Lia as *Mia*. I know I'm going to hear about that later.

Then she said, "This is my friend Billy."

I thought to myself, what's that short for, Billy-Joe or Billy-Bob? "Oh, he's your friend," I said with a sarcastic tone and a stern look.

With the strength of a karate expert Lia elbowed me in my side. I wanted to stop her, but I needed to concentrate on the situation in front of me. The situation was about six foot four and about 275 pounds. I would've been more confident if he had some body fat on his body.

He put his hand out to me. After I examined the oil on his hand, I declined. My uncle would've turned over in his grave if I would've shaken his hand. My aunt slowly passed Ashley to Lia, and that's when I knew I was in trouble. My aunt and my mother are two different people. My aunt is the one who always curses everyone out at the family reunion. She walked over to me, put one finger in my chest, and said, "Let me see your grown ass outside." It was too early to be beefing with auntie, but she knows she's wrong.

CHAPTER 25: Aunt Mae

When you get out here, Mae, please hold your head. Me and my sister will fall out forever if I smack this smart mouthed bastard.

"Now look Ricardo, first off, don't ever disrespect me in my own house. You're not too grown to get popped upside your head. Do you understand me? Don't shake your damn head, answer me, boy!"

No he didn't look at me with those puppy dog eyes. Those are the same eyes that used to melt my heart when he was younger. Nevertheless, I need to let him know that smelling your own piss down here is out of the question.

"Boy! Do you remember when your uncle died? I hope you do because I remember it like it was yesterday. I was washing the Sunday dishes. While I was drying my favorite casserole bowl, a pain shot through my stomach. That bowl had been in our family for four generations, and I dropped it like a paper plate. At that point I knew something had happened to your uncle. To this day, if I see a Cadillac, I get weak in the knees. Your uncle was the single most important thing in my life, but he's gone. It's been fifteen lonely years since that day. You have to remember that he died in another bitch's arms." I had to stop and catch my breath before a tear dropped. As much as I wanted to forget that day, it haunted me. I looked towards the sky before I continued talking.

"When I was in this house day and night, was he thinking of me and only me? Now I've been through this a hundred times with my own kids. Billy is a good man, he loves me and loves the grandchildren like they're his own. What more can a woman ask for? It took me two years to even kiss him and he never left my side. Love is a strange thing, but all people need it." I know it was hard for my nephew to hear me say these things, but I needed to clarify the situation for him and get it out the way. I don't make it a habit of repeating myself.

"What I'm trying to instill in you, Rico, is that I'm happy with Billy. Do I wish my husband were still alive? Hell, yeah! But, God made his decision, now we all must live with it. Especially me."

"Rico, when you called me and said that you wanted to move down here, did I give you the third degree? Did I ask if you were in trouble? Did I tell you don't bring your street life down here?"

"I didn't ask any of those questions because you're my blood, and I love you. Whatever you do in your life, I'm there for you because you are special to me. Please, sweetheart, just give it a chance. Although I don't need you or my trifling kids blessings, but I want them. All of you matter to me. Now they all get along with Billy, so I hope you can do the same."

Without giving him a chance to respond, I kissed him on the cheek and walked into the house.

CHAPTER 26: Born

Once again, my big mouth has me knee deep in shit. I love my aunt so much and I don't want her mad at me. She's always been like a mother to me. I guess a decade is a long time to be alone. Ten minutes is too much for me, let alone ten years. If I can get my foot out of my mouth long enough, I'm gonna try and clean this mess up.

When I walked through the door all heads turned in my direction, including the bright eyes of my daughter. I knew I had to say something, but it was a big lump in my throat. I tried to clear it two or three times, but I still sounded like I was thirteen.

Finally, I apologized to Billy and shook his hand. At the same time I was shaking his hand, I was apologizing to my uncle. I can tell by the bright looks on my aunt and Lia's faces that I did the right thing.

"If my aunt is happy, then I'm happy too, but if by chance you're thinking I'm going to say 'Uncle Billy', you're nuts." I told them with a straight face. The whole room got quiet and I had to check if my foot was back in my mouth. Before I had a chance to get good and scared, they all started laughing.

When I heard that, it made my heart start ticking again. Now that the tension is gone, I asked my aunt, "Where's my room?"

"You're standing in it." she replied, but I couldn't tell if she was serious or not. My. eyes got big as saucers. When I went to ask if she was crazy, the room erupted in laughter. All I could do was shake my head with a smirk on my face. My aunt walked over to me, gave me a love tap on the side of my face, then she escorted me to my new home.

It's strange because as I walk up the stairs, it seems like I'm getting younger with each step. I remember the first time I came down here to visit. I was ten years old and it was three days before Christmas. Although my aunt treated me like one of hers,

I was still homesick. I didn't want anybody to see that. I went into the bathroom and cried for the love of my mom.

I don't know if my mom or my aunt heard me but I'm glad they did, because mid-way into my cry my aunt knocked on the bathroom door to tell me my mom was on the phone. I hopped off the side of the tub, wiped my eyes, and ran out of the bathroom. It's a miracle what that one phone call did for me. I made it through Christmas without another sniffle.

My aunt entered my head by saying, "Do you want Ashley to stay in your room or mine?"

I laughed and said, "I think she will be cool in our room."

My aunt asked if I was sure and I nodded yes. I do know one thing, we still never have to worry about finding a baby sitter for Ashley. My aunt has fallen in love with her already. When I opened the door, I smell a faint scent of weed passed my nose.

My cousin Chicken was a weed head. Every time I call the house he was either smoking or going to get some weed. Since my uncle passed away he's been a handful for my aunt. I must admit that it was no surprise to hear that he got arrested for robbery. To this day I can't understand why rob a pizza man. I guess he had the munchies. Hopefully, when his two years are up, his mind will be right.

"This will do until I can find me and Lia something of our own." Although she's dead set against us moving elsewhere, I told my aunt we had to go because Lia likes to scream my name. She smiled and told me not to flatter myself.

She asked me, "Do me one favor. When Chicken calls, don't tell him you're staying in his room. For some strange reason he want his room to remain the same." She doesn't want to upset him while he's locked up. I can't blame her, but Chicken needs to stop bugging.

My aunt smacked my hand five and told me she would see me later after I settled in. I laid back on the bed and reflected on all the things that got me here. I thought of the bloody night when Tip was taken from me. Then the scene at the airport with me and Black. My heart still can't believe that he left without saying good-bye. Leaving was hard enough before pulled off. It took every ounce of will power and love for my family to get me on the plane.

Before I knew what was happening or where I was, Ashley was beating on my chest. When I woke up I didn't see my mirrors on the walls, nor did I see my camel colored plush carpet. At once I sat up to see Lia looking through our photo albums. The room was spotless and all of our bags were neatly packed away. I guess all the room needed was a woman's touch.

"All of your family are downstairs waiting for you," Lia said when she saw that I was up.

I said, "Like who?" and she turned her mouth up. I guess that was her way of saying that she didn't know.

I looked down at my watch to see how long I was sleeping. To my surprise, it was a whole five and half hours. Between hanging with Black last night and the jet lag, I can believe it. After I came from the bathroom, getting myself together, I scooped Ashley up and started downstairs. Before I made it out of the room, I turned and asked Lia if she was coming. She looked at me and then grabbed my hand and led me downstairs.

From the top of the stairs I could tell that my family was mob deep down there. When me and Lia became visible, the whole room shifted in our direction. WOW! There were people there that I haven't seen since I was a kid. Every aunt, uncle and cousin within a fifty-mile radius was here.

As I walked through the room greeting everyone, I introduced my two queens. I even made Lia happy by saying she was my fiancé. As usual, my drunken Uncle Lloyd wanted to slap box and my cousin Cheryl was being a flirt. That girl's been trying to get in my pants ever since I was fifteen. I'm glad Lia was trapped showing off Ashley. It's been a long day and I don't need any first day scandals.

There were a few people that were missing, but I'd bet a million I'd see them tomorrow. At the same time some loud ass music pulled up in front of my aunt's house. I didn't want to rush to the window because no one else did, but my curiosity was trying to get the best of me.

As I was easing over to the window, the doorbell rang. I was right next to the door, so I opened it. Low and behold, it was my little cousin Aaron. Everyone calls him Ron for short. I don't know why I call him my little cousin he's only eighteen months younger than me.

Without thinking he jumped straight into my arms. I wasn't surprised because he and I were always cool. When he came to New York, I overdosed him on Harlem. What did surprise me was when the guy with him asked for a hug too. Ron turned around and said, "Oh, shit! This is my partner, 'PB'." I stepped up and gave him a serious pound.

"You did say 'PB', right?" I asked after the fact.

"Yeah, 'PB'. That stands for Pretty Black, Play Boy, or Pure Blood. Take your pick." Right then and there I knew this dude was going to be a handful.

I didn't let my face give me away. I just laughed it off and told him I was feeling that. I grabbed Ron around the neck and told him there were two people I wanted him to meet. Five steps later he was staring down the barrel of Ashley's hypnotic eyes. When I introduced him to Lia, I don't think he even looked at her. All he kept doing was making those stupid baby noises at Ashley.

That's until my aunt came in and snatched her up. Before I knew it, the house was clearing out. Even though it seemed like it was still the weekend, it wasn't. It was Thursday night and they had to work in the morning. Ron gave me his pager number and told me to hit him after eleven a.m. tomorrow, that he'll come and scoop me up when I was ready. I asked him if tomorrow was his day, off, and he just laughed and they headed out of the door.

As the house cleared out I looked around for my little princess. She was fast asleep on the couch. My aunt had said good night a half hour ago. The only ones that were left were me and my family.

I told Lia to take Ashley upstairs and I would be up later. Of course, she wasn't going for it. She said that Ashley would get up if her daddy wouldn't tuck her in. Then she told me that she wouldn't mind if daddy tucked her in, too. It didn't take a rocket scientist to pick up on that. To be honest, the thought of christening our new bed with Lia's sweat was appealing. We haven't made love since Tip's death. With that thought in mind, I picked Ashley up and grabbed Lia by her hand and lead her upstairs.

CHAPTER 27: Black

It's been a whole day since I left Born at the airport. I can't believe I did that coward shit. Men just aren't supposed to act like that. I should've just told him what was on my mind. I couldn't see myself crying in front of anybody, especially Born. I can't believe in such a short period of time how my life has gone to the dogs. Right now, if I don't find a spot to get some money, I'm gonna be back robbing crap games and number holes.

It's crazy how soft that money has made me. Before it was nothing to rob a crap game, or an old lady for that matter. Now, it just seems like I don't have the heart for that shit anymore. That crack money was so easy to get. Anything that easy to get doesn't last long. When my mom first told me that I didn't understand what she meant. Now, not only do I understand, but I also had a chance to experience it first hand.

Leroy, the neighborhood drunk, once told me "If life has been a bitch to you, then you will marry one." If Leroy knew a secret when he told me that, then Frankenstein's wife should he beeping me right now.

For the first time in my life, I'm stuck. Not only don't I know my next move, but my feet feel nailed to the ground. Let me check my messages, maybe there is something on there about five foot six and a hundred and twenty pounds that can break my mood. Hopefully Born will be on there also.

I see I do have three messages. I hope they're all good news. Right about now some bad news will make me jump off the top of the Marriott Marquis.

Okay. I'm batting a thousand. So far two dime pieces want to see big daddy today. Oh, shit. That's lil Darryl. He's going to LL's private birthday bash at his mansion. If I'm not busy… hell no, I'm not busy. If I had a date with Sally Richardson, I would cancel for this party.

Let me hit him back to let him know that I'm trying to roll. Damn! What did I do with that card? Shit! I know it's around here somewhere. Oh, yeah. My blue Gap sweat pants. That's where it's at. Alright.

"Hello. This is *Underworld Records*. How may I place your call?"

CHAPTER 28: Born

I rolled over to get me a quickie, but to my surprise, there wasn't anyone to grab. With that early morning shock, my eyes opened wide like a Coast commercial. I felt like a cheap chicken head. She used me for my body then ran out on me.

Really, I hope she's downstairs cooking something for breakfast. I ran my hand up and down the spot I last saw my lover. What the hell is this? A wet spot? What the fuck! I immediately pulled back the comforter to see Ashley's baby bottle soaking through the sheet. I couldn't do anything but laugh. Even when my little princess is not around, she has a way of brightening her daddy's day. I think back on the days when I said if I had a girl I would die. Now I would recommend to any man that the best thing he can do is have a little *mami.* She's been my little stress reliever since she was born.

I guess it's time to get up and see what the crew is cooking. As I rose up the phone started to ring. My instinct almost made me pick it up. I almost forgot I was in a new town and a new house.

When the phone got to the fourth ring, I shouted to my aunt to pick up the phone. The house went back silent and the phone continued to ring. After the tenth or eleventh ring I quickly snatched the receiver up. The voice on the other end said, "You sound winded. What were you doing? Fucking?"

"Who the hell is this?"

"This is PB."

"Check this out, money, don't play yourself out!"

"I was just kidding."

"Oh, yeah? Well, find someone less likely to kill you to play with. Now, what do you want?"

"Aaron told me to give you a call to see if you were up. He might not be up for another few hours, but he wanted me to check on you," he told me, trying to make light of the situation.

I told him, "Thanks," with my attitude loud and clear. "Now, do me a favor. Tell my cousin to call me when he gets up." Then I hung up without saying good-bye. My cousin's got some nerve having his flunky call here on joke time.

Before I had time to finish farting, the phone rang again. I didn't wait ten rings this time because it was clear that I had the house all to myself. I snatched the phone up thinking it was that clown PB and an electronic voice said, "You have a collect call from Chicken…" My face lit up because I haven't talked to my big cousin in a few years.

I pressed the "0" and Chicken said, "Mom, is my son there?" I teased him by staying quiet.

After he said hello twice, I said, "No, your son ain't here champ."

"If you value your live, don't play with me," he said trying to go jail house on me.

"Oh, yeah. I forgot. I'm talking to Monster Cody. What's up, punk. This is Born."

"You mean Ricky Ricardo, don't you?" he replied and we both bust out laughing.

"What's up, Dog? You alright up in there? Did you get the kicks I sent you?"

He replied yes, but he wasn't big on Barkley's or Air Max. He wanted those ugly Bugs Bunny Jordan's. The phone started beeping, so I knew his time was almost up. He asked me if I was sleeping in his room. I stuttered, but I got out a faint no. I guess he knew I was lying because he said if I was, he didn't mind. Then the phone hung up.

For an instant I felt sad. I wasn't sure if it was because he was there or I was one step away from being there. Nevertheless, I got to make it happen for me and my family while I'm out. Right now the only thing I have to do is page Black and get some food in my stomach. Where is Ms. Dee when you need her?

CHAPTER 29: Lia

I hope by the time I'm her age I will have the energy she has. She's been dragging me all over town since eight o'clock this morning. We've paid every bill from the electric to her credit cards. We've done the shopping for the week although it looked like a month's worth. I guess a home full of grandchildren and now Born and me can eat up some shit. Not to mention that three hundred pound monster she's dating.

I did notice one thing, the prices are a lot cheaper down here. She filled up her trunk and her entire back seat for a hundred and three dollars. When I go to Pathmark, I couldn't fill up the glove compartment for a hundred dollars.

Now for the moment of truth. A place I plan to spend a lot of time ... the mall. I hope the mall is just as cheap as the supermarket. I've only been here a few minutes, but I don't see any stores I recognize. I guess Macy's and Bloomingdales might be out of the question.

Every step I take I see somebody watching me. They're acting like I'm from Mars or something. They keep asking where I got my outfit, shoes, and even my earrings. They look so disappointed when I say New York. If I get this much attention from a DKNY sweat suit and some gold balls, what are these hoes gonna do when I put the Versace and diamond studs on?

I wish we still had the BMW. I would really have them talking around here.

After a few hours of running in and out of Lane Bryant and Ashley Stewart for Aunt Mae, I finally ran across a Kiddie World. I told Aunt Mae I would be in Kiddie World when she was done.

As I walked in the older white lady gave me a funny look. I wasn't sure if it was for me, so I kept walking. A minute later she was dead on my heels. I didn't find it strange because a young black girl with a bag always puts a store on alert. What I did find strange was after I examined one or two outfits for Ashley, I noticed they didn't have any alarms on their merchandise. The shoplifting, rate must be really low in Mayberry. I should call my girl Yvonne and tell her to come down and cleanup.

The cloths were reasonable, but I didn't see a whole lot of what I was looking for. Nevertheless, I still grabbed few things. Now, I know the next time I go home to buy out the kids Gap.

Right before I was about to leave, I saw some really cute sun dresses for Ashley. While I flipped through the rack for Ashley's favorite color, a voice from behind said, "You look to young to have any children."

Without turning around I said, "You sound too young for an old ass pick up line like that."

I heard him take a deep breath, so I knew I hit home. I also knew that he wouldn't stop the pursuit. When I turned around to walk to the cash register, I saw him. I must admit he was a cutie. He didn't have that country corny look about him, either. His clothes were on point and his jewelry was definitely on point. His cross was mad icy and I'm feeling that diamond face Movado.

Unless he owns this mall, it's plain to see he's a hustler. He asked me if I wanted him to pay for that. As hard as it is for me to turn down free money, I asked, "Do I look broke to you?"

He stepped out of my way and simply said, "Excuse me."

While I walked toward the counter, Aunt Mae walked in the store. She asked me if I was alright and I quickly said yes. Then I pulled out my American Express and paid for my stuff. When we were walking out I noticed Mae give the guy a vicious glare. I didn't want to ask her, but I saw he wasn't fazed by it.

On the way to the car I asked her if she knew the guy. She immediately stopped walking. She told me he was bad news and to avoid him. She told me that he thinks he's big shit because he's on the tip of everyone's tongue.

"Why is everyone talking about him?"

"The rumors say he's a millionaire," she said with a hint of interest.

"I couldn't tell with that cheap ass shirt he had on."

At once we started laughing. Ashley didn't know why we were laughing, but it tickled her anyway. I told Mae that Born wasn't a millionaire, but he got something that's worth his weight in gold and we laughed some more.

"Ain't that gold, hon. You got this princess."

We put the bags in the car and squeezed in ourselves. As I was putting the seatbelt around me and Ashley, I noticed an all black Lexus LS 400 with *"PRETTY"* on the plates.

CHAPTER 30: Born

I must have showered in that bathroom a hundred times when I was a kid. For the life of me, I can't figure out why it felt so strange today. I know there are a lot of things on my mind, but a shower should be a shower.

No matter how many days get between me and Tip's death, I still wake up trembling. I know this feeling can't last forever. Now that I'm looking good and smelling good, I'm ready to tackle the town. That's if my cousin ever gets here. He claims he had one stop to make and he was on his way. When it rolled off his tongue it sounded real smooth, but that was nearly two hours ago.

It wouldn't be so bad if Lia were here to pass the time with me. Right now, all I got are reruns of Magnum PI to keep me company. When Lia does get back I'm gonna tell her about herself. She could've at least left a fucking note. I know this is a bad time for her to act up, things are hectic enough as it is.

I thought I heard someone pull up in the driveway. I hope its Couso, so I ran to the window. When I pulled the curtains back, all I saw was my aunt's old ass Sentra and a car full of smiles.

As I went to release the curtain I saw a pearl white Q45 pull up behind them I must admit, I was a little shocked to see Couso behind the wheel. Did the Beverley Hillbillies strike oil in real life? I opened the door for the first heatwave to enter. As Lia passed me she gave me a peck on the cheek. I had a mouth full for her before the kiss, but nothing came out. All I could do was smack her on the ass as she passed.

My aunt waved me over to help with the bags. I walked over to the car and saw the whole mall in the back seat. Some things don't change. Lia is still a shop-a-holic. At the rate she's going we'll be on welfare down here. I turned towards the car to hear Lia sexy voice behind me. Don't forget the ones in the trunk. She had to be joking but when the trunk popped open I saw she was serious as cancer. Tonight I must tell Lia that George Washington chopped down our money tree. I kissed her and Ashley and jumped in Ron's car. Ron hit the horn and started to pull off. I yelled out the window, "You girls had your fun, now it's my turn."

My aunt just waved me off. I heard Lia yelling my name over Naughty By Nature. I slapped Ron five and sunk down in the beige leather seat. Ron opened up with a little small talk. He asked if Lia had any sisters. He asked about my BMW, then he broke my heart when he asked about Tip and Black, it made me sink that much more into the seat.

I changed the subject quickly and asked about the machine he was driving. He was beating around the bush, but I could see a lot had changed since the last time I saw him.

"Once we catch up to PB, we are going to kick it," he told me, ignoring the question I asked him.

We pulled up beside a green Maxima with two dime pieces inside. They started honking the horn like crazy when they saw me and Ron. The way they were looking I had no choice but to sit up in the seat. I tapped my cousin on the arm and pointed in the direction of the females. He explained to me that he knew them, but they were nothing but groupies. That made me double take the girls, but more so him. Who in the hell has he become to have groupies? He must have one hell of a story to tell me.

I wish they would've pulled up on my side. They would've got all the rap they could handle, and then some. It's only the first day. Before it's all said and done, my presence will be felt.

One of my biggest flaws is I always manage to have two houses. It wouldn't be so bad if it was just houses, but they always come equipped with two girls. That's the part that always gets you caught up.

As we continued to ride around town, I'm noticing how his Q45 is sticking out like a motherfucker. My mind started to race and I was curious when we were going to catch up with the infamous PB.

"When are we going to catch up to your sidekick?" I asked Ron.

"He's not my sidekick, he's my man (pause)," he snapped at me with a sharp tone.

To keep from flipping on him I just said "whatever" and finished looking at the music selection. I was thinking about calling him Punching Bag. What would he have said then? I love my cousin, but right now, I don't know him. The answer to this mystery is Punching Bag. Hopefully we will be seeing him real soon. Every corner we passed, people waved.

Every car we passed honked. This whole thing was starting to get stranger by the minute. As my head looked from side to side for the wave or honk, Ron said "about time" out loud as he checked his beeper. He told me that PB was at the mall. He pressed on the gas and said, "We will be there in ten minutes." At the speed he was going, we could be in South Carolina in ten minutes. I'm just like that. I hate when other people drive fast because I don't feel safe. On the other hand, I drive like a real New Yorker.

After running a light or two and taking a few corners at 80 mph, we were at the mall. To me it looks more like a shopping center than a mall. Give me a Mart 125 any day.

Does anyone down here work? Because this parking lot is jam packed. As we walked through the double doors Ron spotted PB standing next to the Ms. Fields Cookie Stand. We walked over to him and Ron tapped him on his shoulder, which spun him around. When he saw it was Ron, they greeted each other like they haven't seen each other in years. I can't complain because me and my crew were the same way. That's a sure sign of loyalty; better yet, love.

After all the greetings were over, he got the Ms. Field girl's number and we walked off. I scanned the mall like a bright eyed little kid. To my disappointment, I didn't see any familiar stores. I don't think I'm gonna be able to survive without a Dr. Jay's.

I heard Ron asking PB if he'd eaten yet. I know somebody must have been reading my mind because I'm starving. PB said, "let's go downstairs and hit up Denny's." My face went blank because the only thing I heard about Denny's was that they were racist.

I shouted out, "Denny's? What's up with IHOP?" They both started laughing.

Ron said, "Maybe another time."

"What's wrong with now?"

PB said, "Because we're too hungry to drive sixty miles to Raleigh." Then they started laughing again. This time I couldn't help but laugh with them.

After the humor wore off, I couldn't help but wonder what I've gotten myself into. One escalator later we were entering a restaurant with a big Sambo face on the door. PB and Ron walked straight in, but I couldn't get passed the disrespect to me and my people. What I felt like doing more than eating was throwing a trashcan through the window. I guess down in Hicksville USA a black man can make a fool out of himself and all blacks before and after him is common place. Maybe I'm over reacting but I still think it's these two that's not reacting enough.

Ron came back and said, "One man can't change the south. Especially a city slicker like yourself who don't understand it." He put his hand on my shoulder and walked me to the table.

We sat down to be greeted by a sweet old black lady. That was a little easier for me than a snotty white waitress. She called PB and Ron by name and asked if they wanted their usual. PB said, "No, we're going to let our cousin order for us." It took every reflex I had not to look around to see who he was talking to. I played along with his little game.

I asked Ms. Celia, "Does the plantation have Welch's Grape Juice?"

She looked at me strange from the plantation remark, but replied, "Do country people eat road kill?" I guess that was her way of saying yes because Ron started shaking his head with a smile.

I said, "Give me a T-bone steak with cheese eggs." I folded my menu closed and gave it to her.

She said, "Let me see if my old brain got this all. Three orders of T-bone steak, cheese eggs, and Welch's grape juice."

I gave her the nod of approval and said "You know what? That sounds good."

CHAPTER 31: PB

I can see that this bullshit isn't going to work. Me and Ron have been seeing eye-to-eye since the day we met. He was the point guard and I was to power forward. For two years we worked the pick and roll like Stockton and Malone, except Malone couldn't dunk like I could. We both were all country, but neither of us wanted that life.

Really, we were fascinated with the life that was surrounded with sex, money, murder and more sex. Now we got this clown trying to act like he's better than both of us. I must admit, he did inspire me from all the stories Ron told me. Now, he's in my town and he better recognize that. I know he's looking at this town like it's a piece of shit, but this piece of shit made me over a million the last three years.

Ron was about to pop the question to Rico, but I tapped him and said, "Wait until he finishes eating." Really, I didn't care if the little bitch ate or not. I just wanted to do the honors. Ron's my man, but to be real, he don't know his ass from his elbow. When it comes to business, he keeps his hand on the gun while I handle everything. I told him we're partners, but realistically, he might only get ten percent of the money.

Now, I'm no mathematician, but a man can live really well off of ten percent of 1.5 million. "Okay, check this out Rico. Let me start by saying I've been hearing about you for years. Everything Ron has kicked about you was good. The most important things were that you're loyal to your people, your love for cheddar, and you're a gangster."

"Those three things are the sign of a real man. Now that I've helped blow your head up, let me get to the point. Me and your cousin are taking down some serious dough around here. Now, the only problem is we can't get our hands on enough product. The guys that I'm connected with are so undependable it's sickening. There are times we don't work for two months at a time. Our clientele is the best, but we miss a lot of money during that down time. Money that we all can use." I feel like throwing this nasty ass grape juice in his face for not paying me any attention.

"Now, what I'm suggesting is that we open the flood gates with a New York to North Carolina pipeline. Not just any pipeline, but one with you at the head. This is an offer that no sane man can refuse. You're going straight to the penthouse on a million dollar business. We have the police and the courts on lock, so you don't have to worry about that. This situation is ideal, except for the lack of product. In a nutshell, the more we have, the more we can move."

Rico looked at me, took a deep breath, and said, "I'm sorry. I left my problems in New York not to pick up some new ones. Me and the streets are divorced. So, thanks, but no thanks." Then he got up, dropped a twenty on the table and walked out.

My blood pressure must have shot through the roof. I told Ron to go after him and straighten him out. I think the chump is just playing hard to get so he can get a bigger piece of the pie. That's real shrewd on his part. We can play this chess game as long as I'm the one who wins.

CHAPTER 32: Black

Damn! I feel like shit. I can't fully get over one hangover before I pile it on again. Those industry parties are off the hook. The women in the party are like nothing I ever saw. I couldn't believe that I was sitting with the super model Kenya. She's got to be the finest thing God ever created. As if that wasn't enough, to wake up with Simone in my bed.

For years I had dreams of fucking an R&B chick. The last couple of weeks have been crazy. The only thing missing were Tip and Born. I think as long as they're missing in my life, a billion dollars and that Puerto Rican dancer chick from *In Living Color* couldn't make me happy.

Born has beeped me everyday since he left, but I just can't find the heart to call back. Every time I call his mother, she has nothing but good things to say. I tell her to send my love, but that's it. Before it's all said and done, things will be back to normal. Right now, I'm just living my life because you never know when your number will be called.

I'm going to give Darryl a call to see if he's eaten lunch. Hopefully he's tide up in some million dollar deal that can get us both paid. I want to hit up that new joint the Shark Bar. Every time I go in there I see someone famous. If I keep rubbing elbows like this, they're gonna start wondering who I am. That would be funny if someone asked for my autograph. I'm going to sign Wise from Stestosonics. That's the only person I think I resemble.

Oh, shit! I hear my cell phone ringing, but I can't find it. Where is it? Oh, shit! There it goes. "Hello" the sexy voice said.

I asked, "Who am I speaking to?" but she didn't give me her name.

Instead she asked, "How many girls did you give your number to at Def Jam's party?"

I thought for a moment and said, "Only one that matters."

She replied, "Be very careful before you answer."

I told her, "Why be careful? The truth should, never hurt." She said I was right, then I said, "Hello, Kenya."

CHAPTER 33: Born

It's been about a week since my meeting with Nino and G-Money. I still can't believe he said that was an offer that I can't refuse. If I weren't trying to blend in around here, I would've put two in his head. Don't these clowns know that I can't be pressured? Men do what they want, boys do what they're told.

While I was waiting for Chicken to call and playing Street Fighter, the phone rang. I snatched it up on the first ring. When I picked it up, I didn't hear any recorder. Instead, I heard a snake.

"What's up?" the deep voice said.

I really didn't want to answer, but instead I said, "I'm busy."

Before I could hang up he asked me to give him a minute. I figure a minute wouldn't hurt one way or another. So, with a deaf ear I decided to let him talk.

He started apologizing that our last meeting got off on the wrong foot. He sounds a lot better when he's on his knees. This was the perfect time to hang up, but I passed it up. He really caught my attention when he said that he had six first class tickets to the Bahamas. He said me, him and Ron can take some freaks, or if I like, I could take Lia.

I asked him if this was his way of bribing me. Of course, he denied it. As much as the trip appealed to me, I had to turn him down. I could hear from the tone of his voice he couldn't believe I said no. Maybe it was that nobody told him no twice. Although I told him no thanks I really meant the opposite.

Machiavelli said that a man must be pampered or annihilated. In this case, I'm unsure what to do with this kid. I'll just rock him to sleep until I figure it out. I've always been a firm believer that you keep your friends close and your enemies closer.

"Yo! PB, I don't mean to cut you off, but that's my cousin beeping in from jail." He tried to tell me one last thing, but I said peace and clicked over to the electronic message from Chicken.

We've talked more now than we ever did. I speak to him almost everyday. Even though the calls are only fifteen minutes, they seem to make both of our days.

The phone kept beeping, but I couldn't click over because it would cut Chicken off. Right now, these fifteen minutes are real important to the both of us. As soon as I hung the receiver up, the ring blared through the house. I knew it was Lia. She was calling me from every phone booth her and my aunt stopped by. I could tell she was getting bored with the running around.

I answered the phone saying, "Hello, sweetheart."

The voice on the other end said, "Sorry, I don't play that on the first date." I thought it was "Paper Boy", but it turned out to be my cousin. I really wasn't in the mood to rap with him, but since I gave "Paper Boy" five minutes. I got to give him at least six.

"What's up, Ron?"

He didn't have a lot to say. Well nothing that made sense. When a black man ask you about the weather, they're not coming clean. At that point I figured I would help him out. I told him that me and PB kissed and made up. He tried to pretend that he didn't know me and PB spoke earlier. I knew that was a lie, but I let it ride.

He broke the silence by asking me what I was doing tonight. I didn't have any plans. Lia and my aunt were going to the River Boat for some million-dollar bingo contest. Ashley is fifty miles away at my great aunt's house. That poor girl hasn't slept in the same bed twice since she's been here. "I guess I'm free," I told him. Although a little time to myself to think wouldn't have been bad.

He told me about a party that they go to once a month. I really didn't want to go. Where I'm from it cost money to party. Right now, spending money is low on my list. Nevertheless, I got to get out of the house. Finally, I told him, "Yeah. Pick me up at 12:30."

He said, "What!" in a high-pitched voice. He let me know that this ain't New York. The clubs shut down at 2 am sharp, here. I couldn't believe that bum shit, so I told him 10:00.

CHAPTER 34: Born

I really didn't want to give North Cakalaki too much, but I gave them enough to know that I'm from the fashion capitol of the world. Not only was the Versace in full effect, but the jewelry was turned all the way up. I wasn't sure if they were ready for the Rolex or the carats in the ear. Fuck 'em. I gave it to them anyway.

PB and Ron were all eyes when they saw me. I could tell they were shocked, but not as shocked as me when I saw that 500SL. That was a car in a class of it's own. The back had enough room to put a Yugo in it. Ron had his seat all the way back and the seat wasn't even touching me. My baby was big, but this is huge. I guess this is the club up ahead or maybe not.

As we pulled up the crowd was blocking the street. Even though they saw the car they were more worried about getting in the club. PB got on the car phone, which was burned in the armrest. After he hung up he started counting backward from 10. I couldn't understand why until two motherfuckers about seven feet tall parted the crowd like the red sea.

We eased through with every male and female waving at us. This whole scene was really, starting to trip me out. I guess I can deal with it for one night.

As we made our way out of the car and passed the velvet ropes, I noticed the club was smaller than I thought, but I got to admit, it was laid out. The hanging cage dancers really, caught my eye. Especially the Oriental one.

As we made our way to the bar, the crowd was rocking off of *"Party and Bullshit"*. Before I could order my patented Strawberry Daiquiri, the spotlight hit us. I felt like I was ducking from the police copter. The DJ started to give the C-Note player shout outs. PB and Ron just waved like superstars. Then he said, "To the newest member of the C.N.P. is New York's own, Rico."

I thought my ears were playing tricks on me, but they weren't. I can't believe they thought I would melt in my shoes when I heard my name over the mic. I've been getting shout outs at the roof top for years, and after that, the rink.

These motherfuckers are really trying their hand so I won't hurt their feelings. I won't walk out. I'll just go with the flow and milk it all night, just for one night.

I cut my eyes in Ron and Paper Boy's direction. Before they could get the full effect a red-bone *mami* planted her ass on me. She was riding me so hard she almost knocked my drink out of my hand. It's been a minute since I partied, but I got right back in the swing of things. I rode that ass until I forgot how mad I was. It was last call at the bar before I knew what time it was. It was wild because I still didn't even know the girl's name. She turned and said to me, "Let me be the first to welcome you to North Carolina." She grabbed my hand and led me to the back of the club.

Since it was my first time in the joint, my mind started racing. We came to a sign that had "Handicap Restroom" on the door.

She looked at me with nothing but lust in her eyes and I was erect instantly. We rushed our way in. Miss Thing didn't waste any time. She dropped my pants and gave me a light push. I took half a step back and my bare ass met cold sink. That didn't matter much because I was watching honey drop to her knees. This was like a scene out of one of those B movies. The kind where the white couple are fucking when the killer is on their ass.

She grabbed me in her hand and said, "Did you think mamma was gonna forget about her baby?" I was like putty in her hand at that point. She kissed it a few times, just enough to put those goose bumps all over my body. Once she placed me in her mouth I could've exploded on contact. I knew that would've blown the mood. She had me right where she wanted me with my eyes rolling backwards.

Suddenly, she stopped and snatched open her button down shirt. The sight of her hard nipples excited me that much more. She grabbed my hands and gently placed them on her breasts. I guess that was part of her ritual for getting excited, but I didn't mind. After that, she showered me with nothing but love, until the inevitable happened. Even that didn't side track her train of thought. By this time I was balancing myself on my tiptoes, but loving every minute of it.

Finally when the satisfaction was fully visible on my face she rose from the floor. She looked over my shoulder to the mirror and wiped off some unwanted evidence from her mouth. She concealed her perfect 34C's and put on a fresh coat of lipstick. At this point I had to know her name. My mouth parted to ask her name. Before a word could come out, her slender finger hushed my lips. I guess some things are better left unsaid. She grabbed my hand and escorted me out the way she escorted me in.

By the time we made it back to the dance floor the crowd was departing. I saw Ron standing at the exit looking like he lost his mommy at the mall. I walked right up on him with my mystery girl trailing right behind me. She gave Ron a light slap on the face and walked out. Ron just looked back at me and laughed. I asked him, "Who was that girl?"

He replied by saying "You don't know?"

"If I knew, would I ask?"

He blew my mind when he said, "Your cousin."

I almost fainted. I grabbed him in the collar and asked, "Why didn't you tell me?"

He said, "She's Uncle George's daughter." Then it hit me, George didn't have a daughter. This goofball started to laugh again. Seeing the confusion on my face, he said, "That's George's step daughter from marriage."

I felt the hundred pounds of guilt fall off my chest. Ron told me, "Don't worry. I've been there myself. I think she has a goal to fuck all the men in our family." At that point we both got in a good laugh. On the way to the car he put his arm around my shoulder and said, "Oh, yeah. If you ever grab me like that again, I'll forget I'm your favorite cousin."

CHAPTER 35: Black

"Okay, mom, I'll talk to you later. I love you, too. Tell Born that I love him, too."

I slowly hung up the receiver. I couldn't believe how bad I felt. My second mom always had a way of getting to me. I can't believe Born used her to get to me. I remember when we were younger, I had a dog named Blaze. He was a black Belgian Sheppard. My mom told me not to take the dog out, but Born didn't listen. He convinced me that he could walk a dog twice his size. The end result was as soon as Blaze smelt the fresh air he broke free. There was nothing we could do. He ran into the street where he was stopped cold by a *Mr. Softee* ice cream truck.

All I could do was cry for days. That was the only pet I had from birth. Losing him was like losing a part of my family. I thought I would never forgive Born, until his mom called. She made me see the difference between friendship and love. From that moment on I knew what we had was no ordinary friendship. Not only did she do it that day, but she also did it today.

I knew that today was the day that I'd call Born. I reached in my pocket and pulled out the number. It. was a little wrinkled, but the numbers stood out. I picked up the phone and held it to my ear. I wanted to dial the number, but my finger froze. As much as I wanted to dial, I couldn't. All I could think about was him hanging up for that airport stunt.

Before I knew it, a loud beep took over my thoughts. I nearly jumped out of my skin. I guess I had the receiver up too long without dialing. I slammed it down fast and picked it up even faster. I dialed the number as quick as possible before I changed my mind. The phone started ringing and I took a deep breath.

A familiar voice said, "Hello," I knew it was Lia. Then she said, "Hello?" again out of frustration. I pretended not to recognize her voice when I asked for Born.

I was hoping she didn't ask for my name, but she did. When I said "Black" I could tell she was glad I called, but she let me have it anyway. She didn't say anything about the airport. She asked me what kind of godfather didn't call his goddaughter. I tried to hit her with a few quick ones, but like all women, she wouldn't let it go. I was like a child getting scolded by his mother. All I could think about was did she miss me?

After a few minutes of getting cursed out she said, "Hold your sorry ass on." The next voice I heard was Born's.

He said, "I did have an earful for you when you called, but I see Lia beat me to it."

We laughed for a minute and caught up with what's been happening in our lives. I told him about Darryl and all the parties. He told me about his clown ass cousin. I felt a little jealous because he sounded like he was cool down there. I didn't tell him about Kenya because it was still early. We made up like two brothers would and vowed that this bullshit would never happen again.

CHAPTER 36: PB

"What the hell you mean 'he's in a meeting'? Tell him I don't care if he's meeting with Coca Cola, Sprite, and Moet. Tell him PB is on the phone." While she had me on hold I was getting madder by the second. I felt like hanging up and going down there. I knew if I went down there someone's head was going to spin around like the Exorcist.

The phone clicked and the voice said, "May I help you?"

I said, "Yeah. You can help me by not playing any games with me." I knew by the way he was stuttering that I had his attention. "Don't get so big, Mr. Club Owner, that you don't know where the strength lies. Now let's get down to business. Last month when I had my party at your club, a friend of mine was there. He and a lady friend went into the bathroom and got busy. Now, what I want from you is the tape from that episode."

The trembling voice on the other end of the line tried to convince me that there weren't any cameras in the bathrooms. I didn't feel like playing cat and mouse with him so I cut to the chase.

"Look, fool, I'm going to give you twenty five gees for it." That made him start to stutter more. Nevertheless, part of my plan was complete.

CHAPTER 37: Born

A few months have passed and I feel like things are settling down. I got a job at my man Boobie's barbershop. I haven't cut hair in years, but since I'm from New York, people come to me. I guess they think I know something special.

Since we moved out of my aunt's house, things have been a little tight. I've been scared to spend two dollars. Lia has been on my case about being cheap. She doesn't understand this is not crack money anymore. I bought a Chevy Lumina to shut her up. I was borrowing my aunt's Sentra.

I let her drive to school while I'm at the barbershop. She's trying to learn to sell real estate. I wasn't big on it, but she was nagging too much when we was in the house all day. Now that she has a car, I can't seem to keep up with her. She's always late picking me up, so I catch a ride home with Boobie. Some days we argue about it, other days I'm too tired from standing up all day. I'm down here frustrating myself to death while my man is in New York hanging out for a living. Part of me wants to go home bad as hell.

I just can't believe that five people can die without anything happening. Blacks in America are treated like shit. Who would've ever thought, my man Black, an A & R for a record label. I want to send him this tape I made. He never took my rapping serious before, so I know he won't now.

CHAPTER 38: Detective Sullivan

"You mean after all these months, you motherfuckers don't have one fucking lead? What in the hell have you been doing all this time? Sitting around with your thumbs up your asses? I gave you the killer's months ago and you let them run around. I don't want to hear that bullshit about evidence. You're the detective, make some up. Just do the city a favor and get these menaces off the streets!" His face harden with each passing second. I knocked over my lamp and pencil holder in discuss.

As it crashed to the ground I looked around for something else to destroy. I saw the stack of case files but didn't dare touch them. I knew that could be the difference between them rotting in jail or walking the streets. Knowing that, I just stared at case files.

"What happened to the old lady that saw the whole thing? I bet she can't remember. Her memory would be a whole lot better if it was her son out there dead. Give me five minutes alone with the old hag and she will point me in the right direction," I asked Bryant. I looked around for something else to smash while I paced the floor but nothing seemed worth it.

"Correct me if I'm wrong, but aren't you in charge of the Red Rum Task Force in Brooklyn? Well, it was two hundred and fifty thousand and over a million dollars of cocaine. Not to mention five dead people. Now if that's not a drug related murder, what in the fuck is it?" Click! Those scum buckets are going to pay for this one way or another!

CHAPTER 39: Sara

I wonder who these people are who call the radio station. They sound like they were raised by wolves. They call in knowing that there are thousands of ears glued to the radio. With no regard they talk about other people of other races, religion, or sexuality. Then, tomorrow, when a person bumps them or responds with an attitude, what's the first thing they say? He's racist or she has homophobia. People don't understand that what comes out of their mouths start out snowflakes, but can end up as an avalanche.

I tell my mom the same thing. After a long talk with my mom I can't help thinking I was adopted. She spends half of the conversation trying to get me back into law school. Then she spends the other half telling me how no good my pops is. I love her to death, but some times she can be a little melodramatic. Lisa better be ready when I get there. It's already been a long day. Now she wants me to ride all the way downtown to pick her up. She could've got her nails and eyebrows done closer to her house. She just likes to go down to Big Times to cock watch. She should be like me and do her nails while watching reruns. If she's outside like she promised, we might be able to beat the rush hour traffic home.

Oh, boy. It never fails. Every time I come down here it looks like a car show. The macho shit is such a joke. They must be thinking the car is an extension of their penis. HA! HA! HA! I must admit it's something about a man with a fresh haircut that turns me on.

Look at me sounding like Lisa. Speaking of the devil, there she is. She's outside like she promised. It must be going to snow. I hit the horn two times to get her attention. She waved at me and so did Boobie. I was hoping he didn't come over to the car with his lame ass lines.

WOW! Who is that? Now that is what I call fine. At the same time he sticks out like a sore thumb. Not in a bad way, it's just something about him that's pulling me. Hold your horses, Sara. Are you forgetting how you just wasted two years on Chuck and his bullshit? The last thing I need is a man in my life. I would make an exception if he's a mechanic. I really need some body to fix this lemon I got.

Damn! I think he caught me staring at him. I turned away and motioned to Lisa to bring her ass on. Boobie passed her a piece of paper and she jumped in. She slapped me five and we drove off. All the way out of the parking lot I watched the stranger through the rear view mirror. I hear Lisa running her mouth, but I was more concerned with him.

Lisa said, "Oh, yeah," and before she could hand me the paper I said keep it. She's always get with Boobie because he's got four barbershops. I don't care if he's got money.

I got my own money. What I do care about is that he's a whore. He pulls up on these country hoochies in his BMW with his gold smile. From there he expects you to drop your drawers. Not this girl. This might be silly, but I'm waiting for my Prince Charming to drive up and take me away from all this.

Lisa is still running her mouth about some guy and his 4-Runner. That's my girl and I love her so much, but she worries about material stuff too much. That's why her heart stays broken. I tried to make small talk with her and then she slid in a few questions about the new dude. Without any notice I said, "Who was the other guy with you and Boobie?"

She started screaming, "I knew it!" at the top of her lungs.

My defensive side kicked in and asked her, "What are you talking about?" She claimed she saw me watching him from the car. Of course, I denied it, but my red cheeks were giving me away. She claimed there weren't any guys like that in law school. All at once we started laughing.

There were a few lookers back at school, but the nerd thing was a turn off. Too bad she didn't know much about him. All she knew is that he was from New York and his name was Born or Rico. She said, "Some people call him Rico and others call him Born." I told her that I liked Rico.

A real live New Yorker. That explains the look. These country boys don't know what style is. I've never been to New York, but if all the guys look like that, I have to go.

Lisa asked what I was thinking about.

"Nothing," I said, but she knew me too well. She said that I had a smirk a mile long on my face. Me and Lisa have been through so much together. She knows me better than anybody else. The first time I ran away, I went straight to her house. She hid me from her mother for two days.

That's my best friend. Just at that moment I give the witch a compliment, she starts singing, "Rico and Sara, sitting in the tree, K-I-S-S-I-N-G."

I gave her an elbow and said, "I'm going to tell Mama Betty that you're teasing me again." Two can play the kiddie role. We laughed so hard my stomach started to hurt. I can always count on a good laugh when me and Lisa are together. I needed it too before I go see Mommy Dearest.

"Where is my godson at?" I asked Lisa while keeping my eyes on the road.

"With his dead beat dad."

Jason's not a bad guy. The reason they're not together is because he won't put up with her shit. That's a touchy subject, so I just stay out of it. I've known Jason for a long time. When I see him I do the same thing.

Lisa elbowed me and said, "Don't look now, but your Prince has arrived. Rico is one car behind us." I could see him without turning, so I didn't. She tried to convince me to flag him down. I asked if she was crazy. It's something about hitting on a guy that I can't do.

Finally, I saw him out of the corner of my eye. I found it strange that he was driving a Lumina. Not that it mattered, I thought everybody at Boobie's spent their last on a nice car. The light turned green and he was about to pass us. Lisa leaned over and started to hit the horn frantically. Lucky for me he had his window up and music on. After I got her crazy ass off the horn, I was glad he didn't hear her. Then I noticed a devilish grin grow on his face and I knew he had heard her. He made the next left and tapped the horn. I was so embarrassed I turned two shades redder.

CHAPTER 40: Born

I can't believe how different girls look all over the country, but they're all the same. It doesn't matter if they're black, Spanish, white, or green. They're so predictable. If they're not stealing your beeper number from their man, they're flagging you down when you ride by. Nevertheless, the day of the shy girl is long gone. In a way it makes my job a lot easier, but part of the thrill, sometimes, is the chase.

I have to admit, Shorty that was driving did look right. I never messed with a preppy before and I doubt I'll start now.

As I pulled in my driveway I wondered if Lia was inside. I told her I wanted to spend the weekend with her and Ashley. I've been feeling like me and Lia were drifting apart. I haven't been able to put my finger on the problem, but I think it's the long hours we both have been putting in at work and school. When we were back home, neither of us worked. That meant that we were at each other's beck and call. Now we can't even go to the movies without me falling asleep. Not to mention, we went from three times a week and endless quickies to once a week if that.

I walked in the door to see my baby's toys all over the place. That let me know the monster was on a terror. I bent around the corner to see Lia laid on the sofa with the phone under her chin. She saw me and said another word or two, then she hung up. I was looking at her wondering why. She sat up and said "What?"

I didn't reply by choice I asked, "Was that my aunt on the phone?"

She said it was some girl from her school. If I knew the tension was going to be like this, I think I would've stayed at work. I didn't push the issue, I just scooped up my little princess and blew burples on he neck.

Lia shouted out from the kitchen "Did you pick up the stuff from the market?" I slapped my forehead and hated to say I forgot.

I smoothed it over by saying, "I didn't get it because I was going to take you out to dinner."

"No thanks, sweetheart. Me and Ashley just got out of the tub."

"Well, I'm going to the market and pick up those few items."

She didn't say anything else before I closed the door. I was glad to hear her call me sweetheart. It's been a while, since that pretty face said anything sweet. Maybe this weekend has a chance after all. Maybe if I close my eyes and count to ten the old Lia will reappear. I think I got a better chance for peace in the world.

Ten minutes later I'm walking through the automatic door of the farmer's market. It's kind of packed in here, but I'm not going to let it stop my flow. I'm here for five hot items. I should be in and out in a blink of an eye.

As I walked around with my chromed out hooptie. I noticed how out of place I felt. These other women are flying up and down these aisles like they were born in here. Even the grannies are like speed racers. This and malls are the one thing I'll never get used to.

'Okay. Here are the tomatoes,' a little voice in my head said… *Don't get the ones in the bag*. Lia always has her way of drilling things into my head. I picked up two and examined them like I knew what I was doing. I grabbed the third one and the whole mountain came tumbling down.

I stood there with my mouth wide open as they rolled all over. As I bent down I saw a sexy pair of toes in some open-toed sandals. They were small and French manicured. It was something about that white tip that drove me crazy. The way to some men is through their stomach, but mine is feet.

I followed the mile long legs up to a familiar face. She asked, "Is this your first time shopping?"

"Would you believe me if I said no?" I said, and we laughed.

She shook her head no. Then she bent down and helped me chase down the run away tomatoes. I knew I'd seen her somewhere before. Then it hit me. She was the girl honking at me earlier. I started laughing and asked, "How's your hand feeling?"

She looked at me with a strange look and said, "Fine, I think."

"I thought you might have broken it from hitting that horn so hard."

She punched me in the arm and said, "You didn't have to go there." She tried to spin off, but I grabbed her hand. She turned hot pink and had the devil in her eyes.

I apologized and asked, "Could we start all over?" The tension in her arm returned back to normal.

"Yes, we can," she said reluctantly

She helped me finish picking up a few things and I pushed our bags to the parking lot. I looked at my watch and saw that we were inside for over an hour. I knew Lia was waiting, but I didn't want to let Sara go. I asked her if she wanted to go somewhere for a cup of coffee.

She asked me, "Do you drink coffee?"

I said, "No, but that's what they always say in the movies." She giggled like an angel, but agreed. We went to *Bennigan's,* across the street.

We sat there and talked for hours about everything. We didn't have a lot in common, but we were interested in what each other knew. It was refreshing because Lia hasn't listened to me in a while. As much as I hated to do this, I told Sara "I'm running late for an appointment." I saw the disappointment in her face and I felt it in my heart. I asked, "Can I give you a call tomorrow?"

She said, "I thought you weren't going to ask." We exchanged numbers while I walked her to the car. We stood there for a couple of seconds, speechless, gazing into each other's eyes. I could look at those green eyes forever. They were calling me in a hypnotic way. On impulse I placed my hand on her shoulder and pulled her closer. Never once did our stare break.

As our eyes got closer, it was like peaking into her soul. I gave my lip a quick lick and planted a soft kiss on her cheek. I whispered, "Thank you" in her ear. I opened her car door and watched her back away.

She stopped and leaned out the window, and said, "That wasn't me who honked at you earlier, it was Lisa. You still going to call?"

"No, I'm going to call Lisa."

She laughed. Then kissed her hand and blew it to me.

I couldn't believe how cool she was. It was like she brought out something in me. This one is gonna be hard to forget about.

It's been about five hours since I left the house. I know Lia is going to try to flip when I get back. I don't even care because she couldn't spoil this mood, even if she wanted to.

CHAPTER 41: Sara

I tossed and turned all night thinking about Rico's soft lips on my face. It got so bad I had to get up and watch *Pretty Woman.* Whenever something isn't possible I watch it. Once Julia and Richard ride off into the sunset, then I feel like anything is possible.

The next day at work I was sitting at my desk still thinking about those soft lips. My girl friend Tennile scared the shit out of me. She tapped me on the shoulder, and when I jumped, so did she. She apologized for scaring me.

"Mr. Smith has been paging you for an hour. Forgive me, but it's not good business to keep the vice-president waiting. Girl, unless you have the Ebola virus, you got it bad for some guy." She said while walking away.

Of course, I told her she was wrong, but she wasn't. This stranger has single handedly stole my heart. Before yesterday I didn't think there was any such thing as love at first sight. Granted it was only a kiss, but it felt so right. Rico is cute, smart, kind, and understanding. When a man is well rounded like that, I say he has the Michael Jordan. God forbid he is good in bed.

I can't believe I'm sitting here thinking about doing it to a guy I only met yesterday. The quickest I ever gave it up to a guy was five months. It's just something about Rico that I wouldn't want to be alone with him. He might mess up my five month streak.

I've got to call Lisa and tell her about this. No, I'm not going to tell her yet. I'm going to wait and see if he calls me first. There's a good chance that I'll pinch myself and it'll all be a dream.

CHAPTER 42: Born

I got my wish… a quite weekend with my family. Things were kind of like old times. The one thing that was different was when I made love to Lia, I saw Sara. When I watched Lia sleep, I thought of Sara. When I picked up Ashley, I thought about how a child by Sara would look.

Lia noticed how distracted I was, but she didn't dwell on it. I noticed she wasn't herself, but it's been like that for a minute. This weekend would've been perfect, except I had tunnel vision and all I could see was Sara. As soon as I get to work I'm going to call her.

The ride to work was wet but accident free. I pulled up in an empty rain-filled parking lot. It was my job to open the store this week. I pulled up the rusty gate and opened the glass door. As my half-asleep brain struggled to remember the alarm code, a finger touched my shoulder. I jumped and spun around with my hands up. Although I'm in the country my spider sense still works.

As I focused on who it was, my eyes couldn't believe it. It was the cause of all my weekend daydreams. It was Sara

"Girl, what are you trying to do? Scare me to death?" She wasn't looking like herself. I guess the rain and her drenched clothes played a big part.

"Sara, what are you doing out here in the rain at eight o'clock in the morning?"

"You didn't call and I wanted to see if you were okay," she said with a look of concern.

I told her, "Thanks, but I'm fine. If a man didn't know any better, he would think you have a little stalker in you." We both laughed and I got her a towel. She apologized a few times and asked me to forget about it.

"Could we start all over again?" she asked while toweling herself dry.

I replied, "Hell NO!"

She looked at me with widened eyes and said, "Why?"

I spun her around in the barber chair and said, "Because I wouldn't trade our beginning in for nothing." She smiled and told me how sweet I was. I asked, "You hungry?" She said yes, but she was late for work. I was disappointed that she had to leave. She promised to see me later and every day after that.

After she left, I spun around in the chair thinking about her. Although I felt showing up in the rain was a little strange, overall I was feeling her and couldn't wait until the next time I saw her.

CHAPTER 43: PB

"Can't you leave me alone for five minutes without stressing me about sex? Don't you see that I'm busy? Just because that broke-ass chump you live with don't have shit, don't run over here every day trying to stress me. I got money to count, calls to make, and people to meet," he said in the coldest voice possible.

"I know your main goal is to turn me out and try to get your hands on half of my shit. I got news for you missy. I ran through a thousand girls like you and you see I'm still single. Not because they didn't try their best, but because I'm game tight. Although you rank up there with the best, I'm not falling for it. The head is out of this world and you ride me like you're busting a bronco, I'm just not ready to give up my freedom to no sluts."

She looked up at me while she rubbed me to attention and said, "You can talk to me anyway you want, but I'm not leaving this dick."

Groupies are all the same no matter where they come, from. They just want to be in the limelight. Even if their main purpose is being a handy dandy dick holder, when it comes to women, I've seen enough to make a grown man cry.

Although I'm smooth ... *oh I love when she puts her tongue there* ... I don't *trust* women as far as I can throw them. This one here has a way to make me think she's a keeper. She's trying her best to spin my head around and if I'm not careful, she just might do it

CHAPTER 44: Born

I thought my life was crazy before I moved down here, now it's crazier than before. Lia and I haven't spoke in weeks. Our sex life doesn't exist anymore. There was a time when I couldn't keep this girl off me. Since high school this girl has been a "borderline nympho." Now it's like living with a nun.

There is something wrong with our relationship. The reason I can't figure out what is because all I can think about is Sara. I don't know what this girl has, but I'm hooked on it. I've never been this intrigued with a woman before, then again, I've never dated this kind of woman before.

I'm going to spend some time with her tonight. I told Lia that I was going to see my uncle in Durham, so I would be getting in late. Not that she cared, but I felt I still owed her something, even if it was a lie.

I think I better step on it so I won't be late.

CHAPTER 45: Sara

I've been running around this house like a chicken with no head. I've been trying to convince myself that it's just another date. We've been on two dozen dates already. Then why can't I convince my body that it's just another date?

My nipples have been hard for the past two hours just thinking about him. This is the sexiest man I've ever been with. Not just his body, his voice and his laid back personality made me change my Victoria Secrets.

Rico makes me hot just by holding my hand or placing his hand on my face. This guy has me wrapped around his finger. But what drives me crazy is he won't make a move. He's been a perfect gentleman since our first kiss. That's good because we became friends before lovers. That's important in a marriage.

Tonight what I need is a good spanking. He's got all the points he's gonna get for being a nice guy, now what I need to see is his naughty side. If I keep thinking about his chest, I'm gonna have to get back in the shower. The phone rung and on the other end it was my night in shinning armor.

"Girl, are you on your way?" I'm starving my ass off," Born said through the phone.

I wasn't ready but I said I was, not to escalate his mood. I hung the phone up. Then I grabbed my bag and shoes and ran to the car bare-footed. I elected to fix my make up in the car.

CHAPTER 46: Born

As I stood in front of the restaurant I saw my goddess pulling up. She was looking good enough to eat as she parked the car and walked over to me. Before I could say hello, she gave me a kiss that put goose bumps all over me. That wasn't the first time we kissed, but there was more passion in that one than the rest.

As I reluctantly pulled our lips apart, I asked, "What did I do to deserve that?" She just smiled and escorted me across the street.

I said, "I thought we were going to eat dinner?"

She giggled and said, "We are and some dessert." I didn't understand, but all at once it came to me. I looked up and saw Howard Johnson's Hotel and Restaurant. I started to get excited just thinking that this could be the night.

I've thought about this night since our first date. We walked in and didn't make the left to the dining room. I was really puzzled when we walked right past the front desk. We stopped and stood in front of an elevator that read, Floors 12-25. Could my little preppie angel have a devilish bone in her body? I didn't say anything because I would die if she changed her mind.

The bell rung, and the two chrome doors opened up. She wrapped her arms around mine and walked me inside. We rode the elevator up to the seventeenth floor and marched out. I could tell she scouted the room before this. She led me down to room 317. She pulled out the electronic key and slid it across the lock until the light turned green. When she opened the door and stepped back, my eyes couldn't believe what I saw.

There were rose petals all over and more candles than I could count. I never had a woman go through this much trouble for me. Nevertheless, I was flattered and was prepared to show her a memorable time.

I turned around to see if I was dreaming, but she was there. I scooped up her hundred and twenty-eight pound frame into my arms and carried her to the bed. I wasn't trying to rush her, so I watched her eyes with every step.

When I made it to the edge of the bed, she gave me a kiss of reassurance. That was my cue to lay her down. She took it upon herself to undress me. She surprised me because she didn't go for the pants first. She unbuttoned my shirt first.

Once it was open, she caressed my chest like it was the first one she saw. Her soft hands felt so good rubbing my chest. I didn't want to rush her, but this foreplay was driving me crazy. All I wanted to do right now is return the favor.

Finally, she took off my pants and underwear. I was standing on a bunch of rose petals in my birthday suit. She stood up and kissed my chest. I untied her sash and opened her jacket up. I couldn't believe my eyes. She was standing there in a French cut number from Victoria Secrets or Fredericks of Hollywood. Whatever it was, it looked perfect. I felt like a real virgin. There was no way I was going to be able to control myself.

I started peeling off her bra first. I slid the strap down first to give her shoulder a gentle kiss, and then I unwrapped the rest of the package. When I opened the bra I saw two pink nipples that were hard and inviting. As bad as I wanted them in my mouth, I chose to see the rest of her first. I slid her panties past her thighs. Her hair was so straight and the color was a perfect match. I ran my fingers through it and she shimmied. I knew it was time to get it on.

I laid her down and let my instinct take over. I kissed her from her lips down to her toes. I stopped somewhere in the middle to make sure she was ready to enter. She was grinding on me like a sex-starved woman. Before I knew it she aggressively reversed our positions. Now, she was on top staring into my eyes.

Her first act of being on top was to give my lips some attention. She was a good kisser, but I wasn't too interested in that right now. She must have read my mind. She started to slide down my body while leaving a trail of kisses. Just like me she stopped in the middle also. I could tell after a few seconds that she had no experience, she was just returning the favor. Like all gifts, it's the thought that counts.

I didn't want to make her more nervous by watching her, so I just watched the ceiling and stroked her hair. I didn't want to give it away that it wasn't that good. She made her way back up where she was straddling me. The heat between her legs was calling me.

Before I knew it, she had me inside of her. Now I was no longer faking. She had me opening and closing at an alarming rate. She was riding me like there was no tomorrow and I was loving every minute. Her riding made up for any mistakes she had made. I give her two thumbs up.

I caressed every part of her red skin. This evening was well worth the wait. I watched her shadow on the wall as the candle made it flicker. I've been with a lot of women, but she had this certain warmness about her. Her eyes were closed. I wonder what she was thinking. She had a way of letting out these faint moans that made me pulsate inside her. I could tell by her expression that she felt every one of them.

With every stroke, her breathing got deeper. I was almost sure that she was about to unload. With that in mind, I sped up the strokes. With every thrust, she got closer and closer. I'm not going to be satisfied until I push her over the top.

I paid closer attention to her breasts, knowing that would add to her excitement. She switched the excitement by reaching behind her and grabbing my two friends. This girl must have known me in another life because she went straight to my spot. When a girl massages me there, well…

I felt myself about to reach my climax, but I didn't want to be alone. I told Sara that I was about to cum and my eyes urged her to meet me there. I could see that the thought not only intrigued her, but excited her also.

After a moment or two of campaigning for the inevitable, our bodies collided. We clung to each other like we wouldn't see each other again. Once I felt her body shake involuntarily, I knew I did my job. She kissed me on my cheek and whispered into my ear "I love you."

For me, the first time I sleep with a girl it's awkward for me. Those eight letters just made it worse, but I tried not to show it. I rubbed her back and watched our reflection on the wall as one.

CHAPTER 47: Born

I woke up in a strange bed with a strange woman, and my life still feels like shit. I called Lia as soon as I got to work and she didn't even mention me staying out. Is our relationship that far gone she doesn't even care if I stay out or not? I thought for sure I would get a beep from her about midnight.

Is the rotating barber chair making me dizzy or is it my life? Last night was great, but Lia is all I could think of. There was a note on my mirror from Boobie saying that he must talk to me with emergency in capital letters. What else can go wrong that already hasn't?

Damn! I spoke too fast. Now Black is beeping me 911. I can't take any more bad news. I need a minute or two before I call him back. Even if it's not bad news, Black can be a little much to handle. Especially right now.

CHAPTER 48: Black

Before, when I was in the streets, I never got any mail. If some did come, it was just some coupons or a department store trying to advertise an ugly plaid sofa. Now, things have really picked up. I make it my business to go to the mailbox. Now, I'm scared that I might miss something. Without fail there's always a pre-approved credit card or a party invite. I might be on at least ninety different guest lists, so my box stays flooded with VIP invites.

Mary J. is having her album release party at the country club. If Born hurries up and calls me back, I'm going to see if he wants to go. Okay, that's the phone. I hope it's Born.

"Hello, what's the deal big dog? What the hell took you so long to call me back?" I asked Born, happy as hell to hear from him, but he sounded like something was on his mind, and was rambling on and on about nothing.

"Born, what's the matter with you? You sound like your dog just died. Are you thinking about Tip again? Look kid, I miss you and so does New York. It's been almost a year since that madness. Why don't you come home?" I listened as Born silence worried me.

"Things are lovely now. I can plug you right in with Darryl. He's put me in charge of this new group called "9 Lives." They're alright, but Darryl likes the way you sound. I played an old cassette of when we were clowning around in my mom's house. He told me I was trash, but you were alright,"

"That's sound good kid but rapping has been on the back burner for so long," Born said in a depressed tone

"I was going to tell you all of this when you come up for Mary J.'s party. You're bigger than that country shit. So, what do you say? Are you coming up this weekend or what?"

"I'll think about it but if I do I won't be much fun," Born said sadly

"What in the hell do you mean you will think about it? Homeboy, this is your home up here. My brother is not supposed to be shaping up no clowns for a living. That's like John Gotti shining Sammy the Bull's boots. I can hear it in your voice. You're stressed and fed up with that place. Grab Lia, Ashley, and that old ass Lumina and bounce."

"Grabbing Lia is the problem," Born said angrily.

"What do you mean Lia is the problem? Big dog, I'm late for a hot date with Kenya, so I can't get into it right now. Take my advice, if Lia is a problem, cut her off. Believe it or not, there are girls at these parties that make Lia look like Nell Carter. Worse comes to worse, Kenya can hook you up with one of her model friends."

"Model chicks are good but family is better," Born responded in a low tone.

"Born, you've been wanting to be a rapper since we were kids. Now, get your head out of your ass and take advantage of what's going on up here. On top of all the other shit I've said, I still got a big surprise for you. You get a week to make up your mind. Leave me a voice mail and let me know what you're going to do. I love you, kid, don't let me down."

I didn't want to tell him the whole thing, but Daryl has been pressing up on me for the past week. He really digs the way Born flows. He said that he reminds him of *DOC* from *NWA*. That tape was nearly eight years ago. I know he's gotten a little better since then.

I don't know what Dee is all hyped up about because I don't see it. I just want him to come up here so Dee can see he's wack. Then I'll get him a job with the label and then I'll have him back in New York. That's if he even comes up. Hopefully he'll do the right thing.

CHAPTER 49: Born

This is the type of shit that gets me heated. All the customers have been gone and I'm sitting here waiting for Boobie. I could've been at home at least a half hour ago. That's if I still have a home to go to.

Boobie could've told me this shit over the phone. He was acting like the world was coming to an end. He probably wants to tell me about his new freak. Okay, here he comes.

When he walked through the door, I saw a look I never saw before. He looked like the doctor just told him he has AIDS. He gave me a strong handshake and started to sweep up. Maybe it's just me, but I thought I was waiting here for him. He's not acting like a man who has something important to say.

I gave him a chance to sweep from one end to the other. He was really starting to worry me. Usually he's the coolest man around, now he looks like he's hiding from the mob. I got up and grabbed the broom. He couldn't even look me in the eyes, and I found that strange.

"Whatever it is, it couldn't be that bad. Just spit it out and I'll try to help you get through it."

"Okay, but it's not my problem," he said with a concerned look on his face. I looked at him with confusion wondering what he was talking about.

"Rico, I don't know how to tell you this, so I'm just going to spit it out. I was at the after hours joint last night. I slid into the bathroom to take a leak. While I was in the stall, I heard some of those fake ass C-Note Players come in," he said, a nervous look spreading across his face. I was still confused as to why he would think I would be concerned about them.

"Look man, this must be between me and you. My name can't get mixed up in this shit. I can't stand PB, but I know how dangerous he is. A lot of people have come up missing fucking with that cat. Give me your word, this is between us."

I gave him my word that I would keep shit tight, but on the real this dude was starting to scare me a little bit. I didn't know what he was about to say, but lord let it not be about Lia.

"Okay. I heard the dudes talking about this new girl he's hitting. The only reason I listened is because I thought it was one of my chicks. Anyway, from what I gathered, it sounds like your shorty. They mentioned a tattoo of a rose on her lower back next to her ass. I don't know if this means anything to you, but if so, check her. The worst part of it is PB let's the crew watch the tapes afterwards."

I had to sit back down. I couldn't believe my ears. Boobie was ripping my insides out with every word. I'm trying not to show my pain, but I can imagine the blank look on my face. I've been on the other end of this scene all my life. I've taken another cat's girls from them and never even thought twice. Now, the shoe's on the other foot and I can't take it. I want to kill her. I want to kill him. I want to kill both of them while the whole town watches.

They really made a sucker out of me, but before I flip, I need to catch them in the act. I need to get through the night first. I'm going to need help from the man upstairs not to strangle her on sight. The first thing I must do is call her school to see what the deal with that is. Then, the hunt will begin.

CHAPTER 49½: Born

It took all I had to keep my secret tucked away last night. I purposely fell asleep on the couch so I wouldn't have that freak touch me. The next morning I had Boobie pick me up. Instead of going to the shop, I had him drop me off at my aunt's house. I borrowed her car and shot back to the crib. I parked about a half a block away, but I still had a good view.

I couldn't believe what I was doing. I was acting like some kind of stalker, but I needed to know the truth. Once Boobie told me about the rose, I knew he wasn't lying, but I needed to see for my own eyes.

I watched as Lia dropped off Ashley at the babysitter. As soon as I'm done with Lia and company I'll go and scoop Ashley up. Alright. Let the games begin!

Lia is pulling out of the parking lot. Hold up! Instead of making a left, she made a right. Her school is in the other direction and she's headed straight for me.

I ducked down so fast that I hit my face on the stick shift. I was hoping she didn't see me or recognize the car. I've got to see for myself or else.

After five minutes of lefts and rights she got on the overpass towards Schwab. Only a bunch of rich white people live in Schwab. The police out here are supposed to be prejudiced as hell. They'll pull a brother over for looking wrong. I better get my license and registration out right now.

Boobie wasn't a chump, but he sounded scared to death of PB. Just because a man has money doesn't mean people are scared of him. He must've done something to earn that fear. What ever it was, I'm not taking any chances. That's why I grabbed the gun out of the shop. I know Boobie is going to be mad, but fuck him. The rule in New York is you'd rather be judged by twelve than carried by six. If this big motherfucker gets loud, I'll make him famous. Then I really will be judged by twelve.

After two more lefts and a right turn she finally pulled into a driveway. She got out, grabbed her red Gucci bag filled with clothes hanging out. She rung the bell and Pissy Boy appeared at the door with just a robe on. She kissed him right in the mouth and walked in. That was the first time my heart ever dropped like that.

So, that's what women and men spend their whole life trying to avoid. Now I see why couples know the truth, but won't seek it out. The truth can set you free, but it also can make you homicidal.

At this point, my mind was racing out of control. I didn't want my next move to be my last but, I knew I had to get inside. A sane man would've seen enough and drove off. Right now, I'm a lot of things, but sane isn't one of them.

As I peeked in the front window, I didn't see any movement. I wanted to just ring the doorbell, but I would lose the element of surprise. I've come this far to surprise them, why not give them what they live for. I looked over both shoulders to make sure it wasn't an old lady peeking at me. It looked clear to me, so I slid around back. I saw jet skis, a motorcycle, and plenty of cars. This was a man that really knew how to play. The only thing was, now he was playing with my emotions and that wasn't safe.

I made my way around to the patio. It was pleasing to me to see the door unlocked. The first thing I heard was Sade playing throughout the house. My temperature went up even higher because I knew that she was Lia's favorite. She's really made herself at home over here.

I made my way through the house with nothing but ill intentions in my head. At the same time, I couldn't help but notice how plush his crib was. I peeked around every corner, but there was no sign of the lovebirds. It wasn't any trail of clothes leading upstairs like the movies. Nevertheless, upstairs was my next course of action.

When I got to the foot of the stairs, I listened for any noises. The only thing I heard was Sade. With every note I got even madder. I slid up the stairs like I was a cat burglar. There were three doors at the top of the stairs. I guess I needed to open all of them to find them.

The first knob I touched sent a chill up my spine. The thought of seeing Lia in bed with homeboy was horrible. I opened the door anyway to see gold faucet fixtures and a toilet. It was safe to say that they weren't in there. The next door had the same knob, but the door was half open. I heard a sound that came from the last room. That had to be them. As I tiptoed to the door, my heart started racing. I knew from this moment on that there would be a giant hole in my life where Lia used to be.

I eased the gun out of my pocket and gently pushed the door open. It creaked a little, but I could see Lia. She had her back to me, but I could see she was topless. She was putting her hair in a ponytail like she always does before bed. There was no sign of Pissy Boy. I heard her yell back to him about something. Then I knew he was in the master bathroom. That was a perfect time to make my move.

I opened the door and took one step inside. The door squeaked a little, but she didn't hear it over Sade. As the distance between me and her got shorter, I saw our relationship flashing before my eyes. That was the last thing I wanted to see because it was making me think crazy.

A step or two from her she looked in the mirror and saw me. She spun around and was about to scream. I don't know what she saw first, the gun or the pointer finger over my mouth. She was so shocked she didn't cover her breasts up.

"Death would be too good. for you ho!" I whispered to her in her ear with the cold blue steel touching her skin.

I never took my eyes off the bathroom door, but out of the corner I saw tears running down her face. I sat on the bed beside her waiting for Casanova to appear. I cut the music off in hopes to speed up the process. He called to her and asked why she did that.

When she didn't answer him, he came out of the bathroom. He was wearing a towel and a gold cross around his neck. He had a toothbrush in his mouth and some toothpaste in his hand. When he saw me it was too late for anything. He couldn't run or scream. All he did was drop the toothpaste and spit the brush out on the floor. He started saying that it wasn't like I thought.

"My girl is topless in your bedroom, but it's not like I think." I cocked the hammer. One started pleading and the other one started crying. Lia started saying that if she didn't see the tape of me and some girl in the bathroom, this wouldn't be happening. This bitch has got to be crazy. She is honestly trying to blame this on me.

"Who showed you the tape?" I asked her but I already knew.

It bugged me out that she'd seen that night on tape, but it didn't surprise me. I could've put two right in his face for doing that sucker shit. A clown will do anything for a piece of pussy. Out of instinct I raised the gun at him.

"Rico, you know who I am. I will give you money," he said sounding scared as hell. He had a gun in his face and that's all he can come up with?

"Homeboy, I don't want your money. All I want you to do is get on your knees." He pleaded a little more, but he saw I wasn't trying to hear it. He slowly fell to his knees.

"Don't baby," Lia started pleading. How could she call me baby with her nipples hanging out?

"Where is the camcorder?" I asked PB. He tried to say he didn't have one. I put the burner on his nose and asked him again "The same camcorder you been taping this freak with. Oh, yeah. Your man didn't tell you that he let his whole crew watch you suck his dick." She looked at him with sad eyes, but I did not feel sorry for her.

"The camcorder is behind that mirror. All you have to do is flick that switch." I flicked the switch so his whole crew could see how much of a bitch he is. I think if his crew saw him crying and pleading for his life, he will lose some of his power.

I made Lia kneel down next to him so they both would be in the picture. I let the tension build enough where they could only see death. I moved in closer to both of them. I raised the gun to PB's mouth and made him open it wide enough for the gun to fit.

When his mouth was wrapped around the barrel, I told him to close his eyes. He closed them, but I could see he was peeking. I really didn't care because he couldn't see this coming anyway. With all of my might I smashed my knee up under his chin. He was spitting out blood and teeth everywhere.

Lia didn't scream, although I could see she wanted to. I looked her straight in her eyes and said, "Call my mom and we will set up visitation between you and Ashley. If you don't go along with that you won't like the alternative."

When I asked her if she understood, she just nodded. I looked at PB tending to his mouth. I told him if he wanted to see if the man lives up to the myth, I'm the easiest man to find. I backed out of the room and left the house.

I headed to the babysitter to see the only person that could make me smile right now. As I drove through each light and stop sign, New York was calling me. It was calling me in a big way.

CHAPTER 50: PB

"Bitch, stop yelling! Didn't I tell you I got a headache?"

This bitch keeps asking me if I need more ice. What I need is Rico duct taped in a trunk. I want to stab him in his ass about thirty or forty times until he begs me to kill him. If this prick thinks for one minute that this is over, he's crazy.

Lia said that he's on his way back to New York. I know he will feel safe once he's in Burnt-Down City. I'll have a big surprise for him. My long arm can reach anywhere. He is going to pay for what he did to my mouth. I'm going to buy a million dollar smile back. It's a small thing to a giant. I'll just fill up my grill with gold and diamonds and nobody will know the difference.

I do know that all the gold and diamonds won't help his ass. When I tell Lia I'm going to help her get her brat back, she will give all the info I need, including his social security number. Then I'll kick her dirty ass in the street.

CHAPTER 51: Born

As I stared out of the little window over looking the city lights, I was thinking about the last year of my life. It has been an emotional roller coaster. I'm not sure what scares me more, what I might have done if I would've stayed in North Carolina, or me returning home.

It's only been a year since I left. A year going on five. New York is a funny place. I've seen cats go upstate for a skid bid about eighteen or so, when they come home it's like they did twenty years.

The little dudes don't respect them. They don't let them get any money on their block and their stock is scattered all over town. That can't be my fate. With Lia out of the picture, I have to make it happen for me and Ashley. I love New York and I hope it still loves me.

The captain broke my train of thought with his approaching LaGuardia speech. Every time I fly into New York, the plane circles around an extra ten to fifteen minutes before we land. I read somewhere that the U.S.A x-rays the planes in midair for bombs. I don't know who's worse with their bullshit, the US or the terrorists. I've learned not to put anything past either of them. All I know is that more than four hours on the road makes me crazy. Road rage 101 is a motherfucker.

The stewardess broke me out of my trance when she tapped my seat. She asked me to put my seatbelt on and pull the seat upright. It won't be long now before the New York soil will be under my feet.

The landing was a little bumpy, but it didn't wake Ashley. I can hear the two ladies behind me complaining about the landing. I think if two tons comes flying out of the air without killing me and my daughter, it's fair to say that it was a good landing. I gathered up our things and one by one the stewardess said "Good-bye." As I made my way off the plane, my butterflies were on full alert. It's been almost a year since I saw Black and New York City.

As we came through the tunnel, the first person I saw was Black. He was as serious as always, but the bum look let me know he was glad to see me. There was an awkward moment between us, and it lasted about five seconds before we shared a big hug. He grabbed Ashley and woke her up with a bunch of kisses. Even through her sleepy eyes she looked glad to see him.

Out of nowhere, this goddess put her hand on Black's shoulder. She was so fine my jaw dropped. She asked, "Do you mind if I hold Ashley?" and all I could do was shake my head.

Kenya Cooper was a straight up twenty piece. She looked better in person than in the magazine. She had on a simple Donna Karen sweat suit with a cap to match. The thing that set it off the most was the ponytail she pulled through the hat. I love it when a girl does that sporty look. Drives me crazy. I couldn't help but watch her every move. I know she's my man's girl, but it was also a woman I dreamed of before. Hopefully the awe will wear off in a minute.

As we walked to the parking lot, Black mouth was moving a mile a minute about the Rap World. He was really into this. For some reason all that he said didn't hit home. This is my big chance to grab a mic and all I could think of was a woman I left behind.

As we entered the parking lot, Kenya told him to stop being so corny and tell me something. She had a big smile on her face so I knew it wasn't anything bad. Black tried to quiet her, but I could see he was putty in her hands.

He threw me a pair of car keys, but I wasn't in the mode to drive. I told him to drive. He told me that Kenya was just learning how to drive and he couldn't drive two cars. I didn't understand what he was talking about and I'm sure my face reflected that. Black said, "I though you told me that you get goose bumps when you get close to a machine?"

"I do, but you got me lost."

He pointed to a parking spot across from his. I had to look twice because I couldn't believe my eyes. My BMW was staring right back at my bulging eyes. I looked confused, but couldn't look a gift horse in the mouth.

Black said, "Welcome home" and we hugged again. If this was any indication of what was in store, then it was good to be home. Black must be doing alright for himself. I think it's time for me to take this rap shit serious.

It's been a long three days, and I haven't had a good night's sleep yet. Between my mom, Black, Ashley, and Lia on the brain, sleep was a distant fifth. Tonight wouldn't be any different because of my welcome home party. Darryl was nice enough to add my name to the flyer. Even though the crime family took up much of the flyer, I was glad to see my name.

I thought I was dressed and ready to go when Black took me back to his new crib. He had a pair of Ferragamos and a black Prada suit laid out for me. I was sharp, but I had to admit, my wardrobe fell off in the past year.

I went into the next room and got ready. When I entered the room Kenya started whistling at me like a construction worker. It caught me off guard and made me blush a little. Black said, "Alright, Pretty Boy, are you ready to see what life is going to be like?" I was more than ready, but I was still trying to play cool.

As we pulled up on *Club 24*, the line was about two blocks long. They had two big spotlights outside that looked like the Academy Awards. The thought of standing in line made my shoes get tighter.

We parked where it said, "Reserved" and headed inside the club. Everybody was shaking Black's and Kenya's hands. From bouncers to the club's owner were happy to see them. They introduced me and everyone greeted me like one of them. The owner said that he heard a lot about me. He was hoping I could take the stage tonight.

Black cut right in and said, "Not tonight, but real soon." As we strolled in I didn't see any familiar faces. Nevertheless, it was a warm welcome.

Minutes later, Daryl made his way through the crowd. He had two fine chickens on his arm. He asked us, "What are you doing down here? The VIP is what's happening."

Kenya put her arms around both of us and told me, "Your public awaits."

The crowd in front of the VIP wasn't that bad, Of course, we didn't have to wait. Security let us right in.

As we walked in I could see all eyes were on us. It was real laid back up in here. There were a bunch of sofas and a mean glass pool table. I let my eyes scan the room at all the fine *mami's* up in here. In the process a few familiar faces jumped out of the crowd at me.

The first was Wise and his crew from Brooklyn. They were killing them out of town, but they still bust their guns. I knew they were beefing with Pepper, so I didn't think twice about them.

Then I saw the crew from Boss. They were deep as usual. Those kids really know how to keep it flowing. They had a table full of Dom P. and dime pieces surrounding them.

Oh, shit! There goes Quick and his fam. Kenya pulled me to the bar. She said, "This is your night, too. Are you just going to stand around?"

"Two bottles of D.P.," I told the bartender. When I asked him how much and he gave me a smile, Kenya explained to me that the record company has a tab here. I didn't see Black anymore. I guess him and Dee were pulled away.

A circle was formed and the crowd started chanting, "GO! GO! GO!"

Somebody was in there getting worked. I haven't seen anything like this in almost a year. I made my way through the crowd to see the action. All I could do was laugh. It was my man Lil Curt from the Best–Out crew. He was keeping the rooftop alive. He was shoveling some girl right out of the circle. With every chant, he got lower and lower.

The girl was no match for him. He ate that poor girl up. I saw enough now it was time for me to find a seat. I look around and now Kenya was gone also. This VIP is starting to be like the *Twilight Zone*. Every time I look up, somebody is missing. This big motherfucker put his hand on my shoulder. I guess he was security or somebody's bodyguard. He told me that Darryl was over there at his table. I walked over to the table and there were all my long lost friends. I guess I was the only one who didn't know about Darryl's private table.

Overall, it was a nice night, but I still had a lot on my mind. I guess Kenya could see that because every girl she knew she introduced them to me. Black was right, these industry parties bring out the finest hotties.

Although I still got it, I think I will take it slow. I have to be at the studio bright and early. I got to show *Underworld Records* that I'm the shit, I got joints that Black hasn't heard yet. I got a surprise for them. When I run in there it's going to be like L.L. in Crush Groove.

CHAPTER 51½: Sara

I knew it! I fucking knew it! I've been beeping Rico, I mean Born. No! What do I mean? I slept with this man and I am not even sure of his name. *Sara, why didn't you listen to yourself?* I see now why men get into so much trouble when they think with their little head. If I would've made him wait I would've seen what kind of man he really was. I need to calm down. I'm still in love with him. I'm sure he has a good reason for not calling me back all damn day. When I get to the barbershop he'll be there to explain.

"Up yours asshole!" I screamed at the dude that cut me off. Men think just because you're a lady that road rage doesn't apply. What he doesn't know is this isn't a good time.

"Lisa this is Sara, when you get this message, please call me. It's very important." This ride is feeling twice as long today. I guess when your dying inside the world has a way of slowing down. I'm the one that tried to warn Lisa about this same shit. Now look at me, the pot calling the kettle black.

There's the barbershop, but I don't see his car outside. I could feel my pressure inching up. I got out of the car and looked over the parking lot, but I still didn't see his car. I walked into the shop and all eyes were on me. I looked around to see if he was there, but he wasn't. Boobie started walking towards me with a big smile on his face. I could tell by the look on his face that he thought I was there for him.

When he reached out to shake my hand I didn't move. I asked him where is Rico. His face dropped and he said, "Oh, you're trying to play me."

I didn't feel like explaining what's been going on the past few weeks between me and Rico, so I said, "There is no me and you, so how could I be playing you? All I wanted to know is where's was Rico?"

He raised his voice and said, "Your Romeo is not here Goldilocks."

The whole shop started laughing, even the girl that does manicures. I felt like I was shrinking in my shoes as the laughter grew. I felt like smacking Boobie off of his feet. I knew if I did all hell would've broke loose. Against my better judgment I asked again, but this time with tears in my eyes.

Boobie said, "Your prince charming rode off into the sunset without you. You should be used to it by now. Ain't that the same thing the football player did?"

I couldn't take it anymore, so I stormed out in the shop. There were two guys coming in the shop, but I push right passed them. I heard them saying something, but I didn't pay them any attention. All I knew was I had to get to my car. From behind I heard Boobie scream, "You got my number and I don't mind sloppy thirds."

I almost collapsed right in my tracks. I yanked the car door so hard I broke off two nails. Normally I would've freaked but I was too mad. I opened up the glove box and pressed the little yellow button. I started the car and pulled in front of the shop. I reached into the trunk and pulled out my tire iron. Boobie would to pay for disrespecting me in front of all those people. I marched up to the door and waved to Boobie. I couldn't believe he had the nerve to wave back. That was before I raised that tire iron and his smile slowly faded. I smashed that tire iron through his front window with all my might.

I didn't stop until every piece of the window was on the ground. I ran full speed back to my get away car. As I pulled off I saw the whole shop empty out to the front. I drove down the street with tears in my eyes and a smile on my face. The thought of not seeing Born again made my soul leak out. I picked up my cell phone and called Lisa to tell her what happened. She still wasn't home but it won't take long for her to hear about it. Then I called the radio station. I requested "*Can You Stand The Rain*" by New Edition and cried my way back home.

PART III

"HARD TIMES"

CHAPTER 52: Born

I'm dead tired from shooting the *'Harlem Anthem'* video. Life is crazy. Just a year ago I was cutting fades, now I'm shooting videos with an album that's gone platinum.

In the past year I've hung out with everybody from Quincy Jones to LL Cool J. This year has gone fast, but I wouldn't change it for the world. As soon as I change, it'll be time for my platinum release party. It's going to be crazy. Everybody is going to be there. The Wu-Tang Clan , Mary J, Nas , and Puff Daddy said he's bringing his whole crew. That kid really knows how to party.

I changed in my dressing room and met Black and the crew in the parking lot. Although my mom gave all she could when I was a kid nothing could prepare me for this. This is more then a dream come true. I can't say this is a dream come true cause my dreams never reached this far. The money the streets blessed me with can't begin to compare. Now, I just spent almost four hundred thousand on a video and it didn't even phase me. The paper is rolling in hand over fist. I went from crack slinging to rap singing and its all gravy. I wish somebody had recognized my talents before. Maybe Tip would be alive.

The single I dropped about him is doing okay, but if they knew the man, they could feel it better.

Black tapped me and asked me if I was alright. I looked around and saw the inside of our stretch Land Cruiser. I don't even remember getting inside. I must have really been daydreaming about Tip. Black hit me with a stern "YO!" I guess that was to snap me out of it. I told him I was cool. I was just getting into my party zone. I don't know if he bought it, but it was the best I could do.

He asked me, "What did you think of the video? It was light years from the first one I did in Milbank. All I had was a bunch of little kids playing in the background. This joint here had car chases, fat asses, and a lot of ice in it." To put it plainly, this was a big boy joint.

Black asked me, "What are you thinking about?"

"We made it," I replied with a satisfied look on my face. He nodded his head and gave me a pound with a lot of love.

Club International was the hottest club around right now. There was a mob out front. It was like a Blue Thunder dope line waiting to get in. I knew all these people weren't here to see me, but when I got out lights started flashing. That was a good sign for me, and it helped ease my butterflies.

As I made my way through the line all I felt were hands on my back. These people just wanted to touch me. They didn't care if I saw them or not, as long as they could say they touched me.

That was just the women. The men high fived. It felt like the butterflies were flying to my head. With everyone that left my stomach, my head got bigger. I started to eat this shit up.

I put my hand up to wave at the faceless crowd and the roar got louder. That was enough to make me start blushing. When I turned back around I plowed right into a young lady. I knocked her down to the ground. I almost fell myself. Security went to pick her up to clear the way, but I stopped them so I could help her myself. I felt I owed her that much.

I extended my hand to help her up. When she lifted her head up the butterflies rushed back. She was so fine I was speechless. Her skin was a lovely shade of bronze. She had a sexy pair of chinky eyes. I couldn't believe how good she looked.

I asked her, "You okay?" She didn't answer she just nodded. I could tell she was a little star struck. There was no need for all of that because I felt like the same old Born. When she finally got to her feet, I got the full effect of her outfit. She had on a black mini-skirt with a matching bra top. It made me notice every curve on her body. She was certainly put together.

I noticed the crowd found it amusing that I knocked her down. The girl to my right said, "Next time, get your stinking ass out of the way bitch!"

I saw the lovely girl's eyes shift towards the blimp to the left. I told her, "Don't pay her any mind. She's just mad because I didn't knock her down." We both smiled as I looked her in the eyes. I asked her name.

"Kimberly, but my friends call me Kim," she said in a soft voice.

I said, "What do I call you?"

She smiled and said, "Kim."

I said, "Kim, would you like to be my guest tonight?" She gave me the nod and we continued into the club.

Black said, "Damn! It's about time! I thought you were going to ask her to marry you." We laughed as we strolled through the security.

I just sold a million records on my first try. Black and I are Batman and Robin once again. Not to mention, I got a little cutie by my side. I can tell this is going to be a night that I won't ever forget.

CHAPTER 53: Black

I scrambled for my gun under my pillow. The loud knocks were echoing through the condo. I heard that knock many times before and it always meant the same thing, trouble.

I checked the outside monitor to see if my suspicions were correct. When I cut on the TV, I saw four men in suits with New York's finest behind them. I couldn't believe my eyes. Could it be that after almost two years that Brooklyn shit finally caught up to me?

I hid the gun under the sofa and paced back and forth in front of the door. I couldn't really think with them banging on the door. My mind was saying, "Open the door," but my body was not listening. I knew I had to do something before the door came tumbling down.

Before I knew it, I was face to face with a whole doughnut shop. I was surprised when they didn't rush in and throw me on the floor. The first cop pulled out his badge and said his name "Detective Timothy Hall." The other cop said he was plain old Detective Bryant.

They asked me if I had a minute, like I had a choice. I told them, "Yes," and opened the door wider for them to come in. Only the two detectives came in and the rest posted up in the hallway.

As they walked deeper into the house, their eyes darted all around the room. I guess it was a cop thing to be nosey. They asked, "May we sit down?"

I said, "No. I don't mean to be rude, guys, but what the hell do you want?" They explained that they got my name from the owner of *Club International*. I thought to myself "that bitch." They told me they were investigating a murder. When they said that I tried my best to stay calm, but I could feel my heart beating twice as fast.

They asked about a girl named Kimberly Rowan. The name didn't ring a bell. I expressed to them that I didn't know her. At that point I wanted to ask them to leave. I knew that would trigger off a chain reaction.

They showed me a picture in hopes it would refresh my memory. I snatched the picture and saw the pretty girl from the club last night. I thought to myself, *this is the girl that Born slid off with last night.*

They didn't want to get into details of the murder, but they did want to talk to Born. They asked if I knew where he was. I didn't want to say anything because I knew how they twist your words around.

I asked, "Is he under arrest?" They explained to me that they wanted to clear up a few things about the victim. Since they didn't answer the question, I asked it again. "Is he under arrest?"

They explained, "No, sir. He's not."

"Look Detective, I'm sure we can clear all of this up. Born has an eleven o'clock interview with Vibe. As soon as we are done, we'll march down to your office."

I told them to hold on for a second. I went over to my desk and pulled out our lawyer's card. When I passed it to them their faces went blank. The card read, *Frances W. Holt, The BEST Lawyer around.* He's most famous for beating two R.I.C.O. charges for the Pacino family.

They said that a lawyer wouldn't be necessary. I laughed and said to them, "What? Something changed in the last four hundred years?"

They turned and said, "See you around one o'clock." While I was closing the door, Detective Bryant said, "Oh, yeah. Please don't leave town before we have our little talk." I closed the door, took a deep breath, and ran to the phone.

CHAPTER 54: Born

I tossed and turned all night. I don't believe how restless I was. I sat up in my empty bed and clicked on the TV. I ran my hand over the spot where Kim was. I regretted not asking her to stay. I would've loved waking up to her soft body.

I don't know what's wrong with me. I haven't let a woman sleep over since I left Lia. I don't know why, but I feel it's better this way. To keep from thinking of Kim, and especially Lia, I grabbed the Sound Scan listing. I had platinum circled in red ink. '*I'm Focused*' was the perfect name for this album. I didn't think it was hot until Vibe did an article on titles. They said "I'm Focused' was third behind 'Paid In Full' and 'Criminal Minded'.

The phone rang. I guess I was really into the magazine because the phone made me jump. I looked at the clock and saw it was only 9:27. I knew it could only be Black. Nobody else would run the risk of getting cursed out.

I didn't feel like talking, so I said "Hello" in my sleepiest voice. I knew it was Black. He was talking so fast I couldn't understand him. I tried to get him to slow down, but he wouldn't.

I pressed the number one so it could make a loud beep in his ear. I knew it would quiet him for a second. I told him to calm down and give it to me slow. Once he started talking I was wishing I still couldn't understand him.

He was blowing my mind with every sentence. I couldn't believe Kim was dead. After he said her name my mind went blank. She was too young and much too pretty. Black brought me back to reality by calling my name. He said that we had to go down to 1 Penn Plaza for a few questions. I told Black that I would be at his house in an hour. When I hung up, I couldn't do anything but close my eyes and drop my face into the palms of my hands.

CHAPTER 55: Black

After an hour of questions and another hour of the same questions, Sherlock and Watson left the room. Me and Born sat quietly while Mr. Holt ran over his notes. I could tell by the look on Born's face that this whole thing was too much for him. All the gangster rap in the world can't prepare you for times like this.

Mr. Holt advised him through all the questions. He said there wasn't any sign of rape. There wasn't any semen found in or on the victim. On top of that, there wasn't any eyewitness. I'm starting to think that it wasn't them accusing him. It was those horrible pictures of her, they showed him that was eating at him. After about thirty minutes had passed, Heckle and Jeckle came back in. They told Born he was free to go, but make sure he be around if they had further questions.

I placed my hand on Born's shoulder and said, "Let's blow this joint." We all stood and headed for the door.

"Make sure that I'm present at all the talks," Mr. Holt stated in a cocky tone. I like when he talks slick. It makes me feel, like he's worth the thousand dollars' an hour we pay him.

As we left, Mr. Holt told Born not to worry about anything unless he did it. Then he said, "Don't even worry if you did. I haven't lost in eleven years." Born didn't find it very amusing, but I brushed it off by saying we'll call him later.

It felt like a weight was lifted off my back once we got outside. It's something about a precinct that gives you the feeling that you won't be leaving. Born jumped into his car and sped off without saying anything. Times like this he's the easiest man to find. Anytime he gets upset he goes to the studio. I'll give him some room and catch up to him later.

CHAPTER 56: Born

It's been about a week since Kim's death and the paper won't let up. They say that Kim wasn't anything more than a groupie. It really burned me up when I read that. I didn't know her that well, but she deserved better. The girl is dead and all they can think about are headlines.

I know the wolves are going to be all over the awards tonight. I'm not going to let them spoil this night for me. The word is, I'm up for three awards, but only two of them are locked in. Two is way better than none.

When I do receive them, I'm going to keep it simple. I'm going to thank my label, tell my mom, Ashley, and Black that I love them. Then shout out my Dogs. Then give a big Rest in Peace to Tip. I think that will be more than enough.

The front desk called up and said the limo was downstairs. It was about time. It seems like I've been waiting for hours. I know it was either Black's or Kenya's fault. I don't know which one stays in the mirror the most. At least Kenya has an excuse. Then I laughed to myself.

As I walked through the lobby, Ben the security guard said, "Pick a girl up for him." He was a really cool dude. We played like that all the time.

Just as I thought, as soon as I opened the front door, the reporters hit me from everywhere. I pushed my way through the cameras and mics into the limo. Black said, "I tried to warn you, but you didn't pick up your cell phone." I didn't answer, but I wish I had. I watched the crowd in front of my crib get smaller and smaller as we drove off. I told Black, "If you think that is bad, wait until we walk the red carpet." Kenya sat quiet the whole ride like she can feel my pain.

As we pulled up in front of the *Felt Forum*, the crowd was unbelievable. New York City's finest had the horses out tonight. They think that hip-hop can't do anything without drama.

As we pulled up in front of the red carpet, lights started flashing before the door even opened. The driver walked around and opened the door. The first one to grace the runway was Kenya. She looked great. She was the epitome of a woman. She had it all and never acted like she knew it. She truly was beautiful inside and out. I don't think I could say that about one other woman besides my mom.

The crowd ate her up, and then she pulled Black out and gave him a big kiss. I think that was to let all the hoochies know he was taken. Then it was my turn. The butterflies were flying around at a mile a minute. My life has been like this for the past year, but I still can't get over the jitters.

As soon as my head rose from the limo, a roar came from the crowd. They started to clap and yell at the top of their lungs. The flashes were blinding me from both sides. I was on cloud nine to know after the last week that my people still have me.

I high fived both sides of the crowd and walked inside. The show was off the hook. I strolled off the stage with my second award. I couldn't help notice my escort. She was a perfect "10" with the brightest smile I've ever seen. I couldn't help but ask her what she was doing after the show.

She shocked me when she said, "Whatever you're doing." There was no way I could pass up that invitation.

I told her, "We're in limo number zero-zero-four. Meet me outside after the smoke clears." I hope she didn't mind tagging along behind me to *Club Remix*. I got twenty grand to slide in for a few.

As the forum started to clear, I looked around for the lovely girl. Damn! What in the hell was her name? That's a damn shame I don't even know shorty's name. I didn't see her so she missed out. I knew it would be just as easy to pick up something at the club.

I put my arms around the two lovebirds and walked out to the limo. Kenya said, "It looks like the cat gave you your tongue back." I guess she meant I was looking better. She was right about that. I had to admit it has been a hell of a night.

Kenya started teasing me about not saying her name when I got my award. She was only teasing, but I felt guilty anyway. I told her, "Next year I'm going to get three and I gotcha. As a matter of fact, I will wear a Kenya T-shirt on the stage." We all got a big laugh out of that.

"What will Ms. Thing from the stage have to say about that?" she said jokingly referring to the honey that handed me my awards earlier this evening.

I laughed and said, "Oh, you saw that. You know I'm a hoe by nature. Anyway, I told her to have her happy ass at the limo. As you can see, there ain't nobody there."

"When are you going to settle down?" Kenya asked me with raised eyebrows.

"When I'm old and ready to die."

"Trifling...." She replied jokingly as we all laughed, and prepared to get in the car.

We opened the door to get into the limo. I heard Kenya say, "Oh, shit!" Me and Black stuck our heads into the car. I saw Kenya and Ms. Thing laughing. I guess she scared her and they were laughing about it. We got in the car and we told the driver to bounce.

"You almost missed the boat," I told Shorty with a bright smile on my face, happy that she was able to make it.

"I'm glad my happy ass got here in time," she said, making herself comfortable. I started to like her immediately.

With all that's going on I couldn't have some stranger riding even if she is fine. On top of that I wanted to know her name. When I asked, she said, "I thought you would never ask. It is Peir." I heard Kenya whisper "trifling" under her breath. I gave her a nudge with my leg.

"Peir is a nice name," I told her, still checking her out. The rest of the ride was spent sipping on some Don P.

The club was a madhouse, but it was my kind of party. When we step from the limo the people went from two formed lines to a tight circle around us. I don't want to act funny but some times the attention can be a little much. At this stage in the game I'm like the white folks the show must go. Security then came and cleared a path and rushed us to VIP. When we got upstairs it was all good. The Don P was on ice waiting to be popped. The groupies was undressing me with their eyes trying to get my attention. Right now all I wanted to do was get back to the crib and dock my boat in pier. When we got upstairs, we didn't waste any time. We went from the kitchen sink to the sofa. Then from the shower to the bedroom. I tried my best not to think about Kim. The way Peir looked she commanded attention. Attention that I didn't mind giving.

When it was all said and done, I was alone again. I just wasn't ready for an overnight guest. She wasn't too cool with leaving, but she got with the program. I cut my CD on and rapped myself to sleep.

CHAPTER 57: Detective Bryant

I've been looking at their files for about eleven straight hours and what do I got? A bunch of nothing. I don't have one drop of evidence that connects him to the dead girl.

Now I'm working twice as hard because this is the second time this kid's name has come up in connection with a homicide. Now I got the files and witness statement from that scumbag in Pepper's case. Between his files and the ones of Ms. Rowan, I can't see my desk. It doesn't seem right to me that these detectives close these cases without a fight.

I made a promise to the Rowan family that I won't drop the ball. I know that once the trail comes to light it will lead back to superstar. The one thing that I'm having trouble with is what would be the motive.

I'm pretty sure groupies are the same all over the world. Their main goal is to fuck as many stars as they can. From all the info I have about him, he is a star. With all the money and assets alone, he doesn't seem like the kind that would have to pay for some pussy.

Not to mention he is a handsome kid. All of that would rule out the lack of theory. I can tell just from the first week that this case is going to make me lose the rest of my hair.

If this guy so much as jaywalks, I'm going to put him in jail. Before I jump the gun, I need to find at least a hair follicle to connect him. What happened to the days when the nosey old lady saw everything? Now you can't get a statement, let alone get somebody to take the stand.

Before I get a stray bullet in the back I need to retire, get fat and move to Miami. Miami ... now that's a good thought

CHAPTER 58: Born

I took my headphones off and glanced around the room. I thought I heard a noise behind me but when I turned around it was nothing. I turned the music up and zoned out on the beat. I write my raps better when the music is on blast. I'm not big on writing the words down, so I memorize verse for verse.

I was nodding my head to every beat when a sharp pain knocked me out of the chair. I grabbed my head and felt the warm blood in my palm. The blow wasn't enough to knock me out, but it had me dizzy as hell!

I looked up, but I was seeing double. Although the face looked familiar, I couldn't make him out. I closed my eyes really tight to try and stop my head from spinning. After a few seconds I opened my eyes to see PB. I couldn't believe what I saw, so I closed them again.

When I opened them again the sight didn't change. He was standing over me with the devil in his eyes and a big ass gun in his hand. He caught me sleeping, now I'm at his mercy. I hope he makes the mistake and let me get my gun.

The blood was leaking into my eye. I didn't feel like he had the nerve to kill me, but why did I feel like I was about to die?

He told me to get up. He wasn't a fool because he gave me plenty of room as I picked myself up. He threw me a pair of handcuffs and pointed to my chair. I didn't want to put the cuffs on because I knew I would be helpless. I didn't want to force his hand and make him do something he doesn't want to do

Once I was cuffed to the chair he asked me, "How does it feel?" He smiled and gave me a good look at the damage I did. His teeth broke up in the worst way. Some were missing and others were jagged on the edge. He started talking to me, but I couldn't understand what he was saying. I wasn't sure if the gun fucked up my hearing or was it him? I didn't know and that was starting to scare me.

Waving a big ass gun and sounding like a sci-fi creature, he paced back and forth in front of me with rage in his eyes. I could tell he was a man in need of a hug. One thing I've learned from my tour in the streets, when a man talks this long, he's trying to talk himself into killing. Nine times out of ten, he never finds the right words. In my case, I should walk out of here pretty beat down, but alive.

I tried to talk him out of the ass kicking, but he wasn't listening. He was ranting about me showing his boys the tape of him crying like a bitch. He walked over to the sofa and grabbed a pillow. He told me that I would love this. He opened his zipper and pissed on the pillow. This kid really had problems

Before I knew it he smashed the pillow into my face. I couldn't believe it. I moved my face from side to side to try and break free. It didn't work and the taste of piss on my lips reminded me of that. He laughed out loud like a man slowly losing his mind.

At this point I was mad as hell. I tried to break the cuffs, but I wasn't that mad. After this bastard stopped laughing he said, "Do you have any last words?" Could this be the end? Did he have the guts to look me in the eyes and pull the trigger?

He cocked the hammer on the gun that was looking more and more like a 45 cal. He raised the pissy pillow to my face to muffle the blast. I wanted to scream for help, but I didn't want to give him the satisfaction.

I held my breath until I heard the blast. I jumped with sweat on my face and a damp t-shirt. Someone was trying their best to beat down my door. They were banging like somebody was after them. It must be Veronica here to clean the house. She must have been banging for a while.

I jumped up and put my robe on. I ran to the door and swung it open to stop the banging. Once I did I was rushed by a bunch of cops. The two detectives that questioned me downtown pulled up the rear. The white detective said, "It looks like you had a rough night."

I tried to ask him what this was all about. They said, "We need to ask you some questions." I didn't have anything to hide, so I said, "Go ahead."

"No. Downtown." they said to my surprise. I really wasn't in the mood, but from the looks on their faces, I didn't have a choice. I threw on a Polo sweat suit and let them lead the way.

As we walked into the precinct all eyes were on me. I'm used to that, but these eyes looked at me differently. These are the eyes that I'd seen when I walked into Tiffany's for the first time. These eyes didn't trust me and didn't care how much money I had. These eyes not only stereotyped my skin, but they also didn't care for the generations before me. I wasn't handcuffed, but I felt more trapped now then before. We went into a different room and the first question they asked was, "Is there anything you want to tell us?"

"No. Not without my lawyer."

"We knew you'd say that. That's why we've already called him."

After a few minutes of awkward stares, Mr. Holt busted in. I could see he was a little winded, but I was glad to see him.

"Where's Black?" I asked him, wondering if they got my homie, too.

"In the lobby because they wouldn't let him in." When I saw the look on his face I knew things had gotten worse. Then he asked the detective for a few minutes alone with me. My heart just dropped when I heard that.

After they left he told me what was going down. I couldn't believe what my ears were hearing. No way in hell Peir could be dead. I can still smell her scent on my body. What the hell is this? Another nightmare?

He told me not only is she dead, but they think I did it. Anybody with a GED can tell I was being framed. He told me to calm down, but that was easier for him to say. The Bopsie Twins walked in right as I was about to ask the million dollar question.

"Am I under arrest?"

When they came in one of them threw some pictures near me. I wanted to look down bad, but they might be more flicks like the ones of Kim. They asked me what I knew about it. Of course, I said nothing, but I didn't look at the flicks.

They drilled me for hours on end. The same questions over and over again. I guess they got tactics from *"Menace to Society."* The only difference is I wasn't Ole' Dog and I wasn't lying.

The questions stopped and they left the room. I couldn't believe somebody was trying to ruin me. I tried not to look at the pictures of Peir, but I felt like some giant was forcing my neck down. Satan or curiosity was getting the best of me.

Before I knew it I was looking at the breathless body of Peir. I could feel my whole body get weak. I couldn't believe how she looked. She looked so sad, it was like she was sleeping. Her face was so pale she looked white and too hard to bare. What kind of monster would do this sick shit?

My jaw was shaking so bad I could barely talk. They asked me some more of the same questions, which I only nodded to. Detective Bryant got face to face. He was so close that I could smell the coffee on his breath. He told me that nothing would give him greater pleasure than reading me my rights. He told me if his senses still worked that it wouldn't be long yet.

"Since they wanted to play hardball, "Do me and my client a favor, don't come to his residence without a warrant. Also, don't ask him to another one of your tea parties without arresting him. If, by chance, the arrest isn't valid, I will let your department buy me that house in the south of France I've been wanting," Mr. Holt told the detectives jumping right up to my defense.

He tapped me on the shoulder and I rose right up. He packed away his notes in his briefcase. We all exchanged unpleasant looks and then about faced. As we walked down the hallway, the eyes were burning my back. When I made it past the water fountain, I saw Black. I could tell by the way his face lit up he wasn't sure if I would make it back out. We hugged like I just came home off a twenty year bid. We walked out again like deja vu, but this time my life was on *Def Con 4*.

I couldn't wait for the long arm of the law to pull me out of this mess or wait for Lady Justice to turn a blind eye. No matter what the odds, I wouldn't bet on either one.

CHAPTER 59: The Killer

Today is the day. I can feel it. The timing couldn't be more perfect. The mood is just right. I'm sure Mr. Casanova is home borderline suicidal right now. He's probably hitting his head against the wall as I speak. I've got to hear the panic in his voice. Can the lady's man stay cool with all the ladies dying around him? HA! HA! Let me call and see.

"Can I speak with Mr. Born?"

"Who's this?" he asked, trying to catch my voice.

"You want to know who this is? I thought you would know by now. Since you're too stupid to figure that out, let me introduce myself. I'm your worst nightmare come true," I spoke into the phone menacingly. I wanted to laugh so bad it was killing me…no pun intended.

"Why don't you take that fake ass voice box off and state who you are," Born said getting more upset by the second. I was close to pissing on myself I was laughing so hard.

"You want me to take the gadget off the phone so you can recognize my voice?"

"Yeah, coward! Be a man about the shit."

"Oh, now I'm a coward. Did you learn that in psychology 101 or did you come up with that all by your lonesome?"

"Man, what's the purpose of this call?" Born replied, his frustration evident. That was exactly what I wanted.

"When the time is right you will hear my voice and see my face, but not a moment before. You're gonna pay for what you did. I promise you that!"

"What the hell did I do? Yo, who the fuck is this?" at this point Born is practically screaming into the phone, and I'm enjoying every minute of it.

"Now doesn't that beat all? You don't even know what you did. Well, let me be the first to tell you that it doesn't even matter. You're going to pay dearly and I will have the pleasure of tasting sweet revenge. Oh, yeah. Before I forget ... how is your daughter?" then I hung up the phone.

I waited a few second after I hung up and call backed. I knew his blood would be boiling by then. My suspicions were correct because he started yelling and I hung up again. I knew then I had him. That's just how I need him, in a panic. When your prey is scared or nervous, it's at its most vulnerable point. Everything that he cherishes will fall and then he will fall after it. Like the "*Art of War*" says: "Destroy your enemy from within" and that's what I plan to do.

CHAPTER 60: Black

This is some shit straight out of a Stephen King book. Born is being stalked by a serial killer and the cops don't even believe him. They think it's all a trick to get the weight off of him. They won't even tap his phone. They said the prosecutor on the case won't authorize it. She sounds like she's a real bitch, but aren't they all?

There is nothing for us to do but watch our backs. I'm glad Kenya's in Paris right now working, and Born sent mom and Ashley out of town. I think that was a good move after he told me what that creep said. I could use a vacation myself. Too bad we're locked in to do this video with *Wu-Tang*.

I know Born is not feeling up to it, but a deal is a deal. They were there when he needed them for the "Harlem's Finest" video. That's how the industry works. One hand washes the other. This early in his career I would hate for the industry to frown on him.

CHAPTER 61: Born

On my way here all I could tell myself was that I didn't feel like partying. That's all video shoots are, especially a *Wu Tang* joint. I must admit when I got here they took my mind right off my troubles. There were hoochies from all over the world on the set. There were a few there that looked a little exotic. I don't know if hard nipples were part of the requirement, but they all had that in common.

The whole video was done around, or in, the pool. That was one of the reasons I agreed to do it. When they said the BK freak *"Sincere"* was directing the video, I knew I wanted in. As it turns out, I'm not disappointed.

Every time there is a break in the action Peir or Kim comes to mind. I can't help but believe that their deaths are my fault. The extras and video girls don't give you much time to yourself. What we call acting freaky, they call networking. Their act doesn't stop there. They want to be in all the videos, if possible.

Sincere walked over to me and threw me a towel. We weren't on speaking terms, so I knew he had business on his mind. He beat around the bush for a minute, and then he asked me about the girls and which ones I liked. He made them bend over and kiss each other.

They knew he had the power to get them in a video. If they made him mad, that could be the end of their career. Then out of the blue he asked me when I was going to drop the "Tip" video. I knew he was being too friendly. I told him I didn't think he would like to do that style of video.

He laughed and said, "I don't only do ass videos."

We both laughed and I told him, "Please don't stop doing that." As I said that Jessica, the goddess with the hour glass shape, walked by. We slapped hands as to say she was off the hook. The security guard walked over to me and told me that there was a young lady at the front for me. I asked him her name. He said that he forgot, but I wouldn't be mad.

Sincere said, "Fuck her, we got more than enough women for, the video."

With all that was going on I had to see who she was. I got up, put my shirt on and headed to the front. When I got there, my eyes popped out and my jaw hit the ground.

I couldn't believe what I was seeing. The guard was right. My eyes weren't disappointed. She was a solid "12," but I knew what was under that red skin. I asked, "What in the hell are you doing here?"

She replied, "Is that anyway to talk to your baby's mother?" I hope she wasn't expecting an apology. With a straight face she said, "Didn't you send for me?"

Then it hit me, it must've been Black. He asked me about her a few days ago. He said Ashley was looking more and more like her. He must have gotten soft on me and sent for her.

Some little bow legged Pecan Rican called me. She said that Sincere needed me for the next shot. I told her to tell him I'll be right there. When she turned around, she gave me a perfect view of the dental floss she was wearing. I could see in Lia's eyes she was steaming mad. It was good to see she was still jealous.

"I need a minute to get this straight. Go to my trailer and wait for me. Do not touch anything, especially my beeper or phone." I told her, then quickly turned my back to her and walked away. She rolled her eyes and spun around. Before she got too far I said, "Oh, yeah. And don't answer my door either." She made a funny gesture with her hand and switched off. When I walked in I saw the impatient look on Sincere's face.

"Sorry. Now, let's do it."

The shoot went on for hours and every minute was spent thinking of Lia. During the last scene one of Luke's lovely ladies had me pinned on the side of the pool. She had her hand down my shorts, but I couldn't get in the mood. I needed to hear the director say cut so I could head back to my trailer.

After a few minutes, and a disappointed Luke dancer, I slid out of the pool. I put my robe on and told Sin that I would be in my trailer. I also told him I needed to take care of my pain in the ass baby's mom.

As I started to walk, a few hoochies tried to tag along. I wanted them to come as bad as they wanted to go, but now wasn't the time. I asked them if they would mind if I sent for them in a few. They all said, "No" at the same time. As soon as I get rid of Lia, I will see what else they can do at the same time.

I walked over to my trailer and opened the door. I walked inside and couldn't believe what this bitch has done. The trailer was a mess. Shit was thrown all over the place. She had the nerve to trash my trailer. Then she wonders why I don't want her in mines or Ashley's life.

I sat on the couch and tried to calm myself down. I noticed Lia's pocketbook was still there. I guess she was trying to get out of here before I caught her ass. That was a good idea because I would've killed her little ass.

I heard a light knock on the door. I screamed, "Not right now! I'm busy." I guess they got the hint because they didn't knock again.

Sitting here mad at her and Black for sending her is not getting me anywhere. What I need to do is get this chlorine off me and see what girls are left. I dropped my robe, got naked, and walked into the bathroom. I took a quick look at myself in the mirror. Everything was still pretty tight, so I headed for the shower.

When I pulled back the curtain I almost fainted. I fell back between the door and toilet. I wanted to scream, but nothing would come out. I couldn't believe my eyes. I tried to get up, but my legs wouldn't allow it. Lia was lying in the tub in a pool of blood. The burning tears were making it a little hard for me to see her. I knew I had to get up. This wasn't possible. She wasn't dead. I had to help her. I had to call an ambulance or something.

"Born, get it together! Get up and get it together!"

I heard my name, but I was still trapped in a daze. Each time I heard my name I followed the voice to the light. After hearing it a few times, I looked around to see where I was. The funny smell made me turn my nose up.

When my eyes scanned the room I couldn't see anything that looked familiar except Darryl and Black. I saw a nurse walk passed in all white, and she made me think of Lia. I grabbed Black and asked him, "Where is Lia?"

He looked me straight in the eyes, but didn't answer me. I shook him while I asked him again, but all he did was drop his head. That was enough. I knew she didn't make it. I knew from the way my lips were shaking that the tears weren't far behind.

The doctor walked up while Black had his arms wrapped around me. By that time, the faucet of tears was turned all the way on. The doctor interrupted us and said, "I need someone to identify the body."

Black said he would do it, but I had to tell her that I'm sorry. This whole thing is my fault. I told Black I would be right back. He wasn't trying to hear that, but I insisted. As the doctor and I walked down a long hallway I thought of Ashley. How was I going to look into those beautiful brown eyes and break it to her?

We walked through these two steel doors. When I walked in I heard hundreds of dead people banging to get out. I didn't know which door Lia's voice was coming from. The doctor walked over to door number sixteen. He pulled her out and all I saw was a white sheet that read "Property of NCCH."

When he pulled the sheet back I saw her pretty face. Although I heard her asking me to step closer, I couldn't. I wanted nothing more than to hold her hand, but I couldn't move.

"Is that her?" the doctor asked me, but I couldn't answer him. I shook my head and wiped the tears from my eyes.

CHAPTER 62: Darryl

For the first time in a long time, I'm caught between a rock and a hard place. Born is bringing me and *Underworld* too much bad attention. I don't believe he did it, but the media is having a field day with this bullshit. Yesterday's headlines read *"Born to Kill."* They had him convicted already.

After all the progress we gained from the rap summit last year, they are wishing this to be true. My people at Sony call me every hour. I can hear the panic in their voices. This is the perfect thing that can get me dropped by them. I don't want to turn my back on Black or Born, but if I don't, I'll be back selling bootlegs on Sunset Blvd. I've come too far to go back and I think I need to cut my losses.

As hot as Born is, right now the last thing he is worrying about is a contract. As soon as the smoke clears, every major and independent label will be after him. Not to mention me if he goes for it. I hope he understands.

CHAPTER 63: Born

I rode around all night with tears in my eyes. Although me and Lia weren't on good terms, I never wanted this for her. This whole shit is driving me crazy. The whole time I drove around all I saw was Lia, Kim, and Peir. The bloody pictures were everywhere I turned. They had me to the point where I almost crashed a few times.

Then matters got worse when I got to my crib. I tossed and turned until the sunlight came through the window. I wasn't sure if I rode around longer or I tossed longer. What I did know was that dreadful day was gone. The bad part was the pain still followed me. I've had a lot of pain in my life, but this could not compare. I know this was something I would be fighting for a long time. I just hope I wouldn't be fighting it in Attica or Sing Sing.

With that thought I knew it was time to head to the studio. I jumped into my car and headed for my sanctuary. I turned on Ed Lover's and Dr. Dre's Morning Show. I thought they might be able to get me through this rough spot. Instead, I was the joke. I didn't expect anything less from them. I guess nothing is sacred when it comes to comedians. I made a mental note to myself. Make sure I punch him in the face.

I was about two minutes from the studio. I wanted to call Black to let him know I was alright. I changed my mind because I know he would come right down. I'll let someone else let him know.

Although it was early in the morning, it was too quiet for me. With all that has happened, I guess I'm a little jumpy. I clicked off the Hot 97 Morning Show and grabbed my bag off the front seat. I took one step out of the car and all hell broke loose. Cars came screaming around the corner. I knew who they were. I just didn't want to believe they were there for me. They had the block cut off and me surrounded.

They had their guns drawn and their eyes locked on me. I've been out of the streets for a minute, but I knew this wasn't the time to reach for ID. It wasn't hard for them to make you feel like a criminal, even though deep down inside I knew I was being framed.

After a series of "Don't move!" and hammers being cocked back, I knew my life was over. I didn't see the two detectives that hauled me to the precinct before. I couldn't see them, but I knew when the smoke cleared they would be there.

They moved in and slammed my face onto the hot hood. They were acting like I was public enemy number one. I wanted to tell them that I was innocent, but I knew it wouldn't help. I kept my mouth shut while they forced me in the back of the cruiser.

I sat there while they tore my Benz to pieces. There was a time when that would've made me nervous, but now I know there isn't any coke or guns up in there.

As I watched the cops tear up my hundred thousand dollars machine, I heard a light tap on the window. When I turned to my left I saw Detective Bryant. He had a goofy smile on his face and was waving at me. Then he hit the top of the car and it pulled off.

We whipped through the city with no siren, but more than enough escorts. I gazed out of the window and said to myself that this might be the last time I race through the city. Damn! I haven't seen the Tombs in about seven years, but my streak has come to an end. A very tragic end.

CHAPTER 64: Black

Mr. Holt went at it all morning with the judge and Ms. Bitch, the prosecutor. She didn't want Born to get a bail. She said he had too much money to keep up with his whereabouts.

There was a time when the judge was with Holt and then he sounded like he was with Ms. Liriano. Just by watching her she looked like she was taking this case personal. She was a very attractive white lady in her late forties. On the outside she had it all, but something was missing. She was a lady with a black heart. In my opinion, that is the worst kind of lady to cross paths with. A hurt woman is worse than a wounded animal. I think all she needs is some good loving and her whole outlook on life will change. Then again, she might rip it off if a guy isn't careful.

I would say Mr. Holt has his hands full this time. For Born's sake, I hope she doesn't break his winning streak. Finally, the judge banged his gavel down to stop the cat and dog fight.

"After further consideration, I have a ruling. I think that with the evidence before me, I think your Ricardo Smith should get a bail. He is too big of a star to hide anywhere," he said, and continued to take notes on a note pad.

He must have heard me clap because he said, "Before anybody gets excited, the bail will be one million dollars plus property." My heart almost stopped when I heard that number. The wicked witch went crazy when she heard it. She's too emotional to have this case. That's going to be the first thing I tell Mr. Holt.

While Mr. Holt packed his briefcase away he told the judge he requests a speedy trial. Before Ms. Liriano could shoot it down, the judge granted it. It looked like he was being spiteful to her from the break. I left them giving each other the killer stares. Mr. Holt should go ahead and give her a little taste, maybe that will loosen her up a little. I hurried out of there. I didn't want Born to spend another minute in that place.

CHAPTER 65: Born, The Trial Part I

These four walls have been driving me crazy. I only left this house three times since I got bailed out. All I've done is ordered out and rented movies. I think I watched *"Scarface"* and *"The Color Purple"* a hundred times. I don't know which made me madder. Angel getting killed or them beating up Harpo.

Mr. Holt had me in mind when he said, "Don't leave the crib." He was right, you can't frame a man that has a concrete alibi. Now it's time for me to plead my case in front of a jury. I had on a basic black Armani suit with matching glasses. I was trying to look innocent and smart at the same time. I walked in with Black on my right side and my one man dream team on the left.

I waved to my mom and Ashley. Kenya was there also with her little sister. There were a lot of friendly faces and fans. Where there is good, there is always evil.

Bunched up in one section was the hate club. Leading the way was Detective Bryant. Lia's family was there, also. Senator Smith was also there. I know she's dying to take some bad news back to the rap lynch mob.

As I walked by, some hoochie stood and said, "Give that bastard the electric chair!" I thought this was America, people. What ever happened to "innocent until proven guilty?" I see how they're getting down. I've got to beat this without a shadow of a doubt.

As we took our seats, I saw a very attractive woman to the left of Mr. Holt. I knew this couldn't be the Ice Queen Black was telling me about. She didn't look mean at all. In fact, she looked kind of familiar. She never raised her head out of her notes until the judge dropped the hammer. That's when the war broke out. She pushed her glasses up and went right for the juggler.

Her opening argument was harsh and to the point. She accused me of everything under the sun. She claimed to have witnesses to place me at the scene of the crime. She also said that once she got a guilty verdict that she will push for the death penalty. I heard my mother scream "NO!" over Lia's people's clapping.

The judge quickly gained order while I stared at the jury. The young ladies that looked sweet and innocent when we picked them. Now they look mean and bitter, just like her. She must have known all along that opening statement was going to send them on a witch hunt.

Once Mr. Holt took the floor I don't even think they were listening. It was their turn to stare into space. I've been on the opposite side of the law most of my life, now I'm forced to trust in it. That is a feeling that is hard to swallow. My lawyer was up there beating a dead horse.

Once Mr. Holt closed out, Ms. Liriano called her first witness. It was Mr. Russell, my old English teacher from high school. When I saw his name in the discovery, I couldn't believe it. Then again, I could because he was a faggot then and is still one now. He wanted to see me fail in high school and he still does. He was still the best at wearing cheap suits and talking with a Shakespearean accent. Once he was sworn in and sat down, the flood gates opened.

He told his version of me being a hoodlum, troublemaker and, most of all a violent teenager. I noticed the jury trading looks between me and him. I didn't know if it was because he was hard to follow or they wanted to believe in me. Nevertheless, it felt like a plus for me.

As Ms. Liriano asked him a question, Mr. Holt stood up and objected. The judge granted it and gave her a warning for leading the witness. She didn't ask him about our fight yet, but I knew that would be her next question. I could see from the redness in her face that she was steaming mad.

She said, "Let's skip all the pleasantries and get down to business." Then she asked about the fight. Damn, I'm good. If my rap career is over, I'll see if Dionne has room for me.

Mr. Russell took his glasses off and wiped them with his tie. He crossed his legs and placed them back on. From being in his class for two long years, I knew the theatrics were about to surface. He turned toward the jury and began to sink my battleship.

He told how he didn't do anything and I attacked him. I wanted to jump up and call him a lying bastard. Black felt my anger rising and he placed his hand on my forearm.

"He's lying like shit," I whispered to Mr. Holt.

"After I finish with him, you'll want to give me a bonus," he leaned over at me and said.

All he thinks about is money, but I'm curious to see what he has up his sleeve.

After a long hour of Mr. Russell's bullshit, Ms. Liriano spun around and said, "No further questions." She had a slight smirk on her face and I knew why. He single handedly smashed my character. Mr. Holt didn't seem worried, but I was very worried. Mr. Holt slid from behind the table with his thousand dollar suit to cross examine the witness. He introduced himself and asked Mr. Russell, "Have you ever heard of me?" Ms. Liriano objected and the judge ruled in her favor.

The judge said, "Your superstar's status isn't relevant in this case, Mr. Holt." The crowd got themselves a laugh from that. Mr. Holt quickly moved on to the next question.

He asked, "Mr. Russell, are you an alcoholic?" You heard the crowd take a deep breath all at once. I wasn't surprised because I told him Mr. Russell used to come to class smelling of vodka.

Mr. Russell took offense and said, "Hell, no!"

The judge smacked the hammer down and said, "There will be no profanity in this courtroom."

Mr. Holt said, "Are you drunk right now?"

"No," answered Mr Russell

Mr. Holt said, "Since you are not an alcoholic, when was the last time you had a drink?"

He said, "I had a date last night and we went out for drinks. "

Mr. Holt said, "Drinks! How many is 'drinks'?" Ms. Liriano tried to object, but the judge quickly denied it. She plopped down in her chair.

Mr. Russell said, "Four or five."

Mr. Holt asked, "Did you have a hangover?" Then Mr. Holt waved to the back of the courtroom to Phillip, his private investigator.

He walked to the front with a middle aged guy with grayish black hair. He stood where he was visible for all to see. A buzz came over the courtroom because everyone was curious as to his identity.

Mr. Holt said, "Now, Mr. Russell, I am going to ask you the question again. When was the last time you had a drink?"

Mr. Russell looked over to Ms. Liriano and shook his head. He took a deep breath and said, "Nine o'clock this morning." The buzz from the crowd turned into a roar. The judge banged and banged his gavel to try and get control over the crowd.

Mr. Holt went to his briefcase and took out a big yellow envelope and slid it to Mr. Russell. After a minute or so, he took it back. He showed it to the judge, Ms. Liriano, and finally the jury.

After the envelope made it back to him, he asked, "Mr. Russell, have you heard of me?"

Mr. Russell said, "Yes" and dropped his head. That was the second time Mr. Russell lied under oath.

Mr. Holt turned around to look at Ms. Liriano and said, "No - further questions."

She called her next witness. It was the girl from Harrisburg, Pa. I knew she was going to have a lot to say. Some kids tried to fake on me and my crew at the show. To this day I don't know what really happened. I know they tried to bum-rush us and it backfired. In the process, Ms. Thing got broke up. Of course, the only face she knew was mine. I wasn't surprised, but I was glad the charges didn't stick.

Once she was on the stand she pulled down her miniskirt and sat down. Ms. Liriano started right with the questions. The girl, in between smacking her gum, said she was pleading the Fifth. She said she was advised by her lawyer not to talk about that night. She said she picked up a lawyer three days ago and decided to sue. I guess she figured this could be her payday.

At this point she was the least of my troubles. I could see that Ms. Liriano had fire in her eyes. She had a look that could scare the biggest guy. The more I looked at her, the more she looked familiar. I hate it when my memory runs out on me. Before it's all said and done, I'm going to place that face. I hope it's not when twenty five hundred volts of electricity is going through my body.

Mr. Holt chose not to cross examine, so she got off lucky. The way he ate Mr. Russell alive, I don't envy the next man.

I was pumped up after the Mr. Holt show. I was waiting for the next victim. I thought Ms. Liriano stood up to call on her next witness, but she didn't. Instead, she asked the court for a lunch break. I looked down at my watch and saw how time was flying. I wasn't mad at her because I was hungry as hell.

CHAPTER 66: Born, Recess

We walked into *Jackson Hole* about twenty deep. All eyes were on us. I wasn't sure if they were fans or if they were staring because of the negative press. Either way, I could care less.

Like always, *Jackson Hole* was really busy. Those huge ass burgers were flying from table to table. From past experience I knew it wouldn't be long before I had one in front of me. Everybody laughed at Ashley's puckered lips from the pickles on the table. They hurt her feelings and she began to fake cry with no tears. That was my cue to pick her up and bite her neck. She loves it when I do that.

She looked over my shoulder and pointed to the grill man going ninety miles an hour. I walked her over so she could get a better look. I let her sit on the counter so she had a perfect view. A little cutie in a business suit walked up and want goo-goo over Ashley.

On top of being sexy as hell I could tell she had a good job. That is the most attractive thing about a woman.

She introduced herself as Denise Parker. I was about to give her my name, but she said, "No need. You can tell me this princess's name."

She almost melted when I said "Ashley." She thought that was a perfect name. I thought she was playing when she said there was no need for me to give her my name. I like it when girls play tough. It really turns me on when you find one that doesn't know you.

As it turned out, she did know me. She said she was the second assistant to Assistant Liriano. I quickly took Ashley out of her hands. I said, "What you mean is ... you're her flunky." She got upset, but I really didn't care.

She replied "That wasn't called for," and maybe she was right. She grabbed her bag and was about to walk away when I apologized. That stopped her in her tracks.

She turned and said, "Oh, you do have a heart?"

I put my hand out and asked, "Could we start all over?"

She confessed to me that she did follow me down here. The word groupie flashed before my eyes. I guess she read my mind and said, "No, I'm not a groupie. Ms. Liriano really has it out for you."

"Tell me something I don't know," I said to her. She said that in a weird sort of way. I didn't understand what it meant, but her eyes were starting to scare me.

With her wide eyes she looked behind me. When I looked she stuffed something in my pocket. All I saw behind me were two police officers.

I guess that was enough to make her leave. I reached into my pocket and pulled out a card with her name on it. How would it look, the prime murder suspect calling the DA's office? What do I say, "Hi, this is Jack the Ripper. May I speak to Denise?"

As I read the card, Black walked up behind me. He said, "You must be losing your touch because she practically ran out of here." I told him who that was and what she said. I told him it sounded like a set up to me. He didn't agree. He said that I should call her and pick her for info, he liked the fact that we had eyes on the inside.

I told him, "Moles can be double agents, too." Then we went back to the table for lunch.

CHAPTER 67: Born, The Trial Part II

We rushed through the courtroom door without a minute to spare. All heads turned when the doors opened up. The buzz took over the courtroom again. From the look on their faces I guess they thought I skipped town. As I took my seat the judge dropped the hammer. He cleared his throat into the mic in front of him.

"This is a courtroom, not a concert. Those are a jury of your peers, not your adoring fans. Please don't disrespect me, the jury, or this court of law by being late again. If it happens again, I will revoke your bond and put you where I know you won't be late."

I was not trying to hear that bullshit, but he certainly got my attention. He pointed to Ms. Liriano to proceed. She stood up and asked, "May I approach the bench?" The judge told both counsels to approach the bench. All I could see was Mr. Holt's hands moving up and down. I thought I knew that was a sure sign of trouble.

They were up there for about ten minutes before the huddle broke. Mr. Holt came back to the table and went right for my ear. All he kept saying is we got them. I asked him what he meant. He said, "We got them. I'll fill you in later."

The judge stood up and said, "This court is adjourned until nine am Monday morning." I didn't know what was going on, but I was glad court was over. I gathered my things and started towards my mom and Ashley. I put my hand in my pocket and felt Denise's card. When I pulled it out I noticed there was a number on the back.

CHAPTER 68: Denise

I sat at my desk filing away the paper from today's trial. In the process I was watching Ms. Liriano. The only thing that separated her office from my desk was a crystal clear glass wall. I pretended I wasn't looking at her, but I was. She was pacing back and forth talking to herself. I've been her assistant for a year since she came to town.

She really climbed the ladder in such a short time. She's a good example for all women to watch. The only problem is, this job looks like its driving her crazy. She wants this conviction too damn bad. That's what I was trying to explain to him. She is obsessed with putting him away. I hope he has enough sense to call me, so I can give him the low down.

I don't want to lose my job in the process. I don't know what would happen to me if that came out. Even worse, what if I'm wrong and he is the killer? If so, I will lose more than my job.

CHAPTER 69: Born

I wasn't sure if I'm being watched or not. Instead of taking the chance I did some real Mission Impossible shit and slid out the back. I drove straight to Yolanda's. I had Black talk to Louie earlier. He let us rent out the spot for the rest of the night. Black told me how much he charged, I couldn't believe it. For that price, we could've bought the whole store.

We pulled up in front and the joint was pitch black. My first thought was "they're not here yet," until I saw the company van. The front door opened up and Big Rock stepped out. He waved us inside. I walked in to see Denise at a candle lit table in the back with Black. I walked over and spoke to them. She stood up and shook my hand.

I could tell from the relief on her face that she was a little uptight. I guess I would be also. Black took romance to another level. There was only one light on in the whole joint.

I guess he wanted to make it look empty. Black walked off and we both sat down at the table. I asked if she was hungry and she said no. I knew it was going to take a minute to loosen her up. Louie brought me a meatball hoagie with extra marinara sauce. I really was in the mood for some king crab legs, but I guess this will have to do.

I couldn't help but notice how good she looked. The candlelight flickered off her golden brown skin. Even the baggy sweat suit made her look good. I like a woman that can turn you on no matter what. She watched me inhale that sandwich without a sound. Once I was done, she said, "You might have broken a record." I laughed and she smiled.

"Now, tell me, what's the deal with your boss?"

She didn't have much to say. I could tell by the way she stumbled through it was just a hunch. She doesn't have anything concrete, but she believed in what she had. She sounded like a lady that lived next to The Stephens in Bewitch. She always knew something was going on but couldn't put her finger on it, but knew it was going down.

I can't knock her because I cherish my sixth sense. My gut feeling got me out of a lot of sticky situations. I let her get it off her chest. Ms. Liriano seems like a real bitch, but that's not a crime.

I must admit, when she said she talks to her daughter's picture, I was shocked. She might have a few issues, but I can't see where any of them can help me.

She told me a few stories that made her suspicious. I made it my business to stare. That was my way of talking to a woman without saying anything. When she was done she took a sip of water. She said, "You don't believe me, do you?"

I was shocked by her question. I told her, "It's nothing to believe or not to believe. I do believe that you want help me. Now, let me ask you a question. Do you believe I killed those young ladies?"

She paused for a minute and said," No, I don't."

I told her that meant a lot, believe it or not. I placed my hand on hers and said thank you. I waited for her to pull away, but she didn't. I saw a flash appear out of the darkness. Someone was lighting a cigarette. It was too dark to tell who. Before that I forgot that Black, Rock, and Big Harv were there. I wasn't sure if it was the darkness or did I get lost in her eyes?

I looked down at my watch to see the time. The hours were really flying fast. The conversation was better than I imagine once she got going. I haven't sat and had a conversation since Sara. Some days I think about calling her, but I wouldn't know what to tell her.

Denise asked me what I was thinking about. Although it was Sara, I told her, "You." And she asked how many times I said that on a date.

"I hope I wasn't doing anything in your mind I wouldn't really do," she said flirtatiously. I gave her a devilish look. She smacked my hand to let me know I was being naughty. She was right, my mind was in the gutter. I knew getting close to this girl could mean her death. That was the last thing I wanted for her.

I knew it was getting late, I heard some snoring coming from the darkness. Now, the key to this trick was to get Denise back home safe. I pulled Black to the side and told him, "Me and Rock are going to go out the front. Then you take Denise out the back and get her home safe. Let Big Harv stand watch out in front of her building. Tell him if he sees anything crazy, don't hesitate."

Black shook his head and said, "Don't worry about it. I've got everything." That sentence was pleasing to my ear.

I told Denise that I had to go. I turned and headed for the door. I heard my name leap from the darkness. When I turned to see what she wanted, there she was.

For some strange reason I could see her eyes in the dark. She grabbed my hand and said, "Can I see you again?"

I don't know if she could see my smile, but it was there. I asked, "You sure that's what you want?"

She squeezed my hand tighter and said, "Yes." I reminded her about the bad luck I've been having. She said she didn't care.

At that moment neither did I. I told her yes and gave her a peck on the forehead.

Getting back into my crib was just as exciting as getting out. The biggest regret was Denise wasn't on my arm. I knew I couldn't be seen with anyone until this maniac was dead.

CHAPTER 10: Denise

I went to bed thinking about him. I had a dream that he was holding me tight. Then, when I got up, I was hoping he was there. To my disappointment I woke up to an empty house and hard nipples.

My mind kept saying, "Denise, you're not in school anymore," but there wasn't anything like him in school. You just can't fall for a man because he kissed your forehead. Especially a rapper. How many foreheads has he kissed?

I've got to calm down. I don't t know if he even likes me that way or if he's worried about his case. I know one thing, if he liked me so much, he should've kissed these soft lips.

Look at me sounding hard up. It's been a while since I felt the warmth of a man, but I can't let them see me sweat. It's not because I was short on offers, it's my choice. I refuse to settle anymore. This time Prince Charming must have the white horse and everything. I hope he calls today. If not, when I see him in the court I'm going to feel so stupid.

CHAPTER 71: Born

After tossing and turning all night with Denise on my mind, I knew I had to see her today. This time I took her to Soho, to a little restaurant called *"The Warth Rat"*. The joint was kind of like *The Blue Oyster* in Police Academy. The important thing was I wouldn't see anyone I knew or knew me.

It was already shortly after twelve o'clock when we walked in. I had my shades on with my fresh blue Yankee cap low. All I saw were Mohawks and colorful spiked hair. This wasn't the type of joint that you waited to be seated.

We took a seat way in the back, away from the prying eyes. Once we got passed the nagging waitress we were into each other's head again. This time even deeper than before. This time it was personal.

I showed her some pictures I had of Ashley. I was surprised when she said she didn't have any kids. I told her it was hard to believe with hips like that. She blushed, but I just wanted her to know I was admiring her.

With all that was going on, I felt a little strange being out on a date. I was trying not to disrespect the memories of Lia, Kim, or Peir. I was just trying to keep my sanity. I know tomorrow is going to be crazy with Ms. Liriano coming at me. Her actions in the courtroom already had me scared of her. Now, with all the new shit Denise dropped on me, she really has me shook.

Denise touched my hand to bring me out of my daze. She told me, "I put in for a. vacation when the trial is over."

I told her, "You deserve one. Was that a hint or general conversation?"

She smiled and said, "I hope you don't miss all the curve balls I throw at you." That made for a good laugh between us.

The nagging waitress from hell was back. It looked like the pimple on her nose got bigger. She brought us the check and asked if there was anything else. We were thinking hard about some dessert.

The waitress shouted at the couple to our right. She told them to go get a hotel room. I wasn't sure if it was because they were men or did the kissing exceed restaurant policy? Nevertheless, that made up my mind about the dessert. I paid the check and slid out the door with Denise.

Lunch lasted a little longer than I thought. When I'm with Denise, time flies. It was almost five o'clock when I made it to the back entrance of the studio. I had to come back in this way because I knew the cops I left out front was still there.

I took my electronic passkey out and slid it through the lock. The light did not turn green. I tried it again and again, and the screen said "Access Denied." Could this be somebody's idea of a joke, or has the worst nightmare of all come true?

MTV said there were rumors of me being dropped by the label, but Darryl denied it. I guess I should have known that when the smoke cleared the only people standing would be my family.

CHAPTER 72: Black The Trial Part III

After an hour of fighting off hungry reporters, we entered the courtroom. The junction was finally granted for Court TV to enter. It was like a video shoot up in here. Everyone had on their best dress. I guess they were afraid Mr. Blackwell would see them. Even the evil ice princess stepped it up.

I noticed Mr. Holt had on the Rolex. Born and I kept it simple with the black suits. Born didn't look like himself this morning. He didn't say much on the way over here. He even clammed up when the reporters shoved the mics in his face.

As we made our way to the table, I scanned the crowd. I saw a lot of friendly faces. When I locked eyes with Kenya, she blew me a kiss. That perked me up like a shot of black coffee. She had a special way of doing that. That's why when this is all over, I'm going to pop the question.

Right in front of her was Chuck Chico from the *Source*. I guess he's going to grace the pages with our names. He always showed us love anyway. Even when that chicken head was running around saying Born did this and that. He called her in for an interview and screamed on her. The green-eyed bandit is here. Spike Lee is here with Toya.

I looked over my shoulder to see if Darryl was here. I knew that coward wouldn't show up after the bullshit he's done. He couldn't even tell us to our faces that he was dropping us.

Whether he knew it or not, he did us a favor. Now, we don't have to pay him that seven hundred thousand. Me and Born are family. We shouldn't have had that clowns that close anyway.

I see Lia's mom talking to that fake ass detective. Speaking of detectives, I can't believe Sullivan hasn't showed his ugly face. I wonder if that crazy bastard has an alibi. The judge strolled in, so we all rose. Now that the crowd was divided, good versus evil, let the games begin.

Ms. Evil, herself, called her first witness. I didn't recognize her myself, so I leaned over to Born. He explained to me that she was the gofer on the set of the video. She was a little dumpy looking girl. She was trying her best to squeeze into that skirt, but she was sticking out from every angle.

Since I met Kenya, I try not to be as hard on women, but she's trying to kill my man. Once she sat down, Liriano asked her a bunch of questions that didn't make sense to me. Who gave a fuck if she has kids or not? She asked her to reenact the day of Lia's death.

Mr. Holt objected and said "Speculation."

Mr. Holt had his head down the whole time scribbling notes on a piece of paper. I guess he was getting his come back together.

Liriano rephrased the question. She asked if she'd seen Born that day. She gave a nervous pause and said, "Yes." She went on to say what he was doing. The ice princess even had a way of making fun sound like a crime.

I could tell they had dumpy under pressure. The good thing is, she's been talking for a while and hasn't said anything to hurt Born. I looked over Mr. Holt and he still had his head down scribbling on the paper.

Liriano just asked the girl about when she knocked on the trailer door. She took a deep breath and started spilling her guts. She told what she thought was happening and Mr. Holt objected. When she told what she thought she heard, and Mr. Holt objected again.

Finally, she told what Born shouted through the door at her. Mr. Holt didn't object, but why should he have? I could see Liriano was fed up at the judge ruling in our favor.

Out of pure frustration, she said, "No further questions."

Mr. Holt didn't move, nor did he look up. The only thing on his mind was that paper. The judge cleared his throat in the mic to get Mr. Holt's attention. He rose up, fixed his tie, and slid the paper to Born. I saw Born start to laugh, but put his hand over his mouth. What in the hell was on that paper?

Born slid it over to me and I couldn't believe it. I had to put my hand over my mouth to keep from screaming. The whole time I thought he was over there writing down questions. He was bugging!

On the top of the page it said, "We got this bitch!" Then it was a picture of him beating her down with a baseball bat. I'm not sure if it was me or his drawing, but that really did look like her.

I turned the paper over to keep from laughing. Mr. Holt walked over to the witness stand and cleared his throat. He asked her, "Did you see Mr Smith strike or do bodily harm to the victim?"

She dropped her head and shook it, "No."

Mr. Holt said, "Thank you. And no further questions."

My face went blank with disbelief. I thought he was going to attack her. As soon as he sat down, Born gave him an earful. I wanted to scream on him myself, but Born was between us. I knew I would have my chance at recess, so I didn't sweat it. This is my man's life he's playing with. There will be another murder if he doesn't shape up.

Denise was sitting right behind Liriano. She was trying her best not to look at Born, but every now and then she would fail. She would take a quick glance and return her head to the front.

After the coroner was examined, cross examined, and examined some more, it was time for lunch. The judge recessed us all and we headed out.

I followed behind Born as he made his way to the door. He tried to be real cool with it when he waved at Denise. When he waved, she blushed. When I turned around, Liriano's hawk eyes were dead on them. She tried to turn away real fast like she didn't see anything, but I knew. I knew she saw them and I had to tell Born. On second thought, why even tell him? She can't do shit. Even if she did, I hope it eats her alive.

CHAPTER 73: Born Recess

As much as I hated it, we went downstairs to the court cafeteria. The food and the hard chairs reminded me of high school. As bad as I could taste that pizza burger from Jackson Hole, I didn't go. My mother didn't want me to run the risk of being late again. She felt the seriousness in the judge's voice like I did.

Instead of a pizza burger, I settled for a microwave slice of pizza. I bought my mom a slice of meatloaf.

Before I could pick my slice up, Denise and Ms. Liriano came through the door. Just seeing her walk through made the cafeteria look like Tavern on the Green. I couldn't take my eyes off her. I heard my mother talking in the background of my daydream, but I couldn't understand her. All I could do was watch Denise float across the floor.

Ashley tapped me on my wrist with a cold spoon. That brought me back to earth. Denise and Ms. Liriano sat on the other side of the dining room. We were like two high school kids. We played eye tag for the whole hour. To be honest, it turned me on.

Mr. Holt beeped us when court was about to start. He didn't want us to be late anymore. I gave everyone the nod and grabbed Ashley. We headed for the door, but paused when I was halfway out. I turned around to get one last look at Denise.

As soon as I turned around, I locked eyes with Ms. Liriano. If looks could kill, I would've been dead on the spot. I broke eye contact and headed out of the door.

CHAPTER 13½: Mr. Holt

This is going to be the final test. If I can make it through the grieving parent, I should be able to keep him off death row. I stayed away from them the whole recess on purpose. I didn't feel like answering any questions about my court tactics.

There are a lot of lawyer things they don't understand. They can't tell when I'm overcharging them. How can they question what I do? They better hope I don't sell them out, and then make them pay an extra hundred grand to appeal it.

Damn! That doesn't sound like a bad idea. But, that would fuck the winning streak up. That's a small price to pay for a hundred grand. Here we go. The itty bitty queen is about to call her next witness.

Lia's mom came down the aisle with tissues to her crying eyes. I thought that was a good touch, but that wasn't going to be enough. She had to bury him, here and now, or we will walk out of here with smiles. After this, the only witnesses she has are Detective Bryant and the pathologist. Both of them got a bunch of inconclusive shit that can't hurt us.

I can tell this is her finale. I could see they had their act rehearsed. She was answering the questions before they were asked. I could see Lia's mother was fragile right now. I could also see she was an honest woman. I've been in this game for a long time and the eyes don't lie. I hate to put pressure on her. I can't imagine how it feels to lose a child.

I have two handsome boys and I would die if anything happened to either one of them. Now, if something happened to their mothers, mysteriously ... I can't say I would be mad.

Let me stop before God punishes me by raising my child support for the fifth time.

I'm not watching Ms. O'Neal too much. My eyes are focused on the jury. Facial expressions are worth a thousand words.

Whichever juror they win over, I have to win back. At the very least, I must raise reasonable doubt.

That's the beauty of capital murder cases. Once you raise that, the rest takes care of itself. Look what happened to young Marlon Brando. When the facts came out, the whole world thought he was guilty. The kid didn't do a day, thanks to reasonable doubt. It even got those two rich brats two mistrials. Reasonable doubt is a thirteenth juror.

I just waited on the side like a tag team wrestler. Ms. O'Neal had the whole court reaching for their tissues. Even Born looked a little misty-eyed. I knew I had to get in before the jury hit the mat three times.

Itty bitty finally tagged me in, but before I had a chance to throw my first punch, she asked for a postponement. She said that her witness was too broke up for a cross examination. I knew what she was trying. She wanted the jury to sleep on Ms. O'Neal's testimony. That's an old trick, but it's very effective.

I guess they didn't rehearse this part because Ms. O'Neal said she was fine and wanted to continue. That was a blessing because I didn't need to challenge my objection streak. Thank God for strong black women.

Liriano tried to talk her out of it, but she wanted to get it over with. The judge hit the wood and told me to start my cross-examination. I started it out by telling her how sorry I was about her daughter's death. I know she didn't believe me, but it was part of the act.

Every question I asked her she answered while looking me in the eyes. That was a good sign for me. That was the easiest way to gain her trust. I asked her a few questions about her family. They never give you the whole story, but it sounds to me like they were pretty close.

I asked her a few personal questions about Lia. I didn't want to go too deep because I knew the floodgates would open. I knew the crying would kill me, not the case, but me, as a person.

I hate talking to a crying woman. I feel so helpless when I see them cry. With every question I could see her eyes soften up. I was glad because I was running out of bullshit questions. I needed to get to the heart of things.

I asked her to tell me about Lia and Born's eight year relationship. I explained to her that I needed her to talk about the things she saw, not the things she heard.

She closed her eyes and started to explain. She told me about the night Born took Lia to her prom. I caught the ice queen shaking her head. I know she didn't want to hear this.

Ms. O'Neal made the mistake of saying they were a cute couple. I knew at that point I had a chance. I let her talk because she was saying all the right things. Before she slipped up and said the wrong thing, I asked about her granddaughter.

What in the hell did I do that for? Immediately the tears started flowing. I should've known better. They'll make it public as soon as the trial is over that they plan on suing for custody. I could tell by her testimony that she really missed Ashley. I had to drop the bomb on her.

I needed to ask her if she thought Born killed these women. I was taking a big chance, but I needed her to say "No." At the very least, I needed her to pause. I buttered up her with how honest she's been. I told her I admired the strength she's shown under this much duress. I let her know that there wasn't a time limit on this next question. I was wondering if she could read my mind because she started crying for the third time.

I reached in my pocket and gave her a tissue I had from lunch. She tried to stop the waterfall, but it was useless. Liriano stood up in her defense. She asked the judge to stop these man-handling tactics until tomorrow. Ms O'Neal raised her hand in protest. She still had her eyes in the tissue, but she wanted to be heard.

The judge said, "Yes, Ms. O'Neal, you wish to say something?"

She raised her head to show the court her running makeup. She tried to clean up as best she could, but it didn't work. If she would have kept this up for one more minute, I would've taken out my hanky. She got herself together and asked what the question was.

I took a deep breath and swallowed my tears, and then I blurted out, "Do you think my client killed these women and your daughter?" It got quiet as hell. You could hear a pin drop. Her eyes darted from the jury, to the cameras, and Ms. Liriano. I could tell there was a struggle, between right and wrong, going on inside of her. I don't know what would happen to my streak if the devil won this battle.

She looked over at the judge and said, "Do I have to answer that?" That's when the whole courtroom looked at him. He gave her a reluctant nod.

She looked at me and said, "I've known Born since he was a baby. I want someone to pay for taking my little girl, but I don't think it was Born."

"Mrs Owen, are you saying that you think Ricardo Smith is innocent?" asked Mr. Holt.

The courtroom erupted and Liriano banged on the table. Her assistant looked, surprisingly pleased. The judge banged and banged, but the courtroom wouldn't quiet down. It seemed like the whole courtroom knew this trial just turned in our favor.

After several more bangs from the judge, the room got quiet. I thanked Ms. O'Neal. I helped her off the stand and watched while she made it back to her seat. I felt so sorry for her. She probably just made the biggest choice of her life and felt like she betrayed the memory of Lia. The judge stood up and said, "That is enough for one day. I want to see all parties at nine o'clock tomorrow morning.

CHAPTER 14: The Killer

As I sat there and watched Brenda Kipling run her fat mouth, I got madder by the second. I don't know how this old bag became the lead anchor woman for Court TV. She doesn't know a damn thing about the law. If they just needed someone to read the cue card, they could've gotten someone a little better looking.

She said, "After the botched up job, today, there is no way the jury could come back with a guilty verdict." I couldn't believe she said that. I got up and kicked the TV right off the stand. The TV was upside down, but her nagging voice was still coming from the speakers.

I took everything that wasn't nailed down and launched it at the TV. I think the water from the turned over fish tank finally silenced her. The room smelled like smoke from the TV. I looked around at the room and it was a mess. The mirror was in pieces. My gold fish, Abbott and Costello, were gasping for air on the rug.

The only thing that would ease my pain is causing Ricardo more pain, killing him would be letting him off the hook. I want him to suffer every day of his life. Just like I do. This time when I strike, I'll give him a little something to think about.

I picked up the phone to see if Mr. Ricardo was up for a little cat and mouse, and dialed his cell phone. I made sure my voice alternator was on. I could tell by the way he said "hello" that he was in a good mood.

When I said "hello," the bubble in his voice faded. I told him it was much too early to be tasting victory. I let him know I was just watching him on Court TV. "You looked a little stressed out, superstar."

He had the nerve to scream, "What the fuck do you want?"

"It's not what the fuck I want, it's what do you want. Do you want to see another person die for knowing you? Well, whether you want to see it or not, it's going to happen. Even though I know your black ass will never figure it out in time, here's a hint," I paused for effect just to fuck with him. At this point I was beyond pissed, and ready to strike.

"Of course, it's a lady. Perhaps the brightest you know. I'm not going to say how she looks, but I will say she's grown. Do you need more, or will she be number four? Could I be a rapper, Ricardo? Do I have what it takes? I don't think so. I'll just leave the rapping to the scum bags." Then I hung up.

I stepped on my dead fish and all the broken glass in the living room. I went to my bedroom and pealed off my suit. I changed into some black jeans, black sweater, and a black Gap hat. I bent down and unzipped a black Columbia bag. It was where I kept the knives.

The more I looked at the knives, the more I knew it was the perfect murder weapon. It's what most hunters call a Buck knife, but these have an eagle hook on the end of the blade.

I bought five when I started this crusade. I don't think I'll need the last one. That will be my souvenir from this game.

CHAPTER 15: Born

"Of course she is a lady. Perhaps the brightest you know. I'm not going to say how she looks, but I will say she's grown."

When I hung up, me and Black ran out of the house. The rhyme played over and over in my head. I was so scared because I knew this creep was talking about my mother.

I had Black call her on the cell phone while I ran red light after red light. Black said, "The line is busy." My heart skipped another two beats. "There is a guard posted out front."

I don't know if that was supposed to calm my nerves, but it didn't. It did make me step down harder on the gas. I told Black to keep trying the number. He pressed redial over and over again. He didn't say anything, but I could tell from his expression it was still busy.

I couldn't think straight. All I knew was her crib was about five minutes away. When I screeched around the corner, we picked up one of New York's finest. They were hot on our tail, but I didn't care I wasn't stopping until my mother and Ashley were wrapped around me.

Block after block, the lights were still in my rear view. I told Black, "When I get to the building, I'm going to jump out. Try to keep them from shooting me while I run upstairs."

Black said, without hesitation, "Wish for something else because you got that."

I slammed on the brakes in front of the building. I saw Big Rock posted in front. As I ran by I told him to follow me. We took the steps two at a time until we were in front of my mom's door. I quickly opened it up with my key. The door flew open and she and Ashley were in plain sight.

When she saw the panic on my face, she hung up the phone. She ran to me with Ashley trailing right behind. She hugged my neck and Ashley hugged my knees.

She asked, "What's wrong," but I was too out of breath to speak. Before I caught my breath, Black and about six uniformed cops were coming through the door. They had their guns drawn and kill on their faces. Big Rock told them that everything was okay.

I asked my mother, "Who were you talking to?"

She said, "It was my prayer partners from church." I let out a big sigh and started explaining. The police were one step off my ass. The only reason they didn't lock me up was because they recognized me from the trial.

There's always one petty one in the bunch. He sat off to the side and wrote me about fourteen tickets. He could've written a hundred and fourteen, as long as my family was safe.

The house cleared out and I took Ashley to my favorite lounge chair. I played patty cake with her while the rhyme ran through my head. The more I heard it, the more it wasn't my mom. If not her, then who? Who is the brightest girl I know? I know a few ladies with jobs and shit. It's not like none of them are rocket scientists, lawyers, or doctors. Lawyer ... Oh, shit, Denise!

I jumped up and told Black, "Hold things down here."

"Where are you going?" he asked concerned.

I said, "If I'm right, to save Denise's life" as I slammed the door.

I was glad Denise didn't live too far away from my mother's. Once I hit Riverside Drive, it's only ten minutes away. Before I could blink, I was in front of her loft.

When I pulled up, I saw an out of place blue sedan. It was parked on the wrong side of the street. It had white City of New York plates. The only thing it read was City Hall. I guess she drove the company car home.

I rode her freight elevator up to her floor. I tiptoed to her door so I could ease drop at it. When I placed my ear to the door, I knew something was wrong. I heard something crash to the floor.

I quickly went under the mat to get the spare key. I fumbled with the key because I didn't know which lock it was. Luckily it was only two of them.

When I finally got into the apartment, it was a mess. There was shit everywhere. When I turned the corner, my eyes got bigger than a crack heads. Denise was fighting off the killer. The killer had the knife up to her throat. She was already lying in a puddle of blood.

I ran over and dove on the killer from behind. We rolled on the floor. I ended up on top. I cocked my fist back to punish him. When the hat came off, I got a good look. When I saw the face I froze with my fist up in the air.

That was a big mistake because when I let my guard down, I felt the knife go through my leg. I grabbed my leg in pain and the knife out of fear. I flung the knife to my left, and then I began to throw punches at an alarming rate.

I didn't want the blows to be fatal because I wanted some answers. I yanked the limp body up off the floor. I said, "Why are you doing this to me?"

The killer gave out a painful laugh and said, "You still don't know?"

Honestly, I really didn't know. That seemed to piss her off that much more.

She pulled out a picture and asked, "Do you know her?" When my eyes focused on the picture, my breath almost left my body. That was a face out of my past I'd never forget. She told me she was dead. I couldn't believe it. I was thinking that she killed her. I guess she read my mind.

She pulled a gun out of nowhere and said, "She killed herself." I found that hard to believe. Then she said, "She killed herself because you fucked her over."

I didn't want to say anything that hurried her into pulling that trigger. I tried to talk nice to her, but that was making her crazier.

The tears started flowing and I really knew I was in trouble. She went on to tell me that her father was a no good black motherfucker, just like me. It was enough that she was a psycho, but she hated black men, too.

"Her father left when she was six," she said. "I guess that was her attraction to you. I told her, black men are nothing but pimps and drug dealers."

I started to tell her how sorry I was about her sister.

She shot into the floor in the direction of Denise. She screamed out, "You dumb bastard! She's not my sister, she's my daughter!"

That's who she looks like.

Denise was lying on the floor, choking in her own blood. I wanted to go to her, but I didn't want her to shoot Denise, or me.

I was thinking about my next move, and at the same time, staring at Denise. She fired again, this time even closer to Denise. That was her sick way of getting my attention.

The next thing I knew, shots were ringing out. The police came in with their guns smoking. I was glad my hands were up in the air. I just stood there motionless. That was until with her last bit of strength, she fired the gun at me. At first, I was stunned to know I was shot. That was before I started falling to the ground.

Detective Bryant came into the room yelling, "NO! NO! NO! That's the assistant DA!" It was too late because she looked dead to me.

Black was the last to enter, along with paramedics. He ran straight to my side. The paramedics ran to the ladies. Black held me close. I guess he thought I was knocking on death's door. He started crying while saying to me, "Hold on!"

The paramedics came over to me next. Black didn't want to let me go, but he had to. He was looking too scared, so I lifted up my arm, pointed at his face, and said, "I caught you crying again." He wiped his eyes and we started laughing.

The paramedics said, "The bullet went in and out of the shoulder. You will be holding a mic in a couple of days." That was good news because I have a lot to write about.

Denise winked at me as they carried her out. I told Black about Sara being Ms. Liriano's daughter. He didn't believe it when I told him she killed herself. He really could believe it when he found out she was white.

Detective Bryant was standing over Liriano, with a blank face. I wasn't sure if it was because she was dead or because she was the killer all along. I could tell this one had him fucked up. I wanted to tell him to join the fucked up club but I was sure it would go over his head. A lot of good people died over the love of a women and the grief of another.

"When this is all over your record sales are going threw the roof," Black said with a devilish grin. Then he said, "I'm really glad you're okay."

I'm not sure if that's cause of the sales or what. Nevertheless I was glad to hear it. Truthfully the only thing that would make me feel okay was Ashley's little arms around my neck.

THE FINALE

9 Months Later

CHAPTER 76: Born

This is the first time I've been on stage in almost a year. I always get butterflies when I'm behind stage. I was waiting for my cue. As soon as I get it, the butterflies will go away.

Just nine months ago, I couldn't see anything more than walking the green mile. Now I'm about to make rap history. After all that's has went on in my life, the fans and other artists are still showing me love. If it wasn't for them, I wouldn't have the courage to take the stage again.

Now, I'm a part of the First Annual Rap Mania at the Apollo. All the big dogs are here giving the hip-hop junkies just what they need. As soon as I hear my cue me, Jay Z, and Biggie will take this crowd to the next level.

This is the first time the song *"The Boro's Baddest"* has been performed live. The single was number one for five months. Denise and her little sister are in the front row. This is the first time she's seen me rap, besides in the studio.

I wish Black was here, but him and Kenya are home with my goddaughter, Lanetta. I call her Twiggy because it makes her laugh. I can tell by her beautiful smile, she's going to be special.

It sounds crazy, but when I come back, I'm going to ask Denise to marry me. I never thought I would be the type to walk down the aisle. I guess these last few years have matured me a lot. The crowd is on fire out there. I hope they'll always love me like this. When this is over, I have to hit the road for my promotional tour.

This is my sophomore album and I want to sell twice as many as my debut did. I named this one "13 1/2." It means: 12 jurors, 1 judge, and ½ a chance.

A Note from The Author

Who is King Jewel? I would say that that's a million dollar question. If a thousand people were to ask that question there would be a thousand different answers. Would that make me complex or a deep thinker? I don't think so. I'm still the same guy who grew up in the Highbridge area in the Bronx and dreamed of playing in the N.B.A.

Some might claim that I'm an underachiever, but others can piece together my past and tell that there is a God and someone prayed for me very hard. I still have dreams, but now they include my little princess. In the past if someone asked me to describe myself, I would've used words that could have stroked my ego. Now if someone asked me that same question, the only word I would use is FATHER To find out what drives me day after day, simply look at my princess in the back of this book and there is your answer.

Only God knows how many more books I have in me, and how long I have on this earth. Until then I'm going to live them through "Tsion Jewel". So when you're reading this book and you get to a part where Born's love for Ashley jumps off the page, know that some of this book is fact and not fiction. So when the smoke clears and someone ask you who is King Jewel, I urge you to answer, but this time use all the information that you gathered from this book before you answer. Thanks for all the love and support you've given me and New World Publishing. It will never be in Vain!!!!!!!!!!!!

Author's Bio

King Jewel resides in Maryland with his family. Thirteen and a half is his first novel. He is currently working on his second book, ***Can't Change A Player's Game***, and is the co-owner of New World Publishing.
www.myspace.com/Kingjewel

Those mean streets. Those split seconds life decisions we make. Those adversities. Those chances we take. Those self motivated breaks we create.

These are definitions of survival. These are the tools of Black American survivors. They help us realize a plethora of steps we must take to climb this mountain of street life.

It's so confusing when you trust an enemy and stash valuables from your wife. It hurts when you lose someone that you were adjacent to and there's an attempted coop, and the confusions causes you to find another crew.

Street life compares to mildew. You're too proud to submit, you think you're too involved in this bullshit. You believe your demonic and not deific... Until You Sit and Pray and Say...

"Lord...Please Help Me!

Creation Bey

NEW WORLD PUBLISHING PRESENTS
COMING SOON
Cant Change
A Players Game
DEA
KING JEWEL

Moses

I never was one of those men that were thirsty for another man's blood. A wise man told me that sometimes you have to cut off your arm to save the rest of your body. The day I took that advice was the last time I went to jail. I've lived by those few words for ten wonderful years. I need for tonight to go smooth. If everything goes like I planned it will be in and out of the park in a matter of minutes. First things first I need to call Gator and tell him the plan. I really hate calling Miss Evans house because she always brings up my parents. Hopefully Gator will pick up.

After three rings I knew it was no such luck. I found myself locked into a conversation going nowhere with Miss Evans. We talked for a minute before she put Gator on the phone. I told Gator that Moe was the one leaking information. Gator tried to convince me that my information was wrong. I explained to him that Moe was a thief and the penalty was death. He told me he was on the way to handle it. I let him know that I didn't want this to be a mess being though he is a crew member. I want this to be a lot cleaner.

"Do me a favor. Throw him in the trunk and bring him to me and HC. We'll be at Van Courtland Park at 11:00 pm. Oh yeah! Gator no accidents this time. I want to do this myself," I said to him in a tone I hope he understood. Tonight had to go down smoothly. We didn't have a choice.

"Not a problem. I'll see you in a bit."

I had to make a few stops first. Me and Al were about five minutes from the meeting spot. Al was pretty quiet but he usually is before the action is about to start. I pulled behind Gator's old ass Chevy Caprice. I hit the high beams and he walked back to the car. He leaned over into the car and all I smelled was weed. I asked him did he handle the problem and he nodded with his blood shoot eyes. I told him to follow us to the Park. The park was just around the corner. As we passed the *Welcome to Van Courtland* sign we headed for the field in back. It was the quietest part of the park at night.

When we pulled up my mind was on Moe. The first thing Al said was to get him out of the trunk. Gator went over to the trunk with a screwdriver. He pushed it in the hole were the key used to be and it opened. Al and I looked to see if Moe was in one piece. So far, things were going according to plan. Now the only thing left to do was cut out the poison. Al helped Moe out the trunk, and we walked over to the wooded area behind the field. Gator asked me again was I sure about this. I gave him a look that answered all of his questions. Al threw Gator the rope and told him to tie Moe to the tree.

"It's never personal, just business," Gator replied in an Al Pacino tone, putting his gun on his waist so that he could use both hands to secure the rope.

Once he did that I gave Al the nod. In one motion Al raised the gun over his head and knocked Gator out with one blow. I rolled him over took the gun out of his waist. Meanwhile Al helped Moe take the tape off his mouth and hands. Moe said, "For a minute there I really thought my ass was grass". We all had to laugh at that one. Now it was Moe turn to do the tying, but Gator didn't know. After a few smacks across Gator's face he came to life but not for long. He struggled for a minute then he laughed. From day one I tried to show him what family was all about but he could never catch on.

"In a world where there is enough money for all, stealing will always be against the rules," I simply stated. Although my tone was serious, I was a little saddened by what I had to do to one of my closest friends.

Before he could respond I unloaded one round in his chest and one in his head. I gave Moe the gun and the car keys and told him to get rid of them all. He knew just what I meant and headed for the car. Al and I did the same, then we cruised down the Major Deagan Highway I was thinking about M.J. I want a better life for him but I wasn't sure how I would do it. Sometimes undying love is not enough. You also need a full proof plan and a little luck.

Panama

Once our friends in New York clean up the bill I think it'll be time to step them up. The heroin trade is at an all time high in the United States. They're running through twenty kilos in no time. There was a time when that would last them for a month or more, now their calling us in a week or less. They earned our trust a thousand times over. From day one we put an extra five kilos inside and we told them the money was short they paid the difference. We gave them twenty of the worse kilos we could find, but did they complain? It took them an extra two weeks but they paid in full without asking for a discount. These two guys had single handedly taken care of our families. I think it's time we step them up to at least a hundred. With the right price and the right push, I think they can take over New York. My brother doesn't believe a big dog can beat a little dog sometimes. If I'm right we'll have more money than Pablo and his family. If I'm wrong I will kill both of them and the first twenty-five people that comes to his funeral. Then I'll really get mad!

Big Al

It's been a few months since Gator killed Reno. Surprisingly the summer is in full swing and there are no signs of war. There is no good time for war but the summer is the worse. You look forward all winter to the mini skirts and the convertibles. The next thing you know your shacked up with twenty of your best men in a little ass apartment. All you see is guns everywhere and cigarette butts. Waiting for that one phone call to let you know where your mark is hiding and what's about to go down tonight isn't going to result in war but it must be done.

When there is a weak link in your crew you treat it like cancer and cut it out. Once Reno's drunk ass girl started spilling her guts to Tennile the whole thing started to fall into place. Now it's obvious why Gator killed Reno. He didn't want to chance Reno spilling his guts when me or Moses got there. That's also how Reno knew where and how to rob the runners, that son of a bitch Gator was leaking information from the inside. He wasn't actually robbing them, but I am sure he was getting his cut. When I told Moses his voice sounded very disappointed but I was sure he would make the right call. I never really cared for that piece of shit anyway. I was glad to know he was living in his last day.

M.J.

My new school wasn't as much fun as I recalled. If I didn't have Avon and Keith by my side I would've been lost. Everything we was learning my mother had already taught me. I could count to a hundred and knew my ABC's. I've been writing my name since my last B-Day. I didn't understand why my Mom was making me do that but now I do. I use to run to my Dad and show him everything I learned. He would stop and smile from ear to ear. I knew right then my Dad loved me. After a long boring afternoon I had my eyes set on recess. When the bell rang we all ran to the yard at top speed.

I hit the fence like I was about to run threw it. I was so disappointed to see that my Daddy wasn't there. I never knew when my dad would sneak to the back gate and bring me sour balls or jawbreakers. I wasn't sure if he knew how that made my day but now the same thing that made me laugh is making me cry. I looked up and down the block more times than I could remember. I thought to myself, forget school I already knew it all. That was a very sad day in my life. I dropped my lunch on the ground and clung to the gate. I felt the beginning of a major waterfall. My lips started to quiver and my eyes began to water. I didn't want to cry but I wanted my Daddy. Before I could wipe the tear good, Keith and Avon nearly knocked me down.

They were giggling out of control before they noticed I wasn't in the mood. One by one they asked me was I crying. I denied it but they saw my pain. I didn't know then, but I know now that was the beginning of real friendship. As the days and weeks went on I could see life at the *Sussie Carter Grade School* got use to me and I to it. Some things never changed. At three o'clock nothing gave me more joy than seeing my Dad in his car waiting to pick me up. If you asked me life was perfect. I wish I could've stayed that age forever. I knew that I was dreaming but now I wish I wasn't.

Other Books By New World Publishing

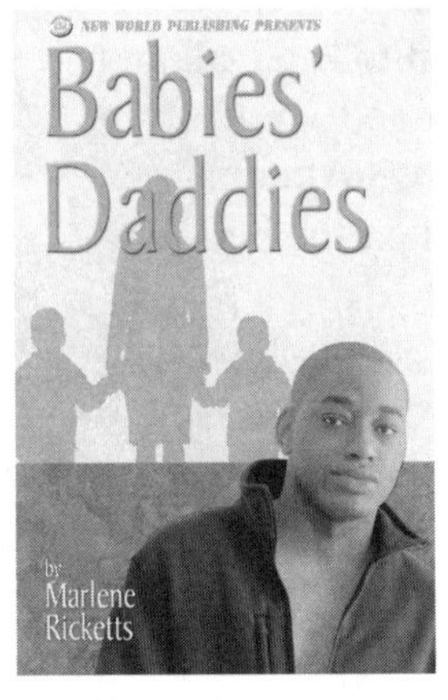

Babies' Daddies By: Marlene
Making It On My Own By: Marlene

Coming Soon

Can't Change A Players Game **By: King Jewel**
Rules Of Da Street **By: Tony Black**
Lookin' For A Lover…Men Need Not Apply **By: Zaria**
Island Breeze **By: Marlene**

Making It On My Own
By: Marlene

Life for Shay Johnson was a party. Between college and friends, she was free to do whatever she wanted. She was on top of her game, and there was nothing you could tell her, she was it! Shay had everything under control until she met Chico, a handsome Spanish guy that swept her off her feet and took her heart. It wasn't until he left her in the street with no way to feed their son and a baby on a way did Shay realized she had a lot of growing up to do. Good friends are hard to come by, and Huey is her prince charming in disguise ready to take her away from life's harsh reality. Will Shay continue to deny herself a chance to love again because of the drama she went through with Chico, or will she open up to a chance at starting over? The struggle of a young girl finding her way to womanhood, and the sacrifices you take to get there are all on the pages of ***Making It On My Own***...because at the end of the day you can only truly depend on yourself.

"Marlene Ricketts brings a fresh face to the literary world. Her characters pop, and her style is sure to drag you in. This book will quickly be on your top ten list of must have's in your collection."

~Anna J.

Author of Essence Best Selling Novel "*My Woman His Wife*"

You will be able to recognize the emotions of yourself or someone you know in Ricketts' strong and intense portrait of a young woman and single mother struggling with the burdens and anxieties of everyday life. Ricketts' creative writing style connects the story line to real-life issues drawing readers in. I enjoyed Shay's "in your face tell it like it is" narrative. Making It On My Own is engrossing and entertaining making for an engaging read.

~OOSA Book Club

Marlene Ricketts delivers a powerful exposé of one woman's struggle while MAKING IT ON HER OWN. I was so caught up in the drama, struggles, love and pain that I was able to read it in the course of one day…
(Amazon.com)

Babies' Daddies
By: Marlene

BABIES' DADDIES was filled with real-life situations; situations that make you sit down and think about the choices we make in life. Marlene Ricketts does a great job of meshing the worlds of the three women, guiding readers through the value of friendship, loyalty and being true-to-self. This is a definite inspiration for anyone whose life has been plagued with disappointments.

~Reviewed by The RAWSISTAZ™ Reviewers

By reading the title, there might be a faint thought of "here we go daddy bashing," but it is on the contrary. Marlene took each man at face value and called it how she saw it, yet she also gave the idea of not all men are alike. There are good men out there. Marlene Ricketts does a great job of mixing three women with different outlooks focusing on one common denominator, motherhood.

~OOSA Book Club

Excellent book. A definite page turner from start to finish. Blu, Ashanti, and Sandra are three women from different backgrounds. Each of the women has high aspirations that land them on a college campus together and form a lasting friendship with one another.

~Keesha of Sisters of Unity Book Club

Marlene Ricketts' novel 'Babies Daddies' is engaging from start to finish. Follow the lives of three women who meet by chance and develop a bond despite varying backgrounds and circumstances. This novel is a "feel good" read without being sappy while remaining true to life. Kudos!

~Angela Wallace, Author of Secret Dramas & 360 Degrees of Drama.

The power behind this novel lies in Marlene's character development and the emotional struggles of each female. Readers are emotionally drawn into their lives. Marlene has a gift for storytelling… I look forward to reading more by this talented author. I also recommend her latest novel, ***Making It On My Own.***

~Amazon.com

www.marlenericketts.com
www.myspace.com/jamgirl3

Manuscript Submissions

New World Publishing is currently accepting manuscripts for consideration. We are looking for African American based mainstream contemporary fiction. We will accept unsolicited manuscripts. Any manuscript that is sent to the company must be in its entirety, typed and double-spaced on regular 8 x 10 paper. Please enclose a self-addressed stamped envelope should your manuscript be rejected and you wish to have it returned to you. Manuscripts are reviewed within 3-6 months When the review process is completed you will be notified. Please be sure to include your contact information.

We would prefer novels with word count of 75,000 words or more.

To send via email please submit to
Newworldpublishing@hotmail.com

Or Send by mail to: **New World Publishing**

Submission Department

P.O. Box 660

Randallstown, Maryland 21133-0660

For more information about the company, please visit us at
www.myspace.com/newworldpublishing

NEW WORLD PUBLISHING

ORDER FORM

Name:____
Registration #___________________________ (if incarcerated)
Address____
City________________State:__________ Zipcode:______
Phone:_________________Email: _______________________

Please send the following number of copies of:

___Thirteen and a half	**By: King Jewel**	**@$14.95 =_____**
___Babies' Daddies	**By: Marlene**	**@$14.95 =_____**
___Making it on my own	**By: Marlene**	**@$14.95 =_____**

***Please send $3.50 to cover shipping and handling. Add an additional dollar for each additional book ordered. We offer a *15* percent discount to inmates.**

Total Enclosed=________

Please make check or money order payable to: New World Publishing.
Send order form and payment to:

New World Publishing
P.O. Box 660
Baltimore, Maryland, 21133-0660

New World Publishing: The streets have just met its match!